D0397211

A
THOUSAND
FIRES

SHANNON PRICE

**TOR
TEEN**

A TOM DOHERTY ASSOCIATES BOOK
NEW YORK

A THOUSAND FIRES

Copyright © 2019 by Shannon Price

A Tor Teen Book
Published by Tom Doherty Associates
120 Broadway
New York, NY 10271

www.tor-forge.com

Tor® is a registered trademark of Macmillan Publishing Group, LLC.

The Library of Congress Cataloging-in-Publication Data is available upon request.

ISBN 978-1-250-30199-4 (hardcover)
ISBN 978-1-250-30198-7 (ebook)

Our books may be purchased in bulk for promotional, educational, or business use.
Please contact your local bookseller or the Macmillan Corporate and
Premium Sales Department at 1-800-221-7945, extension 5442,
or by email at MacmillanSpecialMarkets@macmillan.com.

First Edition: November 2019

Printed in the United States of America

0 9 8 7 6 5 4 3 2 1

For my parents

*

with special love to Nick Gomez-Hall
I miss you every day

AUTHOR'S NOTE

I first read *The Iliad* in college, and the story stuck with me in a way that no other story had before—vivid imagery, unforgettable characters, and emotional struggles that still send shivers down the spine centuries after the poem was written. Years later, while living on the outskirts of San Francisco, I began to devise a reimagining of Homer's epic set in an alternate version of a city that spoke to me with the same vibrant energy.

The Iliad is, unquestionably, a text about war, and contains many varied depictions of violence and brutality. In writing *A Thousand Fires,* I borrowed those same elements and applied them to a modern setting. I do not encourage nor am I a proponent of violence, in any form, and this book is not meant to advocate for the use of guns or violence. It is fiction, inspired by a timeless myth and a city I hold close to my heart.

A Thousand Fires is a story I've had in my head for so many years, and I'm thrilled to finally share it with the world. Enjoy!

Sincerely,
Shannon

Rage—Goddess, sing the rage of Peleus' son Achilles,
murderous, doomed, that cost the Achaeans countless losses,
hurling down to the House of Death so many sturdy souls,
great fighters' souls, but made their bodies carrion,
feasts for the dogs and birds.

Homer, *The Iliad,* I.1–5

1

You turn eighteen, and they find you. There is no other re-cruitment.

Eighteen—old enough to have had your heart hardened, young enough that blood still passes through it.

Not everyone is recruited, of course, but the gangs are smart. They pick people with nothing to lose. The ones who are angry. Those who join San Francisco's infamous Red Bridge Wars do so willingly.

"The bridge isn't red," Leo said once. "It's International Orange. We learned that in school."

He was wrong, I think. I saw the red.

But that was a long time ago, in practically another life-time, and tonight everything will change.

Mom and I sit on opposite sides of the kitchen table. Its surface is marked with old smears of glitter paint and crayon: a record of my childhood. I use my nail to scratch off a bit of crayon.

Outside, streetlamps illuminate the fog like dandelions of orange light in a sea of dark gray. I drum my fingers against my mug of Blue Bottle coffee. Dad gave me two bags of the stuff yesterday before he left on his business trip.

"I know they won't," he had said, "but if they pick you, say no. I don't think they'll come for you, but . . ."

"You have to say it. I know." My heart splintered at his look of relief. Dad's never been a man of many words. Even for me, his shining child. Now his only child.

Back in the present, Mom's mug rests in front of her, untouched. Her usually styled hair is back in a low bun, and instead of a blazer-and-pants combination, she's in a faded lavender robe and yoga pants.

I poke my fork into the frosting of the cake sitting between us. Lyla says it's bad luck to bake your own birthday cake, but I've never minded it. Baking is my one and only solace. I love the rhythm of it: the sharp crack of eggshells, the scrape of the knife across measuring cups to make them level, the whir of the mixer as I watch the twin swirls of the beaters disappear into each other.

Baking fills my hands and, more importantly, clears my mind. Kneading dough is like an exhale for my brain. I'll mix the same ingredients for twice as long as I should, never wanting to stop. Sometimes it ruins the bake, but for the most part things turn out okay. If not, I dump it and start over.

Around us, the kitchen is an explosion of pastries—a tray of blueberry muffins I baked Tuesday morning at 3 A.M. when I couldn't sleep, a plate of meticulously decorated cupcakes leftover from Mom's fundraiser meeting last night, and the dark chocolate and sea salt cookies I sent to work with Dad before his trip. Everyone in his office loves me: the daughter who bakes. They'd think differently if they knew why.

But the Wars are my out. I know it's risky, but it's all I've got. All my research, all my prodding Matthew with questions—it'll be worth it when the Herons choose me. I check the clock: it's already 10:26 P.M. The gangs always choose their new recruits on their actual birthdays. *Come on,* I beg. *I'm ready. Let's go.* I just need to know—am I in or not? Can I make up for what happened, or not?

In Mom's hand is a crumpled note that I knew, even as I was writing it, I'd probably regret. And I do, now. The closet in my room has long been the family storage space for the once-a-year stuff, and Mom just *had* to go into my closet to put away the Halloween decorations.

She found my suitcases, all packed. Mom's smart—she knew what they were for. All it took was the terror in her voice as she called my name from upstairs for me to know what happened. In retrospect, it was stupid of me to leave them there, but there's no changing it now.

"Baby, don't do this," she says. "Finish school. Then you can take a year off. You know your dad and I would be okay with that. Just not this." She shakes her head. "Val, you could die."

"I know, Mom."

"Then *why*?"

I turn away from her. She knows why.

"I won't let you," she says.

"I'm eighteen. Legally you can't stop me if I choose to go."

Mom starts to cry. Even with all my resolve, I nearly break at the sight of her wiping her cheeks—if I keep sitting here, I'll cave. Instead I get up and set the dirty plates in the sink, keeping my back to her. I switch on the faucet. The water is just getting warm when Mom says, "Baby, is this about Matthew?"

"No, Mom. Jeez."

"I know you broke up, but you know the Westons—"

"I want to join, Mom. It's not about Matthew. It's about me."

"Joining won't bring your brother back."

My phone buzzes. Wiping my wet hands on my jeans, I check the screen. It's Lyla. She was supposed to have texted me earlier before she got on her flight, but she must have forgotten. Lyla turned eighteen in October. None of the gangs came for her—like most people, she and her family were relieved. Even if they had, I'm not convinced the gangs would have gotten past her tough-as-nails Cuban grandmother.

I open the text.

STRANDED AT AIRPORT. CAN U COME GET ME?

Tacked on moments later:

DID MATTHEW WISH U HAPPY BIRTHDAY?

Mom blots her eyes with a dishrag. "Who is it?"

"Lyla," I say. "She wants me to go get her from the airport." Even with the waves of anxiety and nervousness in my stomach, I take comfort in my best friend's use of all caps. It's our thing—we never text without it, even if it's something stupid like I FORGOT MY LUNCH or HEY DO YOU HAVE A SPARE HAIR TIE.

I start typing a sorry-but-I-can't reply, but my heart tugs with guilt and I change it to: SURE THING. LEAVING NOW. GIVE ME 45 MINUTES.

Fingers crossed traffic isn't bad.

Mom turns to the clock. It's 10:28 P.M. "Let's go get her."

"You don't have to come."

"I'm not letting you go by yourself."

"The Herons are going to find me whether you're with me or not."

I get up and go to the coatrack by the front door. As I pull my jacket on, my eyes go to a small gold frame on the mantel. Silver wings sprout from either side. Between them, a little boy with mint ice cream on his cheeks smiles a too-big smile, his brown hair the same color as mine.

The Herons will find me regardless—I believe that. I'll have to come back for my suitcases anyway, and then we'll say our goodbyes. Once I join the Wars, I'm not allowed home for a year. The gangs have a lot of rules to avoid an all-out crackdown from the city, and having members stay away from their families is one of them. As is the choice—they can seek you out, but you can say no.

"I'll be right back," I tell Mom.

"Val, please. *Mahal kita.*" She gets up and hugs me tightly.

Mahal kita—"I love you" in Tagalog. Mom only switches to her native language for two things: to talk with my uncle and to make me really pay attention to what she's saying. *Mahal kita* is ours. We save it for special occasions, like before she goes on a long business trip or before the first day of school.

Mom saying it now means a lot of things. The Wars are one of those things parents both believe and don't believe. *The Wars are real,* they think. *But it won't be my daughter. It won't be my son. My child won't sign up, I won't let them.*

Every minute I'm still here, the more my spirit wavers, like sand eroding against an angry tide. I pull myself out of her hug and grab my keys from the basket by the door.

"Bye, Mom, love you." The door slams behind me, muffling Mom's shout.

There was a time when Mom would have followed me with fire in her eyes and a maternal determination that could topple city walls. But that was before Leo, before she shattered. I love my mom—which is exactly why I need to leave her now, even as the pain claws in my rib cage the same way guilt has torn at my heart since that day two years ago.

Outside, my city is cool and still, and I tug my fleece tighter against me. I beep my car to life, its lights blinking into the mist. I open the door and am about to slide in when I hear my name.

Matthew jogs toward me. His dark hair is messy and put-together at the same time in the incredibly sexy way only he can pull off—no, no. *He broke up with YOU. You're not allowed to think anything he does is even mildly attractive. He is your friend and that's it.*

"Happy birthday," he says.

"You, too."

Neighbors since we were seven, I always thought it was cool that Matthew and I had the same birthday. That didn't change as we got older and I learned about the Wars. No matter what happened, I felt our stories were intertwined. I loved that. I still do.

"Are you okay?" he asks, eyes filled with concern.

I nod. "Yeah. Just a fight-ish thing with my mom. It's fine."

He props an elbow on the roof of the car. "Where are you going?"

"SFO. Lyla's stranded."

"That sucks."

"Yeah. I'm just going to get her and be right back."

"All right." He sticks his hands in his front pockets and shivers. "I take it that the Herons haven't been by?"

"No. You?"

He looks relieved. "No."

Thank God. If Matthew hasn't heard from them yet, then I'm fine. He's going to be a Heron, no question—both of his brothers were and his whole family has been associated with the Herons since the beginning. We'll be together the whole year.

After leaving Mom and everything else, my brain doesn't have the capacity to really wonder what that will be like, given all our history.

"I'm coming right back," I say again. "Be sure to act surprised when the Herons come to your door."

"There's no guarantee."

"Oh, please. You're like, the prince of the Heron throne, thanks to Alex." Matthew was so upset when his brother Alex joined. They'd always been close, both in age and just in general. Matthew's other brother—Aaron—is much older and a bit of a black sheep. He lives alone in a cabin in Tahoe and never comes to the city, not even for Christmas.

But Alex—Alex is different. He's the hair-mussing, let's-shoot-hoops brother you see in the movies. Seriously. The night Alex joined the Herons was the first time Matthew ever cried in front of me. I think he was afraid his brother would be killed.

It's a fear I never bothered to have.

"Believe me, I know. I've got Heron blood." He raises his pitch and draws out the word *blood*—a perfect impression of his mother. She's good-hearted and usually means well, but only so long as her image is intact. I've never seen her with so much as an eyelash out of place.

"Heron blood. Wish I had that," I mutter.

"No, you don't."

"Yes, I do. Then I'd know for sure if I was going to be recruited."

He doesn't say anything, just stares at his feet. He's holding something back—you learn a thing or two about a person after being friends for years. *And* dating.

Matthew and I had only been together six months when he broke it off. But those six months were bliss. Lyla said it was like Disney magic, how it all worked out. "A guy and a girl can't be friends for so long without getting feelings," she told me after he asked me to junior prom. "This is your destiny. This is fate."

But that was all the way back in March, before Matthew came over in late July and just ended it. Then and there. He said he wanted to focus on getting ready for college, which I called BS on because I had a feeling he was thinking about the Wars. He said sorry about a hundred times until finally I screamed at him and told him to get the fuck out of our house.

Rage became a close companion—anything to hide how hurt and confused I was. Lyla got me through the tears-and-ice-cream phase, and Matthew and I avoided each other for the remainder of the summer.

Then school started and we still hung out here and there, both of us silently resolved to move past it by never, ever bringing it up. I spent more and more time with Lyla and the theater kids, grateful for their openness and for the darkness of the backstage loft where we'd watch the rehearsals.

Still, the memories are never far: making out at his family's cabin high up in the mountains, the time we walked together past *Cupid's Span* down by the water, or the way he still smiles at me from across the classroom . . .

A hand on my cheek pulls me back to the present. Matthew leans in, whispering my name just once—softly. Desperately. Then he kisses me.

His lips are rough—and I *love* that they are. There was no pre-kiss ChapStick application, no practice for this moment. It just is. I breathe him in as deeply as I dare, and the distance between our bodies disappears. He pulls back too soon and my heart thunders in my throat.

"Sorry," he says. "I didn't—"

"It's fine," I reply, avoiding his gaze so he doesn't see my smile. "Totally fine."

"Look, I know breaking up with you the way I did was shitty," he says. "But I didn't really want to. I just thought it would be . . . better."

"What?"

"It doesn't mean I don't love you," he finishes. "Because I do. I love you."

I say the first stupid thing my lips seem able to form. "You do?"

We'd never said it, not like this. Not as if everything in his life was preparing him for this moment.

"I do." He's waiting. I'm stalling. My limbs are light and numb and sparkling all at once. Matthew loves me. He didn't want to break up. Then why did he? And why the hell would that matter when—

"I love you," I say.

I tilt my head up to meet the kiss I know is coming. We tighten our arms around each other until there's not even the hope of space between us. When he lets me go, I rest my head on his chest. I can hear his heartbeat fluttering.

"I'll do my year," he says. "I can't say no, not with my family and all. It's always been my plan to join."

I tighten my hug around his chest. "We'll do our year together." A cold shiver lances through me. "Unless you already know something I don't."

"If I knew anything, I'd tell you." Matthew lowers his arms and steps back, leaving only our fingers curled together. He tightens his grip on my right hand, then raises the other. "Double pinky promise."

I lift my hand until my wrists are crossed, opposite pinky fingers interlocked. Leo made this up—he'd make us do it whenever he thought we were playing a trick on him. One pinky wasn't enough for my little brother. He always made us do both. Over time, Matthew and I made it ours, too. It's an unbreakable promise, a sacred vow that means we're being 100 percent honest with each other.

I nod, giving his pinkies a squeeze with mine before lowering my hands. Matthew smiles. "Go get Lyla. I'll be here when you get back."

I nod, still reeling from the kiss. *From everything.* "You better be."

I get in the car and start it, pulse racing, and feeling more alive than I've ever been. I roll down the window. "Hey, neighbor?"

"Yes, neighbor?"

I motion for him to lean down. When he does, I grab the collar of his shirt, pull him close, and kiss him. Hard. I let go. "I love you."

The way he gazes at me is so perfect that for a moment I forget the past, the guilt and the scars and the blood that ran down the pavement like paint.

"I love you, too."

I could die in his eyes right here and now, but Lyla's waiting for me. Matthew thumps the roof of the car again and goes back up the hill toward his house. I regain my senses enough to start toward South-880.

Matthew loves me, and we're going to join the Herons together.

Tonight is destiny, I think, remembering Lyla's words. *Tonight is fate.*

I lean back in my seat as San Francisco whizzes by me. I recount all the facts about the Wars I've spent the past years memorizing, as if that will align the stars in my favor. There's a "fan" site and Twitter accounts filled with internet denizens who keep tabs on the Wars from the safety of their screens. I follow them all and did research of my own.

The Herons were the first of the gangs. From what I've read online, it was originally a club for burgeoning tech start-ups— a place where they could meet up, exchange ideas, and swap condolences when projects failed. Matthew's dad, Richard Weston, was one of the founding members.

Then came the dot-com boom of the nineties. Having the connections—rather, the right money in the right pockets— was everything. Herons funded some of the first supercomputers. Matthew's parents met Steve Jobs and Woz long before they were household names.

Over time, being a Heron went from a bragging right to a point by which people defined themselves. The Herons got so popular that there was a fee to join. The fee doubled then tripled overnight, quickly entering into the hundreds of thousands. Some resisted the change, but most scraped at the pearly gates that was the Heron Club with eager hands. Every company would bring their device, website, and software to the Heron Club altar—aka their investing board.

Tech moguls either were Herons or not Herons—which didn't matter to everyone, of course. But when it did matter, it *really* did. Families grew into dynasties, and people like Matthew have never known otherwise.

The second gang, the Boars, started off as a joke—an "everyman's" club without the snooty air that the Herons had. Where the techies in the Herons come from the South Bay or out of state, the Boars pride themselves on being true San Franciscans. Anyone born in SF can be a part of it. From what I can tell online, they don't really *do* much except petition against the Herons' new building projects and shout at them on the streets.

Then around ten years ago something changed, and the two groups went from arguments in town halls to beatings on the street, armed robberies, and storefronts being burned or broken into. People stopped joking about being in the Boars: if you were one, you were dangerous and proud of it.

Neighborhoods were claimed by one gang or another, the bus stops and trash cans emblazoned with Boar or Heron insignias. Fights started, escalating until the police got involved, and the Boars shrank down to almost nothing. A reporter from the *San Francisco Chronicle* wrote an op-ed suggesting that the police give the Herons more leeway because so many of them donate to police programs. I don't doubt it.

It's not hard to spot the Herons out and around town. They always dress in pristine ivory clothes like they've just walked off the pages of a Ralph Lauren catalogue. That's the Heron color—white. Clean as they want the public to think they are.

The public members of the club—at Facebook, Twitter, and the rest—maintain an ironclad stance that they are not at all affiliated with the group of misguided teens calling themselves the Young Herons. It's the latter that actually take to the streets and butt heads with the Boars.

Where Herons wear white, the Boars' uniform is gray hoodies with red stripes down the side. I've seen folks on BART board a train only to get off when they see a Boar in the same car. People would rather miss their meeting or be late coming home than be on the same train as a Boar.

No one knows much about the third gang, the Stags. The Stags wear black—but then again, so does every other North Face–wearing city dweller. They've only been around a few years. Dad doesn't even think they're real. "Just a bunch of wannabes," he says.

I slam my hand down on the radio dial, shutting it off. In so many ways, the Boars ruined my life—without them, I wouldn't know any of these facts. I'd be like everyone else: worrying what colleges I'll get into, what I want for Christmas, or what color my prom dress is going to be. Maybe I'd still be planning the vacation to the one place I want to go to more than anywhere else. Fortunate as I was to grow up in a house where we took regular vacations, there was one place I had always wanted to go but never figured out how: the Philippines, where my mom grew up.

I envisioned Mom, Dad, and Leo walking with me down dirt paths, breathing in the tropical humid air and catching glimpses of the sea between patches of dense trees. I wanted to experience the chaos of city life, but also the quieter regions and even those that cater to tourists. My phone screen background was a picture of the blue jewel waters of Cebu.

Even though my Tagalog is spotty at best, for a long time I've known that I'm not going to be complete unless I visit. A lifetime of school projects about "what countries are you from" had only fostered that desire to go.

But all my dreams of new horizons died with Leo.

My eyes start to tear up, but I blink it away. *Don't, Val. Focus.*

I come to a stoplight, and the car behind me flashes its lights. My body tenses—I've heard the horror stories of people stopping for a weird reason and getting kidnapped—or worse.

But what if it's the Herons?

The stoplight turns green and I keep an eye on the car behind me. It flashes its lights again. This time, someone waves, a white sleeve out the window.

It's got to be them, I think. How did they know where I was? Doesn't matter—it's finally happening.

The speeding lights of the freeway beckon ahead of me, but I pull over onto a side street. This time, the car behind me blinks its lights repeatedly, which I take as a good sign. When I come to a stop, the other car does, too.

Almost immediately, another two cars swerve out from around it, cutting in front of me and blocking my side. Figures burst from the cars, and none of them are wearing white. Even the first driver I spotted seems to have disappeared into the throng.

"Fuck." I start my car again. This is for sure how people die. "Oh my god." I shift the gear with a hand that's already sweaty from panic. Pressing down hard on the gas pedal, I lurch out of my parking spot only to slam on the brakes— instinct alone saves me from running over the third figure who steps out in front of me.

Someone taps at my window. A pair of mean eyes peers at me from above a red bandana covering the guy's nose and mouth. His hood is up. His gray hood.

He taps the window again just as another Boar tries to open the passenger side, but it's locked. Every part of me trembles.

"This doesn't make any sense." *The Boars would never recruit me. Not after Leo.*

The guy who first approached me pounds the window then twists his hand twice. When I don't react, he slams a gun into the window so hard I am amazed it doesn't break. He makes the motion again. *Turn the engine off.* I nod to show I understand.

Reaching for the key, my car shudders into silence. I check the rearview, looking for a Heron in white to step out, challenge the Boars, and take me to my new home. The irony of my angel-seeking isn't lost on me.

"Come on, Matthew," I whisper. "Please."

The first Boar opens the driver's side door. "Get out."

"What do you want?"

"Out!"

When I don't move, he grabs my hair, undoes my seat belt, and yanks me sideways. He tosses me to the ground like I'm nothing, and my knees scrape against the concrete through the fabric of my jeans.

"Okay, okay!" I shout, raising my hands over my head. I turn to run—but I'm surrounded. The ghostly gray-and-red figures watch me, grinning and nodding toward each other. I tense my muscles to keep them from shaking, but it's no use. "I decline your offer to join," I say. "I do not accept."

The Boars explode into wild, raucous laughter—I'm the funniest person alive. The first Boar-guy steps up, reaches into his waistband, and pulls out a black handgun. He points it at my chest, and I stagger back, screaming.

"No one said this was an offer to join," he says. "Get on your knees."

"Please, don't. W-what did I do? Why me?"

"On. Your. Knees."

"Why my family? What have we ever done to you?!"

He cocks the gun to the side like they do in the movies.

My breath skims in my lungs as my mind flashes through a jigsaw puzzle of memories: a little body splayed on a sidewalk, a nice family dressed all in black, a neighbor who brushed away tears . . .

I'm so sorry, Leo.

There is a gunshot.

The Boar screams and clutches his arm as blood gushes from his shoulder.

The Boars scatter. Moments later someone grabs me, lifting me from the ground. My ears ring, and I look at him—he's not wearing white, but quite the opposite.

"The Stags?" I wonder aloud.

The guy holding me sets me down behind a parked car. "Stay here," he says, pushing a lock of gelled hair back into place. He grips my shoulders as if I didn't hear him. "Don't. Move."

He darts back toward the mixing sea of gray and black figures, staying low. I do my best to do the same, flattening myself between the ground and a blue Honda Civic. I scrape my hands on the sidewalk to steady myself.

This is real. This feeling, these sounds. The Boars. The Stags. All real.

An unfamiliar scent permeates the air. I never knew what gunpowder smelled like.

Just as I root myself into the chaos, the sounds fade to nothing. Blood pounds in my ears as I wait for a Boar to find me and finish what they started.

But nothing happens. Then I hear talking.

Scooting forward, I peek around the car's bumper. The Boar who pulled me out of the car steps forward to meet one of the Stags face-to-face. The rest of the gang members keep still, giving the two a wide berth. The Boar puts away his gun. The Stag doesn't seem to have a weapon at all. The

Stag shoves the other guy's shoulder, but the Boar doesn't retaliate.

Someone taps my shoulder. It's another Stag—a girl—and she looks bored.

"Get up," she says. "No one's killing you today."

A siren wails from around the corner. At the sound, the bleeding Boar and the Stag dart opposite ways, the latter headed right toward me. As he approaches, other Stags emerge from their hiding places, and my head spins as I count them. Five.

"Valerie Simons," says the first Stag. "I, Jax, do hereby offer you a place in the Wars among the Stags. If you accept, you are inked. You are bound for one year. After one year, you are free to leave if you choose. Do you accept?"

My heartbeat drums in my head. Where are the Herons? I back away from him. "What . . . what time is it?"

The leader—Jax—is unfazed by my question. He glances at the female Stag behind me.

"Ten fifty-eight," she says.

Just an hour left. Can I take that chance? I'm trembling again, the worst of Cinderellas, eyes scanning for any sign of the Herons. Blue-and-red lights shine from one street over.

"Do you accept?" Jax shouts.

It's not the Herons, but it's not the Boars either. *There's just one thing—*

"My brother," I say. "His name was Leo Simons. He died in a Boar crossfire. Do you know who killed him?"

Jax smiles, slow and sinister. "Yes."

"Then I accept."

I don't have time to process what I've just done. The female Stag reaches up around me and covers my mouth with a cloth smelling of acid and heartache.

I black out.

2

When I come to, I'm lying on a couch inside a dimly lit living room that smells like coffee and pot. The furniture looks like it was found on the sidewalk—a pair of sagging, orange love seats, a gray swivel chair unfit for the saddest of offices, and a large papasan. The big-screen LED television is new, however. A tangle of black video game consoles and wires spreads out on the floor.

The only other thing that isn't sad and worn is the spray-painted beast on the wall to my right.

The giant stag image faces me, its eyes wide and watchful, with antlers curling up toward the ceiling. The one on the right is jagged, even more than it should be. Thorns. The left antler isn't an antler at all, but a curling feather.

I've seen the image before—tags on BART station walls and freeway overpasses. Everyone in the city knows the gang's signs, even if they pretend not to. The wild slashes of the Boars, the curling wings of the Herons, and the pensive gaze of the Stags.

But this one is different. This is art, exquisite and alive.

I get up and scan the room again, trying to keep calm. My hands go to my pockets.

"Where's my phone?" The light coming through the glass of the front door is a pale blue, so I'll safely guess it's morning.

If I had a watch, I'd check it, but Dad noticed my thing about time a while ago and gets upset when I wear one, so instead I just keep my phone on me at all times. I pat my pockets again, my anxiety churning. "What time is it?"

"Seven thirty-one," a voice answers.

The female Stag from last night stands in the adjacent hallway, a cup of coffee in her hand. Her wavy hair is covered by an army-green bandana, while a white crop top shows off a stomach that would make veteran yogis proud. The tips of antlers poke up from her left hip. Her Stag tattoo—dark ink on dark skin.

"Where am I?" I ask.

"Ingleside."

I place myself on a mental map of the city. Home is in the Marina District—not too far away, all things considered, though nothing in SF is really that far away. "Where's my phone?"

"Destroyed. We'll give you a new one."

"Destroyed?" I repeat. "I had photos on there. Texts. How am I going to call . . . I mean, you can't just do that." *Mom. Dad. Lyla. MATTHEW.* I need to let them know I'm okay.

The female Stag's expression clouds into a mixture of anger and amusement. "Jax does whatever he wants. You'd better get used to that or you won't make it through your year."

One year. That's what I've agreed to, isn't it? It's the same rules that the Herons and Boars have. You serve from the day you turn eighteen to the day you turn nineteen.

"I'm Nianna," the girl says. She pronounces it slowly— NEE-ann-uh—like I'm too dumb to get it on my own.

"Valerie." I take a few steps toward her and shake her hand. Another tattoo reveals itself from the underside of her wrist—a slim, finely rendered arrow with feathering at the end. "How long have you been a Stag?"

"Eight months." She smiles. "Long enough to have seen it all."

Nianna lets her reply hang in the air as other footsteps sound from the hall. A guy and girl—their disheveled hair and clothes screaming "couple"—step around Nianna. The guy is stocky with tan skin. He's just a little taller than his companion, though he slouches quite a bit. Locks of black hair stick out from beneath a backward baseball cap.

"Jesus, don't you sleep?" the guy asks.

Nianna shrugs and sips from her cup. "Coffee's on."

"Oh, fuck yes."

The girl he is with zips up her hoodie. "Valerie, right? I'm Kate." She shakes my hand. "Nice to meet you."

Kate has long Rapunzel-style hair—a shiny veil of gold that moves when she moves. It reaches all the way down to her waist but in a light, casual way. Like she doesn't care, and you can't make her.

"Nice to meet you, too," I say.

"That's Mako." She points at the guy. "You hungry? Babe, cook us something."

"What do you want?"

Kate looks to me for an answer.

"Oh, anything. Anything's fine," I say. "Actually, what I could really use is a phone."

"We told your mom, if that's what you're worried about. Your stuff's here, too. We got it when we drove your car back."

My car. My stuff. They went back to my house without me.

My heart lurches as I picture Mom in that old robe that she used to let me wear when I was sick—so, so alone—opening the front door and seeing strangers. There's no universe in which she didn't cry. No universe in which she did not beg them to change their minds. I suck in my bottom lip. Mom didn't ask for this. She didn't ask for any of it.

"Bacon and eggs will do, Mako," Kate says. "Veggie for me."

"Fake bacon for the lady."

Mako gets to work in the kitchen as Kate takes my hand. "Come on. I'll show you your room."

She leads me down the short hallway, passing a bathroom and shower. Opening a side door, she starts down a staircase leading into a basement. "You get the den."

The *den* is really the garage. It's about as warm as an icebox and crowded with old lawn furniture and cardboard boxes of who knows what. By the door, there's a set of heavy weights and a space for working out.

In the corner between two Japanese folding screens is a twin bed with sheets folded on top of it. My suitcases are stacked beside it, a bright orange paper crane resting on top of them. I don't know what to make of that.

I swallow—I thought I'd be unpacking in a room for a Heron. Clean, safe. Matthew at my side. I push my nails into my palm. The Herons didn't come for me, but I know they came for Matthew. Should I have turned the Stags down?

"Hey, Kate?"

She frowns, eyes to the ground, as her finger examines a pimple on her cheek. "Yeah?"

"How often do the other gangs, uh, meet up, I guess? Like if I wanted to talk to one of them."

She shrugs. "All that has to go through Jax. But we don't usually talk to them so much as fuck with their plans."

"Oh. Okay. Thanks."

"No prob. I'll let you get settled. Ooh." She leans down and rustles through one of the boxes, pulling out a purple vase. She wipes the dust on her shirt. "Feel free to keep anything you find. I don't even know where all this came from. Come up in a bit, though. The boy makes a mean breakfast."

"Okay. Thanks."

Kate leaves in a swirl of blond, the stairs creaking under her bare feet as she goes.

The door shuts behind her, and I shiver. My eyes go to my suitcases, and something other than reason moves me toward them. I open the top pocket of the smaller bag and reach into it. My fingers wrap around cool metal.

The pocketknife feels good in my hand. Steady and just *there*. Underneath the denim of my jeans, a ladder of scars tingles with anticipation.

No. I set the knife back in the pocket. I don't need that quite yet.

Instead, I find a clean-ish rag and a bottle of glass cleaner. Kicking a box out of the way, I go over to the window and scrub the dirt and cobwebs until light shines through. I hear the steps creak again.

"Breakfast?" I ask Kate. Then I turn. It's not Kate.

Jax has his hands in his jean pockets. His freshly washed gold hair falls down to his collarbone, and a towel hangs over one of his bare shoulders. He's at least a head taller than me and walks with his head held high, as if he has no equals. I can't help but scan his muscled torso—slim but toned, like the guys on the swim team. Plaid boxers peek out at his hips by that V-shaped muscle guys have that I've never understood. His Stag tattoo blazes over his heart, proud and unafraid.

I was in too much shock to realize it last night. But Jax isn't just attractive—he's the hottest guy I've ever seen. The slight brush of stubble against his jaw makes his face more angular, and I wonder how much older he is than me.

"Like the place?" he asks.

"Sure," I say. "Yeah. It's good. It's fine. Thanks."

His eyes go to the rag in my hand and he smiles, bemused. "Down here two minutes, and that's the first thing you do?"

"They were dirty." *Stunning opening, Val.* "And it's so dark in here. I need all the light I can get."

Jax takes a step back and flicks a switch on the post by the stairs. White-blue florescent lights buzz to life.

"Oh," I say. *Stupid.* "Thanks."

"Don't mention it," he says. He steps closer to me again. "So. You've wanted this for a long time, haven't you?"

I blush—because how can I not?—and try to maintain eye contact while this very attractive, very shirtless guy talks to me. "What do you mean?"

"To join the Wars. I've been watching you." He fiddles with the zipper of my suitcase.

"Yeah, I guess. I mean, I didn't ask anyone to be watching me," I say. "I'm here for my brother. I want to get even."

"I know."

He does? "Can you tell me who it is? The guy who killed him? I mean, was it even a guy? I know most of the members are guys but—"

Jax shakes his head. "I'm not telling you any of that."

I frown. "But you said you knew who it was."

"I do," he replies. "But you're not ready to know."

"Yes, I am," I say. "Please tell me. I have to know."

"Ah, see," Jax says. "We have to straighten some things out first." He lunges toward me, pushing me back until I'm trapped between him and the wall.

"Hey!" I try to shove him back, but he pins my wrists to my sides and heat rushes to my face—there's nowhere safe to look. So I look at him right in the eyes.

"First thing you need to know," Jax says, "is that you don't give the orders. I do. And you will obey every command. You will never go against me." He lets go of one of my wrists and runs two fingers down my cheek. "You're a Stag now, Valerie Simons. Now tell me you understand."

I wish I weren't shaking. I nod.

"As for your brother—yeah, I know who killed him. It wasn't right, and I want you to be the one to kill him and get your revenge. But if I told you now, you'd run off, do something stupid, and get killed on my watch. Not gonna happen."

"I wouldn't do that."

"Yeah you would. Or you'd go to Weston and have him take care of it. Either way, you'd run. And yeah, I know about Weston."

I swallow. Is he right? I'm not completely stupid—I don't know how I'd find this person once I knew who it was, but I'd sure as hell do *something*.

Jax leans back, easing the pressure off my wrists. "I'm a man of my word, Valerie Simons. I promise to tell you when you're ready. When I know you're loyal to your crew and that you won't run. Until then, you're mine."

Shit. I want to say many things, like how long he thinks it'll take for me to be ready, or what if I promise not to run, but I'm smarter than that. Jax is a leader of a gang—one wrong word and I could wind up on his bad side and then he'll never tell me. *Do this, do it for Leo.*

"I understand," I say finally.

His shoulders drop, and he steps back from me. "That wasn't so hard, right? You're one of mine now. I'll take care of you. You get your tattoo tonight."

"Tonight?" I knew the tattoo was coming—one thing all three gangs agree on is that their members be tattooed. I guess that's standard gang MO, but I think it's a mental test, more than anything. *Once you're in, you can't back out.*

Jax answers my questions with a nod. "You're in for one year. If you change your mind and try to run anyway, I'll alert the other leaders. Then anyone is green-lit to kill you. And even if you get away, there's nothing that says a gang can't make things rough for your folks. And I couldn't protect them." His implication is clear—he wouldn't protect them if I'd been disloyal. "Understand?"

Mom and Dad. They deserve so much better than to be added to the Wars' crimson tally. If my staying here protects them, then I would stay for the rest of my life.

"Yes," I reply firmly. "I understand."

"Good girl," Jax says. "We're not so bad, Valerie Simons. And no one's going to mess with you now that you're one of mine." He smiles. "You hungry?"

Mealtime is . . . surprisingly organized.

Kate and Nianna get the silverware while Mako sets down platters of eggs, bacon, sausage, toast, and even fresh fruit. On top of that, there's coffee and a pitcher of orange juice. My stomach rumbles. The last thing I ate was cake with Mom.

"Sit." Jax points to a seat.

Not forgetting our exchange a minute ago, I do as I'm told. The others jostle around me, and I'm feeling more than a little useless when I hear the slow shuffle of someone who just got out of bed.

"The best of us awakes!" Jax exclaims.

The guy behind me is lanky with short, black hair. He's in faded jeans and a loose green sweatshirt that says BOLINAS, which I know is north of the city but I'm not sure where exactly. His arms and hands are covered in tattoos.

"Hullo," he says, taking the seat next to mine. "Micah."

"Valerie."

We shake hands. His skin is warm from a cozy sleep. As the Stags take their seats, I count them. Five, just like last night. I lean over to Micah.

"Where's everyone else?"

"Everyone else?"

"Aren't there more of you?"

"Just one more here. Jaws. You won't see him much. But you'll know when you do."

"So . . . six?"

"Seven, with you. The other Stags are at different safe houses." He moves his head from side to side as he thinks. "Plus, I guess a few more that are technically out, but we could call on them if we needed to."

"Oh. Okay." That's . . . unsettling. I knew the Boars were the largest group—the reports I've read estimate that there are between seventy and a hundred Boars. The Herons are harder to pin down since they're more careful, but I guess there's at least fifty or so. I would have thought the Stags were at least as big as that.

Looking back at Micah, my eyes travel up the tattoos on his hands and forearms. "Where do you want yours?" he asks.

"Oh." I look down at my body. "You know, I'm not sure."

I wanted the Heron tattoo on my back. The wings spread out on my shoulder blades. Elegant and eternal. I guess the stag's antlers could do the same.

Micah reaches toward me. "Lean forward."

When I do, he touches the soft skin on the back of my neck, right below my hairline. Goose bumps shoot down my spine.

"Here," he says. "That's your spot."

"How do you know?"

"I always do. Artist's intuition."

"It's true," Kate says as she sits. She unzips her sweatshirt and tugs up the loose fabric of her tank top, revealing the stag emblem on her rib cage. "I didn't know where I wanted mine either, but I love having mine there. Micah has a gift."

"Yeah, okay," Micah replies sarcastically, but he's smiling.

"You do the tattoos?" I ask. "I figured the gangs had, like, an outside guy."

"Nope," he says, smiling. "I'm the guy."

Jax sits down at the head of the table and lifts a glass. "To you, Valerie Simons. Welcome home." The others raise their glasses. Next to him, Nianna sips hers without taking her eyes off Jax. Their chairs are close, but neither seems bothered by the proximity.

The five of them tear into the food. I fill my plate once and then a second time. With each bite, my determination returns a little more.

This isn't so bad. It feels kind of like summer camp. Only with older cabin mates who may or may not have killed before.

I can do this, I remind myself. Besides, this isn't about me. It's about Leo. And if I have to play along until Jax is satisfied, then so be it.

After breakfast, the group dumps their plates in the sink and goes to do their own thing. I set my own plate in the dishwasher and rinse the rest. When I'm done, I turn to the others for instruction.

"I guess I'll unpack, then?" I ask Micah, who's the only one still in the kitchen with me.

He finishes the text he was working on and tucks his phone in his pocket. "You want help unpacking?"

"Oh." *That's nice.* "Sure. Thanks."

We go downstairs. A set of drawers just beside the bed doubles as a nightstand. Even when all my clothes are unpacked, there's tons of extra space. I hurry and tuck away all the white and off-white clothing I packed, tags still on them. How could I have never even entertained the idea that I'd be recruited by another gang?

I take out the rest—my makeup, my best jewelry, and all the other absurd things I thought I'd need as a Heron. Micah slides the big suitcase under the bed and gives the smaller one a final shake. My last two possessions *thunk* around, and he raises an eyebrow.

"Just some books," I lie. "Just leave them in there."

"Okay." He slides it next to the other one then sets his hands on his hips. "That it?"

"That's it." My eyes scan the chaotic room, and my anxiety rises in turn. "Do you think . . . I mean, can I clean up some of this?"

"I don't think anyone'll care, if that's what you're worried about."

Micah retrieves some Hefty bags from the kitchen. I stuff handfuls of junk into the bags and break down boxes. There's a little bit of everything—a pair of tennis shoes with dirt caked on the bottoms; a down comforter without a duvet cover over it; a framed photo of some girl with short black hair smiling with the Golden Gate behind her, the setting sun casting light across half her face. I set the last of these in the garbage more reverently—probably some poor girlfriend of a Stag long gone. I wonder if that Stag lived in this very space, and threw out someone else's memento. *Will someone throw out mine someday?*

"So," I ask Micah. "How long have you been in the Stags?"

"Since the beginning," he says. "About three years."

"What?" I say. "I thought gang members just did one year."

"Most do, but I won't leave until Jax does."

"Why not?"

He smiles. "We go way back. He's basically my brother. He asked me to join, and I did."

My mind buzzes with questions, but from his tone I can tell he's done talking about it. Picking up a strand of Christmas lights I'd found earlier, we string them along the wall. It's like decorating a dorm . . . if decorating a dorm was done with strangers and that dorm was actually a basement in a house of criminals. I watch as Micah shoves a pushpin into the wall and drapes the strand of lights over it. Frowning, he takes out the pin and moves it down half an inch.

"Thank you for helping," I say. "I . . . I never really thought I'd be here."

"You didn't think you'd get recruited?" Micah straightens a corner of my new bedspread before sitting down on the edge.

"Oh. No, I hoped to be. I just thought . . . well, I wanted to be a Heron."

He raises an eyebrow.

"It's just . . . I always thought I'd be one," I stammer. "My ex—he's the son of a big Heron family." *He told me he loves me, and I love him.*

"What's his name?"

"Matthew. Matthew Weston."

"Alex Weston's brother."

"Yes," I say. "That's him. How'd you know?"

"The Westons are Herons, through and through." Micah shakes his head. "I'm sorry, Valerie, but he's definitely a Young Heron by now."

Somewhere in my heart and head I already knew, but knowing something and being told it's true are different. It's like hearing about a car accident versus being in one. I hug myself at the elbows and try to remember the warmth of Matthew's body, his kiss. *I wish we'd had more time before I left . . .*

The upstairs door opens. "Jax wants you," Nianna calls to Micah.

"All right." He gets up. "See you later, Valerie. Pick a place." He taps the back of his neck—one of the rare areas on his body that's not tattooed—and disappears up the stairs. Nianna comes and stands in front of me, her hands on her hips.

"All unpacked?"

"Just about."

"Good. Look at me." She raises her chin as I do. "I'll say this once: I don't think you should have been recruited. But Jax insisted. So I'm going to insist on a few things, too."

"Jax already went over this." I wish I didn't sound so defensive.

"This is different."

I grit my teeth. "All right, fine. Shoot."

"First, never cross me or I'll gut you like a fish."

I have to force myself not to laugh. Gut me like a fish? Who says that other than old mobsters in the movies? "Um, okay. Sure."

"Next, don't do anything that could get another Stag killed. Don't be reckless, but don't be a coward either. Do what you are told."

"Okay."

"Last thing." She exhales like an angry bull. "Don't fall in love with Jax."

This time I don't have the control to stop myself from laughing. Sure, he's hot, but the guy is insane. Volatile—it's not one of my favorite words.

"That won't be a problem, Nianna." I tack on her name with bite.

"It better not be."

She goes back up the stairs without another word. The door shuts behind her, and I finish my laugh. *Fall in love with Jax? No way.* There's someone else in my heart already, thank you very much.

I pull a sweater from my new drawers and start to tug it on when the scent hits me. Pausing, I bring the soft fabric to my nose and inhale. It smells like lavender detergent. Like Mom and Dad and home. I shut my eyes as my heart crumples like an old newspaper.

I fall back onto the bed, springs creaking with every movement. Somehow, it makes everything worse. This is not my bed, not my room. Only it is. It is for the next 364 days. I sob into the sweater, letting it muffle the sound.

What's Mom doing now? Dad isn't home yet. God, I hope she's with someone. One of the fundraising ladies, like *Tita* Patty. As long as she's not alone.

My knife beckons from its place underneath the bed, but I fight the urge. Instead, I take out the smaller suitcase and open the main pocket. I root around until I find what I told Micah to leave inside. Pulling out the photo album from a side pocket, I place it in my lap like a gift from some unnamed deity.

I try and steady my breath as I flip through the glossy memories. Mom, Dad, and a seven-year-old me in front of the carousel at the Santa Cruz Beach Boardwalk. A selfie of Lyla and me at a Giants game. Backstage pix with the theater club. Matthew and me with Leo after his Little League team won their playoff game—Matt had coached him. Then another photo of Matthew and me at Ocean Beach, just a few weeks before we broke up. He has his arm around me.

One final photo, hidden in the back. Leo's smile always was too big for his face. Once, when he was still a toddler, Leo ignored me for a whole day. No talking to me, no trying to tug my hair. It was like I didn't exist to him.

Until, as I was leaving to go to a movie with a friend and her parents, he took my hand and laid it on his. My palm to his palm. My wrist to his wrist. The lattice of our veins pulsed our shared blood in time with each other. An hour later in a darkened theater, I could still feel the whispery magic of that moment.

The ache batters around my rib cage then tumbles from my throat. *Leo.*

I put the album back under the bed then curl onto my side. Tightening further into a ball, I wipe my eyes and nose.

I loved my little brother more than I have loved anything before or since.

And then I killed him.

3

A light touch on my arm jolts me awake.

"Sorry," Micah says. He steps back. "How long have you been asleep?"

I sit up and stretch out my shoulder, numb from how I was positioned. "I don't know. I don't have a clock. Or a phone."

"Ah," he says. "Well, I can help with that."

He reaches into his back pocket and hands me an old phone. No apps, no frills. Under Contacts, there are a few numbers already added in. Jax. Micah, Nianna, and the rest. A taxi company. Home.

"It's programmed so you can only call the numbers that are in there," he tells me. "You must answer any call you receive. Read every text, but don't reply unless it's one of us."

"I can't call anyone else? What about texts?"

"Only the numbers in there. No texting anyone else." He must see the disappointment on my face. "Sorry. You can go online and everything, but no social media posting. For obvious reasons. Jax finds out . . . well, you can guess."

I certainly can. "Okay," I reply, nodding. "Anything else?"

"Just this." He tucks his hand into his pockets then tosses me something. I catch it just before it hits me in the face.

"What the—"

He chuckles. It's a good sound, like a firm handshake and a hug at the same time. "Sorry, should have warned you."

I swear when I see what it is. The wad of bills is barely held together by a blue rubber band, like the ones that come with produce. "What's this?"

"Money."

"Well, yeah." I fan out the bills. It's a mix of ones and fives, though a pair of hundreds is hidden in the stack. "I mean, what's it for?"

"Anything you want," he replies. "Jax gives all of us cash here and there. When he feels like it. Here's your wallet, too."

I take it—all my cards are gone except for my ID and library card. "Seriously?" I say, motioning to the latter. Micah shrugs and I start stuffing the bills inside. "Where does Jax get the cash from?"

"His mom."

"Really?" It's weird to think of Jax having family—but of course he would. "And she just . . . gives it to him?"

"Yeah."

"Does she know what he does with it?"

"Yeah. She does. But he's all she's got. There's nothing she wouldn't do for Jax. You'll meet her, probably. Theresa likes to surprise us all with a visit here and there." He taps the phone in my hand. "You want to call home?"

Jax's mom vanishes from my mind—*home*. My fingers shake as I hit the screen. Micah wanders from me and stares absently out the windows. There's not much to see other than a bundle of thorny bushes, but I appreciate the attempt at looking busy.

Mom picks up on the second ring. "Hello?"

"Mom?"

"Val? Oh, thank God. Are you all right? Where are you?"

"I'm fine. Uh . . . I'm not sure I can tell you where I am."

Over at the window, Micah shakes his head.

"All these years, I didn't think . . . I didn't think you'd go. I thought I would be able to stop you." She steadies herself. "But you're safe, right? I was so worried. Is Matthew there? Can I talk to him? Heather was just here."

It catches me off guard to hear Matthew's mother's first name—to me, she's always Mrs. Weston. But that's not the reason my blood stops cold.

Mom thinks Matthew is with me.

She thinks I'm a Heron.

I clap a hand over my mouth. Why didn't Mrs. Weston tell her? Better yet, why didn't Jax tell her when they got my stuff?

Shifting the phone to my other hand, I take a deep breath. "No, he's not here. Mom. I got recruited by the Stags, not the Herons."

"The Stags?"

"Yes."

"But your father said—"

"I know. I thought so, too. They met me on my way to the airport. The Stags did." It's an easy decision to leave out the part where I was almost shot. "I don't know how they knew. But I'm one of them now." I hear her pulling a tissue from the box and wait. "Is Dad there?"

"No, he's still on the plane. He'll be back in a few hours. Please come home." She's crying again. "Don't do this. Please, *please* come back. I can't lose both of you."

"Mom, I'm going to make things right."

"It was not your fault, Val. Not. Your. Fault." She starts to fray. "If anything, it's mine. If we'd been around more, then you—"

I push my fingernails into my palm. "I should have been there." *I should have protected him. That's my job, as the big sister.*

Was my job.

"I should go now," I say.

"Oh, Valerie . . . you'll call again, won't you? I . . . I know you can't visit."

Of all the rules that the gangs have, Mom would know that one. "Of course I'll call again. As much as I can, Mom."

Out of my sight, Micah makes a sound between a laugh and a sigh.

"Val?"

"Yeah?"

She starts up again, but I'm done listening. Jax knows who killed Leo, and that's worth more to me than anything else right now.

"I'm staying, Mom. But I'll call. I promise. I love you, Mom."

"I love you, too, baby. Please, please come back."

"*Mahal kita,* Mama. I love you."

I hang up before I can hear any more. I'm not sure I'd be able to take it. God, I'm the worst person alive. I think of her friends—why don't I know any of their numbers by heart? Maybe I could sneak a call on a pay phone or something.

Dad is coming home tonight. It'll be fine. He'll come home and they'll read my note over again, and they'll understand why I've done what I've done.

Micah says nothing as he waits for me. When I finally meet his eyes, he's fiddling with one of the half-dozen piercings on his ears. "All good?"

"Yeah, I guess." I wipe my nose. "Best as it can be."

"Ah," he replies. "You want to get going, then?"

"Where?"

"Tattoo time."

"Right. Um, one sec."

Opening my meager set of belongings, I root around until I pull out a tan-colored fleece. I hesitate, and swap it for a black running jacket instead. I'm a Stag now. I better dress the part.

I go to the bathroom and toss my hair up into a messy bun then take two seconds to touch up my makeup. It's been a full day since I looked in a mirror and it shows. Frowning at the bags under my eyes, I pat on a bit of concealer then stash my stuff under the sink.

Over in the living room Jax lounges on one of the orange chairs facing the TV. His fingers race over a game controller. "Oh, come on!"

Next to him, Mako laughs, lifting his own controller as he sits up. Sounds of warfare blare from the screen. Nianna sits on the rug next to Jax while Kate braids her hair.

"We're ready to go," says Micah.

Jax nods. "Come straight back when you're done."

"Yes, sir."

I barely have time to slip on my Nikes before Micah ushers me out the door. As we walk out, we pass bunches of dying hydrangeas dotted with rust and wilted roses that have long since bloomed.

We walk down Holloway toward Plymouth. A nearby telephone pole is banded with a yellow stripe and the number of the bus we need. When it pulls up, Micah hands me the fare, and we both pay the driver.

Ingleside rolls by us in a blur of pastel houses, untended gardens, and precariously parked cars. We reach the BART station and get on a train toward downtown.

The train car's steady jolt and whir of acceleration lull me into a welcome calm. Even with the unflattering light and smell of stale air, I take some comfort in it. Grimy and grim— at least I know this. The blue-gray color of the seats is as familiar as that of my father's eyes.

Micah doesn't try to make conversation, but I don't mind. He doesn't seem like a guy who cares much for small talk. I settle into the quiet, feeling grateful at least that it's just him

with me. I'd hate for Nianna, or worst of all, Jax, to see me
squirm at the buzz of the needle.

"Does it hurt?" I ask. "Getting tattooed?"

Micah shrugs. "Less than you think."

"So it still hurts."

He laughs. "You'll be fine. Here." He reaches into his
pocket and pulls out a granola bar. "Eat this so you don't faint."

On cue, my stomach rumbles as I open it. "Oh. Thanks."

We get off at Sixteenth and Mission and ride the escalator
to the street. The Mission District is colorful—literally. Diego
Rivera–esque murals fill the alleyways between buildings and
at intersections. All the gangs leave these murals untouched.
Pink, yellow, and blue railings adorn the exit up toward street
level—an ode to the area's rich community. As we reach the
open air, I hold my breath to fight the smell of the vagrants
congregated outside the station. Most are harmless, even
polite, and heartbreakingly they're as much a part of the Mission as the murals.

As we walk, it's easy to tell which buildings have benefited
from the influx of money and which haven't. The former have
bold, stylish paint jobs and planter boxes bursting with suc-
culents. Beneath the bare tree branches, hip twentysomethings
in plaid shirts hold hands with their big-sweater-wearing
girlfriends, outnumbering the older, more worn natives. They
look like misplaced Barbie dolls next to the Hispanic markets
and Salvadorian restaurants.

We pass a woman holding a cardboard sign asking for
money, a baby strapped to her chest. I pause, find the wad of
bills in my pocket, and extract a hundred from the bunch. I
hand it to her.

"*Gracias,*" the woman says. Her eyes are red and rimmed
with tears. "Thank you."

I give her a small wave then catch up to Micah. He leads

us toward Valencia and beyond. The sky is a wash of pale pink. Clouds stretch in feathery wisps across the skies, but here the wind is mild. All things considered, it's a nice fall afternoon in San Francisco.

A few blocks later, Micah stops at a residential building. I hug myself at the elbows as he punches the intercom.

"Hello?" a voice crackles.

"Hey, it's me."

The door buzzes. Micah holds it open for me. Something in me hesitates. What the hell am I doing? The hallway above me is poorly lit—I can't see the end. There could be anything in there, or anyone. *Deep breaths.* Whatever's in there, I have to take. I *want* to take, to make things right. Matthew wouldn't be scared. He understood exactly what being in the Wars would mean, and so do I.

I take a step and hope.

The linoleum floor sticks to the bottom of my shoes, and I steel myself from asking about the cleanliness of the place. Micah follows right behind me. He greets a guy standing at the top of the stairs in front of a pair of doors.

"What's up, man?" They hug, and Micah thumps the guy twice on the back.

"Not much. Business as usual." The guy holds up a key. "It's just the way you left it."

"Thanks. Is Jules here?"

"Nah, you just missed her." The guy nods to me, his eyes traveling up and down my body in the quick way guys don't think girls notice. "Hey, newbie. I'm Kurt."

I shake his hand when he offers it. "Valerie."

He makes a show of tugging his sleeve until I see the Stag tattoo on his bicep. "This is 2H—second headquarters. Jax isn't that clever when it comes to names."

"Don't say that near him," Micah fires back, and the two

laugh. Kurt looks back at me. "This may not look like much, but it's safe. You've been on like three cameras in the past two minutes. Walls have been reinforced, and we've got stock here."

"Plus one of the stairs is a trick step," says Micah. "Flip a switch and it becomes a slide."

"Oh yeah, totally. That's our biggest defense."

I crack a smile. "Cool. Thanks."

"Anyway," says Kurt, "my number's in your phone. If you ever need me, just holler."

"Great. Thanks."

Micah's unlocked the door and holds it open for me. *This* room is pristine. Afternoon light from the retreating sun illuminates a dark leather chair next to a stool and table. Vials of ink stand like colorful paladins next to a tray of needle guns. On curling papers tacked to the walls, one design repeats itself over and over: a stag with antlers of thorns and feathers.

The Stag emblem's history from rough to refined plays itself out over the length of the room. Closest to the door, the sketches are unpolished—stags with round eyes, then diamond ones. Whole-bodied silhouettes leaping in the air like old-timey heraldry. Closer to the shuttered window, the current one, the official emblem, makes its first appearance.

From then on, it's all the same, with only tiny refinements. Switching the thorns and the feather. Switching them back. An unspoken energy sings through each paper, and the images tremble with a vitality all their own.

"This is amazing," I say. "How did you learn to draw like this?"

"Been drawing my whole life," he replies. "I was *that kid* in all my art classes."

I sense a hint of sadness in his words, but he's already moved on, busying himself with getting everything organized.

"Well, they're wonderful," I say. "How did you learn to tattoo?"

"Early on when the Stags were just starting, we had a lot more time. Found a guy who took me on as an apprentice."

"Well no wonder," I reply. "You're super talented."

He smiles cheerily. "Thank you," he says, patting the arm of the chair. "Glad you appreciate it. Now sit."

I take off my jacket and settle into the chair, and Micah moves in like he's in a trance. He pulls out bottles of rubbing alcohol and cleaner, a roll of paper towels, a large white box he tells me is a light box for tracing, and a few blank pieces of paper. The last of these he shoves into the mouth of a printer tucked below the desk. It's so clear he loves this.

"So, arm, neck, or elsewhere?" he asks, plugging in the light box. Switching it on, he lays a printout on the bottom and the tracing paper on top. He follows the lines, face so close to the page that I wonder if he can even see the image.

The stag Micah's drawn for me demands to be seen. It stares out at me, the feather antler soft yet bold whereas the one of thorns is all edge.

I'm so in awe at seeing a master at work that I forget to respond. "Oh. Back of the neck. Like you said."

"It'll hurt more. On the spine."

"You said it didn't hurt."

"I said it hurts less than you think."

I take a breath. "Back of the neck. Not too big, though."

"I can't go too small. It'll wreck the detail."

"Oh. Okay. Um. Small as you can then."

Micah puts his hands on my neck, measuring it out with his fingers. I picture his brain whirring and flowing with artistic ease. "All right. Give me a sec."

I close my eyes as he does his thing. I thought I'd be more nervous—but no, this is necessary. Tattoos are part of the deal.

"Are you sure you want to do this?" he asks.

"Back of the neck? Yeah, I'm sure."

"I mean be a Stag."

"Yeah."

He takes a moment to respond. "You know there's no going back, after this."

No, there certainly isn't. I grit my teeth. "I know. But I have to do this. I'm ready."

Micah shows me the outline and, once I approve, presses it to my skin, then wipes it away and does it again. I don't mind him taking his time. It's my skin, after all. He presses on my neck again.

"So it'll be this wide, this tall. I've got a mirror if you want to see."

"I trust you. Let's do it."

"All right, get ready." There's a buzzing sound by my ear. Micah's fingers press down, and the first bites of metal tear into me.

He was right—it hurts less than I expected. I smile inwardly. *This isn't even as bad as what I do to myself.* Ah—never mind. That hurts. Oh man. I keep my body as still as possible as the needle gets hot. *Like I'm being branded,* I think, then I roll my eyes at my own stupidity, because that's exactly what's happening.

Micah wipes away the blood and ink. "Still with me?"

"Uh-huh." I focus on breathing—in, out.

By the end of it, nearly three hours have passed. Micah sets the tattoo gun down and rolls the chair back. "You're all done."

"Really?"

Micah peels off his gloves. "Yup."

"How's it look?"

"A masterpiece."

"Someone's humble."

"Hey, I have a gift, remember?" He laughs. "Or maybe Kate was wrong. Maybe I just drew a weird flying dolphin on your neck."

"Please, no."

"One sec." He takes out his phone and snaps a picture. He hands it to me. "Take a look."

"Oh my god." The tattoo is *gorgeous,* delicate yet strong. Even though it's the same design as everyone else's, I can't help but feel that this stag is mine, my own. Crafted just for me the way swords were forged for generals and kings.

"I can't stop staring at it. It's incredible." I turn to Micah. "Thank you."

"You're welcome."

Micah tears off a line of plastic wrap and tapes it carefully over my neck. He packs up his things and gives me instructions on how to keep the tattoo clean. "If you need help, just ask. It's a bit awkward to reach with that placement. Don't brush your hair too much. When you do, be careful."

"Okay." My head feels heavy and my neck prickly as I sit up.

That's it, then. I pause a moment, marveling at how easy it was to choose for my life to be radically altered. It's a Sunday night—everywhere else in the city, kids my age are busy getting ready for finals, or at the mall making lists of stuff they want for Christmas.

But me? I'm on my own, a tattoo freshly mixing into my skin. I'm doing this for Leo. For my parents. And for me.

We say bye to Kurt and head outside. The dinner crowd swarms the streets, laughing and exchanging pretentious-sounding stories about fusion restaurants and places their friends just *have* to try.

Micah tugs on a worn blue beanie, the San Franpsycho logo sticking out from the tag on the side. "Sometimes I miss living here." He points to a hipster-looking couple smoking e-cigs on the corner. "Other times I don't."

"It has changed a lot," I say. "There never used to be so many, like, boutique furniture stores."

"The new businesses are fine. What I don't like is what happens to the people who were here before. If you haven't noticed, it's pretty one-note around here."

I catch his meaning. "The city's still diverse," I say, but it comes out more defensive than I'd like.

"Yeah," says Micah. "But a lot less than it used to be, and we have the Young Herons to thank for that. Everything they do is to get more wealthy people into SF. Which means hell for those who don't have money coming out their ears."

We get on the train, squishing between weary-eyed commuters. The train rocks, and my body tilts into Micah's, but he doesn't seem to mind. We hit Glen Park—one stop shy of ours—when he puts his hand on my wrist.

"Boars in the next car."

"What?" I crane my neck and the tattoo stings. "What do we do?"

Micah's eyes are fiery and still. "It's probably coincidence. Just be on guard." His tone is dark and unusual, like some beast in him has come alive. He takes out his phone and sends a text so quickly I wonder if he even typed anything.

"Jax?" I ask.

He shakes his head. Gathering my breath, I make my expression as passive as possible. The train stalls, and the conductor says something about maintenance on the track. Of all days. I do my best to focus on my breathing, and not on my crazy fast heartbeat or the fact that I'm batshit terrified.

Finally, we start moving again and the intercom garbles. "Balboa Park. Balboa Park station."

"Don't move until the doors open," Micah says.

The train slows. Lifetimes pass. The doors open.

Micah pushes me forward, not bothering to apologize to the cyclist we bump into to get off. I shove my ticket in the turnstile and speed through the barrier. In a move I can't decide is stupid or brave, I check behind us.

Three shark-eyed guys in gray-and-red sweatshirts trail us. I make eye contact with one of them, and he smirks. He stops short and pulls up his sleeve.

On his arm is a name written in red. *Leo.*

I lose all feeling.

Micah's hand finds mine—his warm, mine icy—as he leads me out the west exit. A long concrete overpass connects to Ocean Avenue beyond and a man emerges from the shadows.

He is huge in every sense of the word. His brick-wall frame walks in the opposite direction, and it's only as he passes us that I see the Stag tattoo covering half his skull.

We reach the end of the overpass, and Micah slows. I check over my shoulder again, but the Boars must have stayed in the station. A gentle mist settles onto both of our heads. Droplets collect on Micah's hat. He lets go of my arm, and I wiggle my fingers to get the blood flow back.

"Who was that?" I ask.

"Jaws, the last of our group. Are you okay?"

Blood pulses in my ears. I see rain. I see red. I see a little body and the lights of an ambulance. No siren.

"Valerie?"

"Oh, yeah. I'm fine." I take a breath. "Did you see?"

"The name? Yeah."

"It was my brother's," I say quietly.

"I know. They're just trying to psych you out."

"I know."

"Did they?"

"Did they what?"

"Psych you out."

"No." I stare at the ground. My shoes are dark from where puddle water is soaking through. Bile rises in the back of my throat. "How would they even know about Leo?"

He gazes at me a long while. "People talk," he says, but in a way that makes me believe he's resigned to it rather than in favor.

Then—kindly, gently—he reaches around my hair and touches the pad of his finger to the plastic-wrapped tattoo. Then he turns and walks toward the street, so quickly you'd think I broke his heart.

4

Micah unlocks the door, and we're blasted with a wave of heat and the smell of booze. On the couch, Mako leaps up and raises his hands over his head—touchdown.

"There she is!"

He gives me a hug and kisses my cheek. *Drunk.* Kate appears from around the hall. She's in dark-wash jeans and a black sweater.

Come to think of it, Mako's in all black, too.

"Val!" Kate shrieks. "Come here right now. Shots time."

"Wait, what?" I ask as she drags me into the kitchen, hair swishing around her shoulders in old Hollywood waves—the girl really knows how to use a curling wand. "What are we celebrating?"

"You, obviously," she replies.

In the kitchen, Nianna perches on the countertop, nursing a glass of red wine. Next to her, Jax picks up a shot glass of what I guess is vodka. He puts it in my hand.

"Initiation. Drink. Now."

"What is this?"

"Drink of the gods."

"Vodka is not the drink of the gods," Nianna says, rolling her eyes.

"Don't listen to her," is Jax's reply. "We drink." The air

between us crackles with daring—Jax is a permanent truth or dare. I pick dare.

Lifting the glass to him once, I down the shot. The vodka is ice-cold and horrible, but I finish it in one go. Jax claps and even Nianna looks pleased.

"Another," he says. "Right now."

Two drinks later, my stomach churns. I've had alcohol a few times before—Lyla's sister, Zoe, let us tag along to a few parties—but I can already tell this'll be different. No one's going to be looking out for me or making sure I drink enough water here.

I wonder if Matthew is drinking tonight. If he is, it's champagne and fine wine. My chest aches at the thought of him. Where would he get his tattoo?

My own ink makes me the center of attention for the next few minutes. While I hold the loose strands of my hair up, the Stags *ooh* and *ahh*.

"Oh, my gosh, it's perfect!" Kate gushes. "Nianna, are you seeing this?"

"I'm seeing it," she replies. "Nice job, Micah."

Mako and Kate move on to flirting with each other in the corner while I lean back into the cool door of the refrigerator. I inhale a deli sandwich I find in the fridge, grateful to have something in my stomach.

Micah—who disappeared for a moment, only to return dressed head to toe in black—takes a place next to Jax. The latter claps a hand on his shoulder.

"So how was our little Valentine?" he asks.

"Really good, given the placement."

Jax loves this answer. "Perfect. Fucking perfect!" He roars like an animal then pours another drink. Then another.

"Valentine."

I look up. "That's me?"

"Hell yeah, that's you. This shot's yours."

"Oh, no," I say. "I'm good. I only just ate, so . . ."

He straightens and holds the glass out. "I thought we talked about this. One more. Then we go."

"Where?"

"Drink first."

Reluctantly, I do. My throat and stomach are both wildfires as I nod to Jax, who beckons me forward. As he gives me the finger, his hand lands close to my ass, which I try hard not to notice. At the door, Mako dares Kate to open what looks like a very broken umbrella.

"Don't open that inside," Jax snaps.

Kate mumbles an apology while Mako howls with laughter and says, "Told you he'd freak." I hide my smile. Jax, the big tough leader—who would have thought he was superstitious?

The guy in question leads me out the door. Where Nianna—*When did she get out here?*—waits, a black backpack hanging off each of her shoulders. Smears of neon paint coat the sides and zippers.

"Right," says Jax. "Standard procedure. Don't be seen. Don't get caught."

"Let's do it," says Nianna. She tosses Mako one of the backpacks, and he catches it with ease. Whatever's inside clinks—metal on metal. Jax and Micah follow Nianna. Mako lets out a whoop and slides his arm through mine.

"You're with us, Valentine."

"That's so cute. Valentine," Kate muses from around his other arm. Mako kisses the side of her head.

"Where are we going?" I ask.

"Nowhere," says Mako. "Nowhere and everywhere and nowhere again."

"What does that mean?"

"Honestly, I have no idea," he says. "Just follow me."

The alcohol's hit me, and I throw my hands up. "Okay, fuck it. Let's just go."

The mist settles on our clothes as we go, but I feel warm as ever. We walk for ten minutes, maybe fifteen—I have no idea—skipping at times and twirling at others. The streets are empty, but Mako keeps us out of the headlights of any cars and buses.

Kate stops and points at a wooden fence. It's part of a church. "Babe, this," she says. "Right here. Give."

Mako squats and opens the backpack. Inside are cans of fluorescent spray paint. He picks up two—orange and pink—and gives them to Kate. Next, he unrolls a plastic stencil. With the glow from a nearby streetlight, I can just make out the shape of the Stag emblem. Kate takes the paint and faces the wall.

"Watch and learn," Mako says. He touches the small of my back, and I flinch. He just laughs.

Kate's arms fly across the boards of the fence, leaving streaks of color in their wake. She darts from her canvas to the backpack and back, grabbing at the cans and dropping others to the ground. Washes of color sweep over each other. Left to right. Right to left. The color erodes the dark wood into a sea of pastels that quivers with energy and passion.

She wipes her hands on her pants, adorning her thighs with neon jewels. She grabs the stencil and the last can of paint for three final sprays.

Kate backs away from her masterpiece and runs the back of her arm across her brow. Three Stag emblems stare at us, the navy-blue paint stark against the pastels. Smiling, she reaches up and runs her thumb against my cheek.

"For you," she says. "Lovely."

I motion for her to hand me one of the cans. "What is

this?" I turn the thing over. The words *chalk based* stand out. "It doesn't look like real spray paint."

"It's not," Mako replies. "It's discontinued because of how it runs. But Jax doesn't like messing shit up for real. Says it makes us lazy. This way, we have to constantly refresh."

My brain muddles through his words. The tags aren't permanent, and that's why I see fewer of them around. I teeter on my feet, the alcohol now swirling freely through my bloodstream.

We fly through the neighborhood, down Holloway and beyond. Mako keeps us clear of Ocean Avenue—"Too many people." Instead, we steer up the hill and into the mist.

We color fences, telephone poles, MUNI stops. It feels wrong. It feels amazing, like we're running the city, claiming it with each tag. We're the Stags, and we are here, and this is our city. They let me do my own work, but I can't get it right. Each one is just a sloppy imitation of what they create.

If Kate is the sea, Mako is the sky. Auroras explode from his hands. His strokes are jerkier but bold. Artistic. He lets me do the final stencil, and I pick the very edge to cover the least of it as possible. The paint smells, but not badly.

All our phones buzz at once. Kate doesn't even check it before she stops short and turns around.

"Time to go home," she says. "Holy shit, I have to pee."

The rush disappears like the fog. What I really want to do is vomit. I can feel the alcohol in *my eyes*. I've only been drunk—what, like, twice before? I had the sandwich for dinner, but I've had a lot of liquids . . .

"Damn it, Kate," I shout. "Now I have to pee, too."

Mako—who relieved himself on a fence two streets over—doubles over in laughter. When he recovers, he slaps Kate's ass and spins around the empty intersection, whooping.

"This a'way," Mako says. "Back to Holloway House."

"I like how you guys say that like it's a real place," I say as we stumble-walk down the hill. "Holloway House."

"Well, there are other houses," Kate says. "Like where you got your tattoo. There's another one downtown on Beale Street. But we stay here more often than not. It's the biggest." She hustles ahead of Mako and me, cursing under her breath. "Fuck, I gotta pee."

Neither Kate nor I make it to the house. Breathless with giggles, we each find a dark corner and squat. *Mom would flip if she saw me doing this,* I think. The guilt of leaving her swings back, and I have to force her from my mind.

Zipping up my jeans, I check my phone. Its weight is still unfamiliar in my hand—it's a smaller model than my old one. Kate was right—the text message was from Jax. All it says is "H." Whether that's Holloway or home, I don't know, but I don't question.

We reach the house. Standing to the right of the door is the giant from the BART station: Jaws.

"Oh. Hullo," I say. "I'm Valerie. It's nice to meet you." I hold out my hand. When he shakes it, I nearly laugh—his hand is twice the size of mine. He lets go, and I teeter backward, waiting for his reply.

"Oh, Jaws doesn't talk much," Kate says. She pats his cheek and he doesn't so much as blink. "He keeps all of us extra safe."

"Oh," I say as she holds the door open for me. "Well, thanks. Jaws."

He nods.

Inside, the air is stifling. The TV blasts bass-heavy rap, and the smell of weed winds its way through the halls.

"Valentine?" Jax is spread out on the couch again, a beer held idly in his hand. "Come 'ere."

I plop down next to him, all twirly and out of breath. *Whoa—who am I?* I've never been this familiar with guys I've

just met. Oh wow, this vodka is hitting me. What was I thinking? Oh. Yeah. I've never been *that girl,* whose legs guys run
their hands up and down like Jax may or may not be doing
now.

"Did you have fun?" Jax asks.

"Yeah." I pull my leg away from him.

"Good. Hang on. Stand up for a second."

He shifts his position, half-lifting me until I'm perched
with my legs on either side of his hips. Jax says something.

"What?" I'm spinning. I'm ten thousand miles up.

"You shouldn't crunch your neck," he says. "Not with that
tattoo. Micah will kill me."

"Where is he?"

"He went to bed. Tattooing tires him out." He slides a
thumb under my shirt. I pull back again and this time Jax curls
his fingers so he's holding on to the end of the fabric. Keeping me there. My skin is hot, and so is his.

"We'll get them," he says quietly.

"Who?"

"The Boars." Jax shifts again, still holding me as I try very
hard to focus on his words and not the heat currently between
my thighs. "I know you're mad that I won't tell you. But I
promise, we'll get the guy that shot your brother."

Around us, the room's quiet—and whether that's because
everyone else has gone to bed or the music has stopped or I'm
going deaf, I don't know. All I see and feel and hear is Jax.

"Sorry," he says, noticing my look. "I just wanted you to
know that I know it wasn't right. There was no honor there,
and for that we'll get them back."

"Promise?"

"I promise. That's all we're here for, V. Live fast, fight for
what we want, then die and be remembered for all we did."

"I'll start by fighting," I reply, the words an oath to myself and to him.

Here I am, in a strange house in a part of town I'm not familiar with, no family or friends around, and yet for the first time in two years, I'm actually feeling hope.

This is not how you planned it, Valerie, I think. *But you're where you wanted to be.* In the Wars. Closer to finding the Boar.

Closer to being free.

5

I open my eyes to an unfamiliar ceiling. My cheeks are chilled, and I am in the same clothes I was wearing the night before. Was last night even real?

Sitting up, I grope for the glass of water I vaguely remember bringing downstairs and gulp down the dregs. Pale light from the windows illuminates the room and the smell of coffee drifts down from upstairs.

My pillowcase is dotted with blood and ink. Micah said that would happen. I touch my fingers to the back of my neck, drifting over the ridges of ink and scar tissue. It was real, all of it.

Day one of the Wars, done. I flop back onto the bed, stomach sloshing. *Oh man.* I do not feel good. My mind wanders as I try to motivate myself to get up.

I wonder if anyone else I know was recruited. I didn't have that many friends besides Lyla and Matthew, but I had some. Kids from elementary and middle school. I have a sudden vision of myself pointing a gun at an old classmate or a friend of a friend and the thought makes me shudder.

I finally drag myself out of bed and upstairs. I quickly pee, wash my face, and then go to the kitchen. Nianna's already up, running a sponge in and around a shot glass.

"Morning," I say.

"Good morning, newbie." She gives me a quick nod and motions to the coffeemaker beside her. "Do you drink coffee?"

"I do, thanks."

I find a cup and pour a generous portion. Some of my friends hate coffee, but I love how it pairs with baked goods. Plus, there's the caffeine—I swear I wouldn't have been able to function at school the past two years without coffee to mask the effects of all those sleepless, nightmare-ridden nights.

I open the fridge to look for creamer. Even after yesterday's feeding frenzy at breakfast, the fridge is fully stocked. Inside is a hodgepodge of brands and items, all haphazardly stuffed into the drawers.

"This is a lot of food," I say casually, taking what I need from the door.

"We support the mom-and-pop shops around here as much as we can," Nianna replies. "Even if that means buying more than we need."

"Oh, I see." Okay, it's a little wasteful, but at least they're supporting local businesses.

We fall into an awkward silence—me sipping coffee, her washing dishes. I wonder if she's taking her time just so she doesn't have to look at me. I clear my throat.

"So, are you always up so early?"

She nods. "I try and do yoga every morning."

"That's awesome," I say. "And really impressive."

"Helps me focus," she says.

"Yeah, I imagine." *Okay, so maybe Nianna isn't so bad.* Might as well try to keep talking. "So, Kate and Mako are obviously dating. Did they know each other before the Wars?"

"No," she replies. "We recruited Mako about two months before Kate. They hit it off from day one."

"Oh, wow." I open the cabinets, looking for sugar. I find

some and empty the crumpled packet into my mug. "What about you and Jax?"

Nianna snorts. "You think we're dating?"

"Well, not anymore."

"Definitely not," she says, the hint of laughter dying in her tone. "Jax is . . . too much to deal with. Plus, I'm queer. And damn proud of it. So, no."

"Oh. That's cool. Cool cool," I say. *Come on, Valerie, you know other words besides cool.* "I'm, uh, gonna go shower."

"Okay."

I go back downstairs for my towel and shampoo. Between running around last night and drinking all that booze, I reek.

The bathroom is cramped, but with so many people's stuff, I can't say I'm surprised. Dry strands of gold hair bunch on the floor. Bottles upon bottles of shampoo, cologne, and shaving cream crowd the singular shelf. The trash can overflows with crumpled tissues and—Jesus Christ—a used condom.

I turn on the shower, and the state of the bathroom melts from my mind as the water warms against my hand.

I scrub my face twice, borrowing an apricot scrub and a green tea wash. There's a trio of bottles on the tiled ledge that promise to keep my blond at its best. I go ahead and guess those are Kate's. Not sure what they'll do for my brown locks, but I'd rather borrow from Kate than Nianna. I pull my hair forward to avoid the tattoo and keep it out of the direct stream of water.

I'm washing the last of the suds off my shins and knees when I feel them. Pausing, I run my hand over the ladder of red ridges on my thigh. Hidden skin, the kind you'd only notice if I were in a bathing suit or short shorts, neither of which are often needed in my fog-bowl city.

I switch off the water. Goose bumps settle on my body, and I exhale. *You're fine, Valerie. You're fine. Don't need to cut right now.*

I dress, and quickly tidy up as best I can. After dumping out the garbage can and wiping the floor with a paper towel soaked in 409, I head back downstairs. Blotting my hair with the towel, I look around the room. *Now what?*

Nianna and I seem to be the only ones up. My eyelids are heavy and I could definitely just loaf all day, but I'd hate for my second day to consist entirely of me being lazy.

I settle on organizing the boxes in the garage. Stacking a few plastic tubs on top of each other, I set up my tiny collection of things from home—the photo album, a Kate Spade bracelet Mom gave me last Easter, my pocketknife. I set the last of these down with a *clunk.* I think to myself, *See, Valerie? You didn't need to resort to that.*

The upstairs door opens and Micah shuffles down. He's in sweatpants and the same Bolinas sweatshirt he wore the other night. He cocks his head to the side.

"What are you doing just standing there?"

"Uh, just. Thinking."

Micah absorbs this with a small nod. "Come upstairs. There's food."

Though my hangover makes food sound repulsive, I change my tune when I see the waffles and toast neatly prepared and laid out on the table. Mako scrapes a steaming pile of eggs into a dish just as Micah and I walk in.

"Hey, newbie," he says. "Survived day one."

"Yup, you're stuck with me," I reply. "Thanks for this."

"Eggs and toast, don't thank me too much," he replies as he sits down.

Kate joins a moment later, waving sleepily at me before taking a seat on Mako's lap.

"You sleep okay?" she asks.

I nod, mouth full of buttery toast. "*Yef.* Tank you."

She smiles and leans over to grab a waffle. The coffeemaker hisses and bubbles from the counter. I get up and pour myself a fresh cup. The warmth seeps into my fingers as I wrap my hands around my mug. I'm not sure if it's the coffee or the lingering alcohol in my system, but I'm feeling almost comfortable here.

"Did you have fun last night?" Kate asks.

I nod. "Totally. It's kinda surreal that this is my life now."

"It'll take a week or two," she assures me. "But then we'll put you to work. I'm sure you don't want to wait long."

"What do you mean?"

"Your brother," she says. I clench my mug harder. "I'd be just as pissed as you if that happened to my sister. I'm really sorry that it happened, but I'm glad you're here. So we can help you."

Mako nods. "I feel the same. It shouldn't have happened." Behind him, Micah and Nianna nod their assent.

"Thanks," I mutter, taking steady breaths to keep from crying. "That's really nice of you guys to say."

But it's better than nice. Despite barely knowing these guys, I feel my attachment to them firm up faster than lightning crackles across the sky. It's as if someone had breathed courage into my bones, and something else too—*validation*. Everything I tried to explain to my therapist, to my parents, to Matthew . . . they all wanted me to move on.

But you don't move on from this kind of thing—this depth of guilt that constantly swirls and shifts, restless and unrelenting. You don't move on without action. The Stags see that. It's so shocking and sudden and gratifying that I have no idea what to say.

Down the hall, a door opens and Jax saunters in. He's wearing a faded Giants hoodie and dark jeans.

"'Morning, guys," he says, snagging a waffle from the

table. Without asking, he pours a dollop of maple syrup onto Nianna's plate and dunks the waffle into it. He winks when he sees her glare.

"So what are we doing today?" he asks.

Nianna shrugs. "Showing Val the ropes, patrolling, watching out for the other gangs to—"

Jax shakes his head. "That can wait. We have a new recruit. That's worth celebrating. And by celebrating I mean taking a day off."

"No word from her, huh?" Nianna replies.

He ignores her, running his hand through his hair to get it out of his eyes. An unruly lock falls back in his face anyway. "So, newbie. What do you want to do?"

"Oh, I don't know," I reply. "Whatever you guys want to do."

"That's a shit answer. Come on. Pick something, and we'll go."

Crap. I rack my brain for something fun, maybe something they haven't done in a while . . .

"What about Twin Peaks?" I ask. There's a beat of silence where I panic. "Or, seriously whatever you—"

Jax claps me on the shoulder. "Twin Peaks it is."

"I don't think I've been since right after I moved here," Mako says, and even Nianna nods her assent.

We disperse to go change. From my meager pile of clothes, I pull on jeans, boots, a long-sleeved thermal, and a pair of fleece jackets. Lyla has a saying: if you think you don't need a jacket for a day in San Francisco, you're wrong and you do. And if you look outside and think you do need a jacket, you're still wrong—you need two.

She's a smart one, that Lyla. It's weird to remember that her world is still turning like normal—well, sans me. She's going to class, slogging through rehearsals, and wondering if JB Sanchez is ever going to ask her out.

I know she'll be okay without me, but I kinda hope she misses me as much as I miss her. All things considered, Lyla is a better friend than I deserve. She was there all through Leo's death, the funeral. The whole emotional roller coaster that was—is—Matthew Weston. She's the one who invites me to football games and dances with the rest of her theater friends. They're kind to me, too. I'm the friend who bakes.

Still, it's a battle for me to stay motivated about stuff like that. If she hadn't dragged me to places, I would have just stayed home, studying, sleeping, and baking my life away until I could get back at the Boars. Some days I can't think of a reason for her to stay my friend, for all the shit I give her. I don't know how I'll make it a whole year without her.

I pull my hair into a ponytail, then dig into my small makeup bag so I can slap some moisturizer on my face. Satisfied that I don't look like a complete zombie, I head back up.

Kate and Mako wait by the door, the former finishing off an intricate twist of braids that would make the dragon queen from *Game of Thrones* proud.

Jax waits by the front door, tugging a leather jacket over his sweatshirt. The jacket is dotted with drips of bright paint, and both sleeves are coming away at the seams.

Nianna's the last, wearing all-black sportswear and a purple beanie over her hair. "My god, get a new jacket," she says to Jax, frowning.

"This one's fine."

"It's falling apart."

"It was made for me," he says, shrugging. "Custom."

"Then get a new *custom* jacket."

"You're not the boss of me," he says cheekily. "Now let's go."

Without missing another beat, Jax ushers us out the door. A huge black van sits in the driveway, and as we get close, the

ever-silent Jaws starts it for us. Jax takes shotgun, and I feel a
bit like a kid on the first day of school not knowing where to
sit on the bus. Squeezing in next to Kate and Mako in the
back, I've barely clicked my seat belt before Jaws takes off.

I pay attention to the street names and buildings we pass,
trying in vain to place them against the landmark of Sutro
Tower. The former radio tower's red-and-white stripes are
partially hidden in the fog. The weather makes me worry—
we won't be able to see much from Twin Peaks. I should have
picked a different place.

In no time at all, Jaws makes the turn onto Twin Peaks'
winding driveway. The parking lot is full, so Jax instructs us
all to get out while Jaws finds a spot. To my great relief, the
clouds have parted a little and we have a clear view of downtown. Some clumps of fog hide the Oakland shipyards and
some of the other landmarks, but I'll take it.

"*Wooooo* it's cold," Mako says, hunching his shoulders to
his ears. At the same time, Kate beckons him over and he huddles around her.

"Look at this view, though," says Micah. He's smiling, eyes
wide like he's never seen the city before. "Been a while."

"Wish the weather was a little better," says Nianna.

I pretend not to hear her, but smile when Mako replies,
"It's November in San Francisco, what were you expecting?"

The group of us finds a patch of sparse grass to sit on.
Micah's brought a sketchbook, and while most of the group
talks, I watch him work. He's sketching the others in a semi-
anime style. His eyes flicker to mine, acknowledging that he
knows I'm watching, but he keeps drawing.

"Good?" he says finally, running the pencil over the lines
that make up Jax's profile.

"Really good," I reply. "You're really talented."

"Thanks. Do you draw?"

"Not really," I say. "I was never great at it. My skills are in baking."

"Really?" Immediately, he switches gears and suddenly a large, smiling cupcake is floating above anime-Jax's head.

"Yeah," I reply. "It's a stress relief for me." It's a conversation I've had tons of times with so many people. *Stress relief* is an easy answer. I leave out the baking frenzies as an attempt to soothe my anxiety. I leave out how sweets were the only thing I could stomach in the days after Leo died, my brain's natural cravings beating out my despair. I leave out how I don't make anything red velvet because the color reminds me too much of Leo's blood. "I'll bake for you guys sometime. If we have the time."

He draws a smiley face on the cupcake. "Sweeeeet."

"Valentine." I turn and realize Jax has swapped places with Nianna. He scoots closer, our knees touching.

"So," he says. "Any questions for me?"

"What?"

"About anything."

"Um, what's next?" I ask. "If you're not going to tell me who killed my brother until I earn your trust, then I want to get started."

He gives me an approving nod. "We're in a holding pattern right now."

"*Still* in a holding pattern, you mean," Nianna chimes in.

"Good things come to those who wait, Nianna," Jax replies coolly.

To my right, Micah's stopped drawing. Kate smiles when I catch her eye, but I'd have to be an idiot not to notice that Jax is irritated.

The guy in question's phone buzzes. "Must've said something right," he says to Nianna as he gets up to take the call.

"That's her?" she replies, and he nods as he puts the phone to his ear.

"Who's that?" I ask.

Nianna checks our surroundings before answering. "That's his mom, Theresa." She mouths a word to me. It takes me a moment—and her mouthing the word again—for me to get it.

"Heron?" I mouth back to her.

She nods.

"I don't get it," I whisper, pulling my hood down. "You guys work with Herons?"

"That one, yes." Micah scoots closer to both of us, forming a small huddle. Mako puts his head on top of Kate's. Both of them listen, too.

"Jax's mom, Theresa, is high up in the Heron ranks. Not at the very top, but enough to hold sway. No one in the Wars knows she's Jax's mom."

"And no one's figured it out?"

He shakes his head. "Their last names are different. Theresa hates Jax's dad. He left her when she told him she was pregnant."

"Shit," I say.

"Yeah, it wasn't good. But Theresa is old money. She had Jax in some villa near the coast. Her family kept it hidden from everyone. Theresa resumed her public life and no one was ever the wiser."

"I still don't get why we work with her if she's a Heron," I say. "Isn't that, like, a hundred percent against the rules?"

Micah bobs his head. "Kinda, yeah, if anyone knew Theresa didn't give a shit about the Wars or the Herons. She's a Heron in name only, but their internal politics don't interest her. She only got more invested in their dealings because of Jax. The one thing Theresa cares about is him, and she's happy to help him fight against the Herons."

"Okay," I say. "So what?"

"Theresa gives us intel on what the older Herons are up to, what properties they're trying to buy and build on, et-cetera. The Young Herons do their parents' bidding."

"I still think that's pretty fucked up," says Nianna.

Micah goes on, his large eyes staring at Jax, who's still on the phone. "Anyway, we try to get ahead of it. Herons trying to evict some folks on Such-and-Such Street? We get there first. Jax gives money to the tenants who can't pay rent, then we tag the street. The tenants stay a little longer. The Old Herons get pissed off, and the Young Herons get the brunt of the blame." He says this all in quick, skipping-stone rhythm, his gaze lingering on Jax.

I put the puzzle pieces together. "So I take it you haven't heard from Theresa in a while. That's why you've been in a holding pattern."

"Bingo."

"And what do the Boars do, while you do all this?"

"Whatever they want," Kate interjects, tucking up her hood then lying down on the ground. "Break shit, set stuff on fire downtown. Shoplift from the bougie, Heron-owned stores downtown and in the Mission."

The Boars are the muscle, the Stags the strategy. "So why aren't we and the Boars on the same side?"

"Ah," says a cool voice behind me. Jax stares down at us, the meager light slipping between the clouds illuminating him like a spotlight. "The Boars don't exactly care for me much."

"Why not?"

He stoops down and starts rolling up his pant leg. Scrunch-ing it to his knee, he pivots until I can see the black tattoo on the back of his leg. I'd know the Boar emblem anywhere.

"Because I was supposed to lead them."

6

"I joined the Boars when I turned eighteen, same as everyone else."

We're back in the van, jostling our way home. Jax has his seat tilted back as far as it'll go, so he can keep talking as Jaws drives. I moved up a row and am squished between Micah and Nianna.

"Why did you leave?" I ask Jax.

"I didn't agree with what they were doing. They were picking fights over something that happened years ago."

"Yeah, well," Nianna says, crossing her arms. "Aaron Weston fucked his whole family tree, didn't he?"

Wait, what? Aaron—that's Matthew's brother, the one who lives up in Tahoe. "What does Aaron have to do with this?"

If she notices that I only used his first name, she doesn't say anything. "He started this mess."

My pulse quickens. "What do you mean?"

"You don't know? Aaron Weston and Annie Boreas were a couple."

"Who?"

"Tyler Boreas is the correct Boar leader. Annie was his older sister."

So Aaron dated the Boar leader's sister? "When was this?"

"This was, like, twelve or so years ago. Aaron Weston and

Elliott Boreas—the other Boreas brother—had been rivals for years. Some sort of bad blood between them that started when they were in school together. So when Annie and Aaron got together, it pissed Elliott off to no end. The Herons didn't want to be associated with the Boars, and vice versa. But the two of them stuck it out. They were planning to get married."

Her tone tells me there's more. "Then what?"

Nianna's eyes flicker to Jax, who waves his hand idly like *go on* and looks back to the road.

"Then Annie drowned," she says, shoulders slumping. "Somewhere in the bay on New Year's Eve. Aaron wasn't there, but it was his family's boat, his family's party. Everyone was too busy partying to notice she was missing. Then the coroner's report came back. There were some high-level drugs in her system. The kind you don't just get off the street."

"So sad," Kate whispers.

Nianna nods. "Elliott and the Boars went ballistic. They tore through Heron territory—the Marina, North Beach, down into downtown, and SoMa. Set cars on fire, broke windows, tagged everything. The group that's now called the Young Herons retaliated. They were smaller in number, but they could hire whoever they wanted to find the Boars and hurt them."

I shift in my seat. The Boars sound like me. All Elliott wanted was revenge for someone he loved. "That's not really Aaron's fault, though."

"He got his girlfriend really fucking high, then she drowned," Kate says with a shrug. "I'd be pissed."

"I'd be pissed," Mako echoes.

Nianna goes on. "Once the police got involved, things got even worse. SFPD was—and still is—desperate for cash, and the Herons could give it to them. The Boars felt betrayed by the city that was supposed to protect them. The people's people and all that. They lashed out, Herons retaliated. On and on. That's how the Wars came to be."

"Wow," I say. Here I was thinking it was all about money and status, when in reality the city was undone by something as simple as two people falling in love.

"A few years ago, the Boars recruited that one," Nianna says, pointing at Jax.

The guy in question stares out at the horizon like he owns it. "The longer I was in the Wars, the more I realized the Boars had lost their way. No one even knew Annie or cared about their original purpose. They just wanted to get back at the Herons for how they were changing the city. Which is a worthy cause, but they weren't being smart about it. So I bided my time and waited as I rose through the ranks. After a while I realized the Boars were never going to be the group I wanted them to be, even if I led them. So I left, and took another Boar with me."

Jax's chest rises and falls—it looks like he's going to say something, but instead he shakes his head. "Anyway, the Boars and Herons have forgotten their way, and they're taking the city down with them. So I'm going to do the one thing that they—and the police—can't do."

"Which is?" I ask.

"I'm going to end the Wars."

What? The flatness of his words brings me back to my senses. "I don't understand." *And I'm starting to get real freaking tired of that feeling.*

"Despite appearances, Valentine, you're sitting in a car with a bunch of pacifists."

Wait, what? "Really?"

"*Pacifists* might be a bit strong," says Micah. "With Theresa's help, we get ahead of the Young Herons' plans and stop them from moving forward. We protest, we create chaos, whatever it takes. And when the Herons are stuck, there's nothing for the Boars to retaliate against."

"And every month on the first, Jax sends them both a message asking them to end the Wars," Nianna finishes.

"How do you do that?"

"When I left the Boars, I stole one of their IRIS machines," Jax replies. "It's this old prototype comm machine one of the first Young Herons built—Interpersonal Relay Internet System. When the Boars were founded, the two gangs agreed to use it to talk to each other. Only for official dealings between the two groups. The kid who made it was a genius. Each comm gets a unique encryption, and every time you send a message it routes it across half a dozen connections. You can't see it if you don't know what you're looking for, and it was never on the market, so . . ."

I don't know whether I should be impressed or what, but I am stunned. *What have I gotten myself into?* "But on the news, the Stags are just as violent as the others."

"Well, we don't take shit lying down," says Nianna, like *duh*. "If one of the other gangs fucks with us we obviously fight back."

"I fight back," Jax corrects, his voice rising. "If another gang does something against you, I'll let you handle it. But if it's against the Stags, I take the action."

All the blood stays on his hands. Next to me, Micah turns and looks out the window. "Okay," I say.

"I fucking mean it," Jax snaps, suddenly. "I'll take the hit."

"Okay," I repeat. *Did I say something wrong?* "But my revenge for my brother is mine?"

"Yes," Jax says, with a nod of his head. His word feels like a vow somehow, like it's inevitable that I'll be able to find the Boar that killed Leo.

"Society says we're bad, but we're doing what the police can't and the other gangs won't," Jax continues. "We're what the Boars should have been, but are now too big and disorganized to be. We're smarter than they are, and doing the right thing."

Doing the right thing, just the wrong way.

"Anyway, you'll start your schooling today, Valentine. The binders first. You have to know every face and name in the other gangs."

Binders with faces and names. Riveting.

"Binders, range, following orders. That's your life, until I say otherwise," he goes on. *Until I've earned my place. Until I've earned the knowledge of who killed Leo.*

"Okay," I say.

He takes a vape from his pocket and inhales deeply, cracking the window just enough to let a wave of cold air in and the vapor out. "You know the buses?"

"Most of them," I answer.

"BART?"

"I'm a native. So, yeah. Honestly the only thing I'm missing is more black clothes."

Micah gives me an approving smirk, but Jax is apparently too busy getting high to bother with me anymore. Or at least I think so until he says to Jaws, "Take us downtown."

If you'd have asked me what I'd be doing on my second day in the Wars, I would not have said shopping.

Yet here I am, in a dressing room of some boutique off of Union Square, tugging up yet another pair of black pants. These have a leather stripe down the side—real leather, not the knockoff stuff at Forever 21—which makes me feel like a badass girl superhero. *Sexy,* I think, though it's not a word I usually use to describe myself.

"Well?" Kate shouts from the next fitting room.

"They're good," I say, shimmying off the leather-stripe pants and sliding back into my own. I gather the bundle—two jeans, a pair of black leggings, plus a couple of midnight-colored sweaters—and exit. Kate's waiting for me, a form-fitting running jacket hanging over her arm.

"Grabbed this one for you, too," she says. "Medium?"

"Yup," I reply, but my heart is sinking. I recognize the swirling lettering of the label—that jacket's not cheap. "Wait," I say. She hands it to me. "Kate, this is nearly two hundred dollars. No way am I getting this."

"Why not?"

"Because it's two hundred dollars for something made for me to sweat in."

She laughs—ethereal and eternal. "It doesn't matter what it costs. Jax is paying. Don't forget what we told you about his mama. And besides," she says, "this is an independent business. Jax has met the owner, Kailin. The more we spend here, the more likely they can afford whatever rent the Herons charge here now."

Kate yanks the jacket back from me and tugs the rest of the bundle with it. She heads for the register, and I follow right behind.

Seeing us, Jax gets up from where he was playing some game on his phone. As the cashier rings us up, all I see are numbers getting higher and higher.

"Jax," I say as he counts out bills. "I can put some of it back."

He pauses. "Do you like them?"

"Well, yeah, but—"

He turns and hands a wad of hundreds to the cashier. "Thank you so much." In one smooth move, he hooks his arm around my shoulders—well, more around my head. He pulls me close and kisses my hair.

"Don't worry about it, Valentine. Anything you want is yours."

The Boar who killed Leo, I want to say, but I know he's talking about *stuff,* not information. Not yet.

"Thank you," I mutter, then duck out of his grasp.

"Told ya," Kate says triumphantly. "Now let's go get coffee. Nianna says this place is super bougie but has the best espresso."

We go, Kate texting the others down the street that we're on our way. I rub the sheeny ribbon of the bag—I never thought I'd ever have so much from such a fancy store. Maybe if I saved up and wanted to splurge on something, sure. But not like six things plus the orchid-colored lipstick Kate threw in at the end.

The air is cool, the clouds above us every shade of bruise-blue and impenetrable, like a long curtain draped over the city. I shiver. Coffee is starting to sound better and better. Walking behind Kate, I admire the latest of her fancy braids—a fishtail that somehow blends seamlessly into a regular braid, with a perfect curl at the end.

The streets are as busy as ever. I sidestep a vendor hawking some skincare line and have to quickly pivot out of the way of a man pushing a cart full of garbage bags. The latter's dog follows closely behind, tail low.

If there is ever a place where two opposing forces meet, it's on the streets of San Francisco. Tourists dodge vagrants, then pose for pictures next to the cable cars on Market. At night, concertgoers and theater lovers skirt past discarded needles and sprawled bodies on the ground at Civic Center Station. The situation was bad years ago, but has been made worse by the influx of money into the City by the Bay. The cries for change are louder, but that change often comes at the expense of those without the means to fight it.

I figure, if anything, the city's myriad ailments help the Wars. It's like a cancer—there's no easy fix, and while the state and local governments tangle themselves in red tape, the Wars go on as a newer symptom masked by others.

We pass under the shining marquee of a private hotel and residence, and Kate slows as she studies the map on her phone. The *click clack* of heels on the pavement sounds from behind us, and I wonder why on earth anyone would walk in heels when the pavement still glistens from the morning's rain.

The clacking stops, and I realize Jax is no longer right behind me. I turn around.

Jax is frozen in the middle of the sidewalk, one hand already at his back where I know a handgun is concealed. Squaring off with him is a girl our age with black hair shining down to her waist and eyes I can only describe as blazing. There are two guys right behind her like soldiers flanking a queen.

"Well, look who decided to wander my way," the girl says, her voice purring. She narrows her perfectly shadowed eyes, cocking her head to the side to look at me. "And you came with some friends."

"Holy shit." Kate grips my arm, yanking me back toward her. "That's Camille Sakurai. Leader of the Young Herons."

The ground swells and shakes. We're downtown—of course the Herons would find us. *Matthew!* Is he here? Is he close by?

"Hey, Camille," Jax replies, as if he's greeting an old friend. "We're not here on business. Just passing through."

"Just passing through," she repeats. "Oh, okay. Don't mind us, then." She folds her arms across her chest, the bronze-colored bangles at her wrists gleaming in the light from the storefront. "You never just pass through."

"Showing the newbie what's what."

"Oh, that's right. You got a new recruit, too." Camille locks her eyes with mine. A moment later, Jax steps back in front of me, blocking me from her sight. "Hi, Valerie," she calls. "So lovely to meet you in person."

"How does she know—" I whisper frantically, but Kate squeezes my arm and says, "Not now."

"Tell you what, Jax, I'll make you a deal," Camille says. Her tone is riddled with a savageness that cuts like steel. "I'll forget I saw your face tonight for two minutes with your recruit."

"No way," Jax says instantly.

"You're not exactly in a position to negotiate," she says. "And you're on my turf, asshole."

"And you're on camera, Your Highness," Jax says mockingly, tilting his head toward the hotel. Surely there are hidden cameras all around us. "The longer you stand here the sooner someone is going to wonder why the daughter of a self-driving-car mogul was talking to a couple of punk-ass high-school dropouts."

Camille's look is murder. "Fine. Fuck off, Jax. And don't come back." Turning, she clicks her way into the hotel but pauses on the first step, her bodyguards pausing as she does. "Oh, and Valerie? I'll be sure to tell Matthew everything about this. He's right upstairs, you know."

Upstairs. Without thinking, I look up, wondering which of the glowing windows has Matthew somewhere behind it. Jax and Kate whirl me away from the site of the standoff, Jax's hand on the small of my back.

"You okay?"

"Yeah," I reply. "Are we, uh, safe?"

"Safe enough, but we shouldn't hang out here much longer."

Kate navigates us to the coffee shop. Inside the air is warm and the mood quiet as workers take orders and patrons hunch over their laptops.

Micah's sipping what looks like a simple Americano when he sees us. "What's wrong?"

"Camille found us," Jax replies. "Let's go."

We gather up our stuff and hustle out of the café just as fast as we entered it. The van pulls up and we hop in. This time, Nianna takes the front and Jax sits next to Micah, clapping a hand on his shoulder.

"Lighten up," he says to his friend.

Micah shakes his head. "It was dumb to come here." He adds something else right into Jax's ear. I don't catch it.

"I know," is our leader's reply, and none of us will ever have any way of knowing whether Jax was agreeing to Micah's statement or to what was whispered. I'm just glad to be safe.

I look out the window as we pull away. The farther we head from downtown, the brighter the lights of the hotel seem to burn against the gray cityscape—like a thousand fires reminding us of the Young Herons' grip on the city, and on me.

Matthew is a Young Heron now. And if what the Stags have said is true, then they're our biggest enemy. I should hate him.

But how can I? Even at the peak of the breakup, I didn't *hate* Matthew. Not really. And no matter how painful it was, it didn't erase the years in which we'd forged our bond. *Our stories are intertwined,* I remind myself. Is that still true, now that we're on opposing sides?

I think of Annie Boreas—what was it like for her to forsake the world she knew and dive into the great blackness of the unknown? She left behind her brothers, and probably the rest of her family ties. No matter how strongly her heart was drumming that what she was doing was the right thing, was getting what she wanted most worth the risk?

Hours later, Kate, Nianna, and I sit around the kitchen table. Nianna fidgets like an impatient cat as Kate paints her nails a deep purple. Micah plays video games in the other room while Mako's gone out for a run.

Jax asked to be alone.

Three plastic monstrosities sit before me. I've flipped through each a dozen times, but the memorization is excruciating. I'm good with names and faces but not *that* good.

Besides, I still can't get over what happened downtown, or what the Stags told me as we were leaving Twin Peaks.

How come Matthew never told me about what happened with Aaron? He only ever said that Aaron was the black sheep of the family and that he loved his life in Tahoe. He didn't tell me about Annie, how she died, or the choice she made before she did. Love over family—did she ever regret her decision? *Speaking of . . .*

"What happened to the guy Jax left the Boars with?" I ask. "Am I gonna meet him at some point?"

Nianna and Kate both pause. After a glance at the hallway door—toward Jax's room—Nianna exhales. "Jax didn't leave with a guy. The Boar he took with him was named Brianna. He'd had a crush on her for ages and, well, he's Jax. He gets what he wants. But shit got messy fast. She wanted out of the Stags. It became this big thing, because at that time the Stags were like, *brand-new,* and Jax couldn't let her go home. It'd ruin the small reputation they'd earned so far. Then Brianna was kidnapped by Boars. Fuckers rear-ended her car, and when she got out they swooped in."

Chills run down my spine. There are only a few things that can happen to a woman when she's kidnapped—and none of them are good.

"Jax went ballistic. He tried to meet with the Boar leader, but they refused. Brianna was theirs for who knows how long."

I exhale, shaking my head. "Fuck."

"Eventually, they let her go. She said they didn't harm her, that they were only holding on to her to piss off Jax, but who knows? Once they let her go, Jax never went to find her, at least not that I know of."

"Why not?" I ask. "Didn't he like her?"

"Yeah, he did. And I bet that's why he didn't go. He was furious that he'd let it happen. Jax is as proud as they come, and her getting caught made him look bad. Anyway. Nothing good can happen from being close to Jax, so don't get any stupid ideas about trying to change him or start envisioning what your kids would look like, whatever." She sees my face at the word *kids* and gives a half smile. "I dunno. You straight people are crazy sometimes. Anyway, that's the dirt." She shrugs. "You're welcome."

"Thanks."

"Back to binders," is her reply.

Yes, ma'am. I grab the Boar binder again and search for the three that Micah and I saw on the train, but my thoughts linger on Jax. There's no way he loved Brianna, otherwise he would have gone to her after the fact. Maybe she didn't want him, after all. Not like Jax would ever admit something like that.

Focus, Val. The three Boars.

I shiver when I remember the sight of Leo's name. It looked like blood. But it couldn't be. It was paint and nothing else. Paint that distracted me from the guy's face. The Boar had greasy blond hair and a wide grin—but hell, that doesn't narrow it down much.

"Jimmy Finesman," I whisper, tapping a photo that might be him.

"What about him?" Nianna asks.

"I think Micah and I saw him on BART yesterday. Him and a few others. I think."

"All the way in Ingleside?"

"Yeah."

She absorbs the new information with a nod. "Interesting. I bet Micah told Jax, but if shit like that happens when you're on your own, always report it."

"Got it." I go back to the binders. Jimmy doesn't matter much to me. Time-wise, if he is in the Wars now, then he couldn't have killed Leo. *But then why does he know about it?* Micah said people talk—like my brother's murder was so notable it's worth sharing. *Great.* My throat tightens, but I fight the feeling and turn another page.

It crosses my mind, and not for the first time, that Leo's killer may very well be dead. Logically, it's a possibility.

But no—I can feel he's alive. Maybe it's naive to delude myself into such a hope, but I feel it. He's still out there somewhere, unaware that the point of my joining the Wars was to stop his heart the way he stopped Leo's.

"No wonder the Boars are always on the news," I say, shutting the binder once more. "There's so many of them."

Kate takes the nail polish and touches up her own color. "I heard Jax tell Micah that Ty doesn't even ask them to do half of the vandalism and other shit they do. We wouldn't do shit like that. The things the other gangs do are usually a give and take. Tit for tat, or whatever."

"Retaliation," Nianna clarifies. "The Wars are a big balancing act. At least, it is for us and the Herons. The Boars do whatever they want. Just for kicks, I guess."

"Huh," I reply glumly. Murder people. Ruin lives. Kill

little brothers—for kicks. *Breathe, Valerie.* "Hey, what time is it?"

Kate leans back and checks the clock on the oven. "Three thirteen. Why?"

"Just wondering."

I blink back tears and look down at the binders again. Grabbing the Heron one, I open to the first page. A now-familiar face is first.

In the photo, Camille looks like she could be the long-lost cousin of the Kardashians. The folds of a designer jacket billow in the wind as she exits her car. At her wrists, twin bracelets gleam like polished bronze in the camera flash. Long black hair frames her face, contrasting with a perfect pink lipstick. Her eyes are directed forward, away from the cameras. I can only imagine what kind of glares a girl like her can deliver—like a sword through your chest.

Nianna stretches up and I tilt the binder so she can see.

"Camille is one tough bitch," she says. "Her grandfather's Yakuza or something. She's been leader since the last Weston left."

I study the rest of the Young Herons, my heart rate rising. The photos vary—some direct shots, others more blurred— but I keep matching face to name as best I can. And then—

"I know some of these people," I say. *Charles Davis. Kayla Meyers-Britt.* We'd run around the Westons' yard, playing tag or whatever as our parents sipped wine and laughed too loud. "I haven't thought about them in years. They used to come to the Westons' parties."

"They're on another side now," Nianna says. "Don't forget that."

"I won't."

"How'd you get invited to the Westons' parties?" Kate asks, eyes bright and curious.

"My mom has her own event-planning company. Mrs. Weston hired my mom for some event when I was a kid, and they stayed in touch. Easy to do, I guess, given that we live down the street."

"*Soooo,*" Kate says, "your family's rich too?"

"No no no," I reply. Money is something Lyla and I have talked about at length, a habit that's no doubt going to be fueled by her upcoming years at UC Berkeley (if she gets in, which she totally will). "We're fine, but we're not like the Westons. It's weird to talk about, I know. Because, like, obviously I have privilege. But we're definitely the crappiest house on the block. I went to a really great school, but I didn't get a new BMW for my sixteenth birthday or anything like that."

Kate shrugs. "Still."

"I know. And I'm not saying I'm poor, by any means. I'm really grateful for how hard my parents work for me. But at school, every moment of my day was people reminding me that I had less than them and thus *was* less than. . . . That stuff wears on you after a while."

I think back to the time when Matthew and I were dating. We were hanging out with his friends at lunch one Friday. They were a nice enough group of sporty, Ivy League–bound guys and girls. All intelligent, all beautiful. Some girl came up to us—Melissa something, she was part of the student council—and asked if Matthew had a second to chat privately. I watched as they talked, and after a moment she'd turned bright red, then looked confusedly in my direction.

"What was that about?" I asked when he came back.

"Nothing."

"What did she want?"

"She asked me to junior prom." Then he kissed the side of my head. "I told her no, obviously."

"Oh. Okay." It's not like we were a new couple. Did she

really not know Matthew was taken? Or did she just not
believe it? The confusion that I'd read on her face was laced
with a disbelief and derision I was starting to get used to as
Matthew's girlfriend. The bell rang and I pushed the inci-
dent out of my mind, until now. Matthew never made me
feel like less than—but every part of his world did.

Back in the present, Kate smiles, and a wave of relief
washes over me. "I guess I understand that. If I had a penny
for every time my dad told me my sister was his favorite, I'd
probably be a Heron by now. It's not my fault I'm not good
at school and tests and stuff."

Shit, that's rough. So I say as much.

"'Yeah, well, you're our favorite," Nianna tells her firmly.
Kate gives her a playful shove in response.

"Yeah, yeah."

Nianna gets up, waving her nails to dry them. "Go tell Jax
you're done with binders. He wants to take you shooting before it gets too late."

"Okay."

Kate scoffs. "You're going to ruin all my hard work."

"I'm careful," Nianna replies, deftly moving the binders into
a pile.

"Hmpf."

They keep talking as I go down the hall. Pausing, I listen
for a moment—Jax is still on the phone, voice low. When I
knock, he immediately stops talking. A beat later, he opens
the door, hand raised.

"Hold on," he says into his phone. A girl on the other line
replies, her words lost in a high-pitched laugh. A jolt of jeal-
ously shoots through me. *What the hell?* Nothing to be jealous
of. I don't care. *I have Matthew.*

"What?" he asks.

"Nianna told me to tell you I'm done with the binders."

"Oh," he replies. "Well, go do whatever you want 'til Mako comes back."

Somewhere behind me the front door opens and shuts. Mako's voice echoes down the hall, calling for Kate like the husband on an old sitcom.

"Never mind, then. Give me a few more minutes." Jax puts the phone to his ear again and shuts the door.

Whoever's on that other line must be a hell of a person to have hooked Jax. The ridiculous part of me is disappointed— but it's better this way. Jax is my leader, nothing more.

A few minutes later, he comes back out. I get up from the couch where I was waiting. "Who was that?" I ask.

He ignores me and cups his hands around his mouth, making a mini megaphone. "Yo, Mako?"

"Yeah?"

"Let's take Valentine shooting."

"Yes, sir."

I wait as Jax pulls on a steel-gray thermal and dark blue vest. He reaches behind the door. A drawer opens and shuts. When he comes back into view, there's a shiny black gun in his hand.

"Jesus," I say, jumping back.

"It's not loaded," he replies, a laugh in his voice. "We'll go over the basics here. More light in the kitchen." He makes a shooing motion with his hands, and I scoot back toward the kitchen.

I take my usual seat. Mako produces another gun from a leg holster and puts it on the table. Even Jaws peers at the spectacle from over in the foyer. I didn't hear him come inside, but I don't mind him being there. I'm oddly fond of Jaws: knowing that it's somebody's job to guard us, to be in and to become the shadows, is comforting.

Two sharp taps on the table pull my attention forward.

"First rule," Mako says. "Never point a gun at anything you don't want to shoot." He pulls back the top of the gun. An oval-shaped hole on the side opens up. "Always check it yourself to see whether or not it's loaded. Here's the chamber. Even if the gun isn't loaded, there can be a bullet in there. Always check." He tilts it. "This is where the magazine goes."

Bullets. For a moment I'm not there—I'm in the back of an ambulance hearing a paramedic say there were two bullet wounds . . .

"Val?"

"Sorry." I give Mako a nod. "I'm listening."

"So this is a Glock. Nine millimeter, semiautomatic. Here. Hold it."

I take the thing and point it at the ground. It's heavier than I thought it'd be. I knew joining the Wars would mean learning how to shoot, so I did research online and at the library. Glocks are made by one of the most popular manufacturers, I remember that much.

My fingers run along the metal etching on the grip. I shift the gun a few times until Mako shows me how to hold it properly. He has me grip it with two hands. On the night I was recruited, not one of them held their guns that way.

My skin feels too soft, the pads of my fingers too delicate. *You're new at this. Just be patient.* I shake out my hand and take the gun again, holding it the way Mako showed me, finger near but not on the trigger.

"'Atta girl," says Mako. "How's the grip feel?"

I flex my hand. "Good."

"Fit and grip are really important."

"This is good."

"Okay. Now, lift it up toward the window."

I do. On top of the gun is a small tab with a notch in it. At the end of the gun is another raised bit.

"That's the sight," he says. "To aim, you put the front sight level and in the center with the back one. Try it."

"You sure?"

"Yeah." He laughs. "It's not loaded."

Finding a bit of mold on the window blinds, I level the gun at it until the sights align. I set the gun down on the table again. My hands tingle.

"Got it."

Mako walks me through a few other basics: how to rack the slide, where empty casings are ejected, and how new cartridges are loaded automatically. Finally, he looks at Jax. "All right, chief. Roll out?"

"Roll out."

The three of us pile into the car, leaving me alone in the back seat—as if I didn't feel enough like a child already. Mako drives us a short way down toward Lake Merced. We pass a pair of joggers and an elderly man out for an evening stroll. The streetlamps are just coming to life, their orange glow fading into the lavender twilight.

We pull over at a low building surrounded by a chain-link fence. A huge CLOSED sign hangs over what would be the entrance. Below it is another one labeled PRIVATE PROPERTY.

"Is this it?" I ask as we get out. Beyond the fence there are long rows of grass and gravel. I don't see any targets.

"Yep," Mako replies. "Place got closed down a year or so ago. Jax's mom bought it for us."

"No, no—she bought the *land*," Jax says, his voice low in mock seriousness.

"Yes. How could I forget?" Mako laughs. "The land. That's all."

I stop short, stunned. It'd cost an obscene amount of money to buy such a large plot in San Francisco. Right on the lake, no less. Just how rich is she?

Jax pulls out a key to get us through the gate, then another to get us inside the shack of a building. An alarm beeps to life. Jax types in the code as Mako flicks on a light.

The former gun club is musty and dimly lit. The walls are lined with old flyers and dotted with holes, souvenirs from picture frames that used to decorate the space. There are a few empty shelves, a cash register, and a locked safe bolted to the ground in the back. Jax unlocks it as well and sets a box of bullets on the counter.

We head to the back. Mako goes over the points with me while Jax sets up a target. I can hardly see the faint outline until Jax flicks on a set of spotlights. He walks back toward us. Mako slips two earplugs into my hand.

"Won't have these out in the field," he says. "But I'd feel bad if you went deaf on my watch."

"Thanks." I twist the bits of foam and put them into my ears.

Mako loads the magazine. "She's all yours. Remember how to hold it. And remember it's going to kick back at you."

"Right."

I pick up the gun, rack the slide like he showed me, and level the sight. Closing my right eye, I focus my vision.

"You got it," Mako says from behind me. Jax doesn't say anything.

In the brief moment of quiet, the two sides of my brain take up arms.

Leo died this way. Someone pulled the trigger that sent the bullet ripping through the chambers of your little brother's small heart and—no.

No, you have to learn so you can kill the Boar who shot him.

Nothing matters but that. Now aim. Aim like that paper is Leo's murderer.

Rage wins. I fire.

There is a kickback, but I manage to keep steady. Adrenaline rushes through my limbs. I fire again and again until the clip empties.

I set down the gun and back away like Mako told me to. He jogs out to fetch the target. He holds it up to the light, and I'm surprised at the cluster of holes near the center.

"You're a good shot."

"Apparently." I stretch my arm.

"Do another one," Jax says. I try to catch a glimpse of whether he approved of my shooting. Instead, I see a tiny flame. He's lit a cigarette.

Luckily, Mako's got me well taken care of. This time, he loads the clip then removes it and has me put it back on my own, loading and unloading it several times.

Whatever beginner's luck I had in my first round wanes. When Mako gets the target, he hands it to me more abashedly.

Jax steps up behind me. Apparently, he's remembered this is important. "You'll have to practice."

"Obviously."

"Every day."

"All right."

He nods.

Then, quick as a leaping cat, he takes two long steps sideways, pulling his own gun out from his waistband as he does. The shots come in quick succession. I jump back as Jax fires away, barely aiming. He keeps his weapon steady until he empties the clip.

"Fuck, man," says Mako. "There's never any warning with you."

Jax laughs. "Come on. Let's go home. It's cold as fuck out here."

I nod in agreement, but I don't stop trembling. Not as Mako and Jax finish locking up the place and gate. Not as we climb back into the car.

My thoughts bleed with the reminder that I'm dancing with demons, flirting with monsters. The Stags can help me avenge Leo. Jax said so. I was so giddy with hope that it didn't hit me exactly why it rang so true.

The Stags can help me find Leo's killer, because they are killers, too.

It's nearly nine when we get home, and I'm more than ready for bed. I'm about to say my good nights when Jax calls from his room.

"Kitchen. Everyone. Now."

The Stags do as they're told. When we're all ready, Jax clears his throat and holds up a piece of pale blue paper. It's the old-fashioned kind with perforated tear-aways on both sides. Faint gray text works itself down the page. Jax raises the paper for us all to see. "Ty wants to meet."

Nianna recoils like she's been bitten. "Why?"

"He says he has a proposal for me."

"Sounds romantic," Mako mutters.

"Who's Ty again?" I whisper to Micah.

"Ty Boreas, the Boar leader," he replies to me, then addresses the rest of the group. "Are you gonna meet him?" he asks, shifting on his feet.

Jax nods. "Yeah, I'll meet him. It's through IRIS. He can't fuck with me. It's against the terms."

"Sounds good." Micah tucks his hand into his sweatshirt

pocket, leaning back against the fridge. "You want us with you?"

Jax thinks. "Yeah. It'll give Valentine some experience with the other gangs. I'll let Ty know when and where."

Jax turns to go and the others start to disperse.

"Did the IRIS thing say anything about the Herons?" I ask. I catch myself before the words *Or about Matthew Weston?* slip out.

Immediately the mood of the room changes, and I regret saying anything at all. *Fuck.*

"Nothing from the Herons," says Jax. "Camille keeps pretty quiet. Might change, though. New man in their ranks."

"We expected that," Nianna says. Her eyes settle on me. "We've been watching the Herons groom him for months."

Him. *Matthew.* She knows we're close. Was she watching that night I was recruited? Did she see our kiss? Anger and embarrassment rise in my chest. That was private, only for us.

And what does she mean by *grooming* him? Matthew told me it was always his plan to join, but only because he had to because of his family. Did he actually want to be part of the Wars? He's not like the Young Herons. He wouldn't even join the football team because he didn't like the idea of hitting people, let alone really hurting anyone.

Jax turns away for real this time, and Nianna locks eyes with me. "Don't ask about the Herons again," she says, her voice carrying a strong tone of *What the hell were you thinking?* "Jax tells us what we need to know. Even if there had been something, it's not our fucking business until he says so."

"Sorry," I reply sheepishly.

"Better be," she says. "You really gotta learn."

"I said I was sorry," I reply, eyes starting to sting. Assuming we're dismissed, I go and shut myself in the bathroom.

There, I let a few tears fall and silently blot them with toilet paper.

I'm tired, my arm aches, and I feel as small as ever—not to mention confused. There's no way the Herons have been grooming Matthew . . . so why does a small part of me believe it's possible? Since the breakup, we haven't talked as much. Matthew did quit student council abruptly, and whenever I asked why he'd change the subject or brush me off. I should have been more on him about it. Now that we're apart, I can think of so many other questions I wish I'd asked him, and just as many things I wish I had said.

But I can't change the past, just like I can't shake the one thought that scares me more than anything: if what the Stags say is true and Matthew has been groomed by the Young Herons for months, then Matthew chose not to tell me.

And if he really does love me, then why the hell didn't he?

7

Mako takes me to the range every day. By the end of a week, my shoulders are sore as hell—which isn't helped by the hours of workouts that Jax has me doing. Whether it's hazing or him wanting me whipped into shape, I don't know. But he still makes me do it.

Mako yawns and pinches the bridge of his nose as he waits for me to take my shot. The Stags never seem to go a night without drinking. I'm sleep-deprived myself, but I downed a ton of water before going to bed so the hangover's minimal—even in the Wars, I can't shake my responsible side. Mako didn't have the foresight. I think his headache would have kept him in bed all day if Jax hadn't gone into his room and personally shoved him out of it.

I'm glad my head is clear, at least. I want to be ready for tonight.

Jax agreed to meet with Ty at midnight. They can each bring up to ten of their people. For the Boars, that's about a tenth of their number. For us, that's everyone.

We're meeting at Mission Dolores. It's not neutral territory, as far as I can tell, but Jax was adamant about no violence because it's sacred ground. Mission Dolores is the oldest building in the city and an actual church. *Doesn't get more sacred than that,* I think.

My apprehension about meeting the Boars has only just beat out my thoughts about Matthew. I didn't realize how badly I'd want to talk to him until I wasn't allowed to. We didn't talk for a while after we broke up, but that had been my choice. This—not even having the option—has been torture.

At least I can call home. Every time I do I weigh the pros and cons of it—hearing Mom's voice versus causing her pain because of my calling. She never wants to hang up, and then there's a painful song and dance of when I'll call next.

I remind myself that I'm doing this for us, for our family. It won't be long now. I'll earn Jax's trust, he'll tell me who the Boar is, and I . . .

I'll have to take the shot. It's no longer scary to me—well, at least not like it was before. Having been to the range now, I've learned the rhythm: picking up the gun and loading it myself as if it were a sword I am taking into battle, or a spear sharpened by stone and so polished that it gleams as it flies, catching the sunlight before meeting its deadly mark. Guns are tools, bullets are tools. I have to remember that.

We wrap up our practice and get back in the car to head home. Mako and I are still a ways away from Holloway House when I ask, "Do you know what the meeting's about?"

"If I'm guessing, I'd say it's about the Herons. There's a developer trying to buy a chunk of businesses near Twentieth. That's Boar territory. I'm betting Ty's going to ask us to team up against them."

The prickliness of his words sticks in my gut like a tangle of thorns. Matthew is my oldest and best friend. I love him. He loves me. He can't be my enemy.

He already is, I remind myself.

"I thought the Stags stayed out of the other gangs' business."

"We used to, yeah. But times are a-changin'." He flicks the blinker on. "Mind if we stop for gas?"

"Not at all," I reply.

While Mako fills up the tank, I dash into the Walgreens across the street and buy a bag of peach rings and a bottle of Pedialyte. Mako's cleaning the windshield when I get back. I offer him the bottle.

"Here," I say. "My friend's sister swore this was a hang-over cure."

He sets the squeegee down and takes the bottle, frowning at the bright pink drink. "Isn't this for kids?"

"Technically. I tried it one of the few times I got drunk." I shrug. "Works pretty well. Want a peach ring instead?"

He takes both, and we get back in the car. Mako sips his drink. "Damn this stuff is sweet. Thanks, V."

Back on the road, I sink my teeth into another peach ring and think, *As long as Mako's in a good mood, I might as well capitalize on it.*

"So how long has Ty been leader?"

"Uh, two years," he replies after taking a second to think. "I don't think anyone's stepping up to take it from him. Boars don't have a clear line of succession."

My shoulders sink. "But the Herons do."

"I guess, kinda. Camille seems pretty comfy where she is. I don't know if she'll want out once Weston has a year under his belt."

"Is that how long it usually takes to change leaders?"

"I would think, at least. Right?" he says as we approach a stoplight. "Gotta prove yourself before an old leader would pass off the reins."

"Yeah, I guess so," I reply, but I'm reeling. *So Mako thinks Matthew will be the next Heron leader.* I got that sense from Nianna, too. Have they all known about this, as total strangers?

It makes me feel so stupid. How could I have not known as his friend, and as someone he says he loves? There must have been signs.

We come to a red light, and Mako shifts to grab his wallet from his pocket. He stuffs some loose bills into it and asks, "You buy anything with your cash yet?"

"Well, this," I reply, lifting the bag of peach rings. "Not much else, really. Maybe I'll get a new mattress or something."

He laughs. "Yeah, that one you have is a piece of shit. Cash is nice though, right? Took me a long-ass time to get used to having cash I could just throw around."

"Yeah, I guess."

He shrugs. "Beats cleaning floors, I'll tell you that."

"You cleaned floors?" I ask, chewing slowly.

"That's what my mom and grandma did for a while. They'd bring me along to help. Wasn't until I was older that I realized it was just because they couldn't afford day care."

"Oh."

"Hey, it's fine. Now I'm here," he says, patting his pocket. "Now I can send them cash. It's all good."

We get back to Holloway House, and I head to the bathroom to clean my tattoo. I hold up a compact to the mirror and pivot so I can see the back of my neck. My fingers run down the feather, across the stag's eyes, and up the wild, twisting antler. Micah snags the back of my collar to check on it at least once a day. I don't want to disappoint him by mucking up the healing.

Kate doesn't register me as I go back into the kitchen and drink a glass of water. Her painted nails grip a small, square-shaped paper.

Kate, as I've learned, likes origami—cranes, elephants, foxes, cats, butterflies. I find them on the bathroom counter, crumpled between the couch cushions, or placed lovingly atop the apples on the fridge. There are a fair number of stags amongst the collection, which was only surprising given how difficult the folds are.

"I like doing stuff with my hands," she told me when I asked. There was the beginning of an elephant between her fingers. "It clears my head."

Keep the hands busy, keep the mind clear. It's the same reason I bake.

I check the clock—I have a few hours before we're supposed to meet the Boars. And I could use some time to think.

While the oven preheats, I fall into a routine. Flour and baking soda and salt. Shortening and eggs. Combinations that just go together. The dough forms, and I try to remember the last time I made this recipe. Too long.

Leo loved snickerdoodles. He liked to shape the cookies into balls and roll them in cinnamon sugar. Every batch he'd pick one cookie to roll again and again, until the dough was so saturated it crumbled.

"Don't eat it!" he'd shout when I set the baked cookies on the cooling rack. "Don't eat the Leo cookie!"

I smile—that was a happy memory, but they weren't all like that. If I'm being honest, some days I didn't like Leo. It's horrible to think, now, after everything, but it's true.

It was exciting at first. My friends would come over, and Mom would let them touch the growing globe of her belly, but I knew my baby brother would only kick for me.

Then came the day, in the middle of Spanish class, when Señora Gomez pulled me aside to tell me my *hermano* was coming, and I needed to go to the front office right away.

Then he got older, and things got worse. Seven years is a big gap. I was tugging on training bras as he graduated from pull-ups. He and his snotty friends would yank down their pants and moon me during their campouts in the yard. He'd steal my iPod and make fun of my makeup. He was a pest.

Other days, I felt like I was raising him, what with Mom's fundraisers and Dad out of town a lot. Leo was my brother, but in some ways he was my kid. He cried in front of me. He told me about the kid in his class, Jake, who ran faster than he did but Leo was catching up. More than once, I forged Mom's signature on his field trip forms.

My nose tingles, and I pinch it to fight the tears.

Throwing myself back into the task at hand, I knead the dough again and again, until it's well past blended.

I slide the cookies into the oven and set a timer for eight minutes. They don't take long, and if you're not careful the bottoms will burn.

"Can you come grab me when this goes off?" I ask Kate.

She shrugs. "Sure."

Not quite the cheery answer I expected, but okay. I leave Kate to her menagerie and go to the basement to change into something warmer. Inhaling a lungful of musty air, I flick on the light and gasp. Jax is on my bed next to a pile of unfolded laundry. In his hands is a bundle of red lace.

Underwear.

My underwear.

Embarrassment and shock slice through me. I dash over and snatch them from his hand.

"What the fuck," I shout. This place is getting to me—I never swore so much at home. "Why are you going through my stuff?"

He laughs, his grin pulling to one side. "Calm down, Valentine. Jeez."

I stuff the underwear back in the drawer, my cheeks turning the same color as the lace. I can't stand this guy sometimes. It's like living with an earthquake—throwing me off balance whenever he pleases. "What do you want?"

"Just wanted to make sure you aren't nervous about tonight." Jax sits up. "It'll be your first time meeting another gang."

"I'm not. Nervous," I mutter. "You wouldn't let anything happen to me." My tone is light, but as I turn, I see something catch in Jax's eyes.

"I protect my own," he says, as if that answer suffices. He tugs at the collar of his leather jacket. "Wear black."

I frown, taking in the color and the clean, masculine smell of the leather. "Is that new?"

"Yeah," he replies. "Theresa sent it after I mentioned I needed a new one. What do you think?"

He does a slow turn, only breaking eye contact for a moment as he pivots. The jacket is beautiful. The back is detailed with a kind of sunburst design—five rings of concentric circles, each painstakingly embroidered with a bronze-colored thread that shines ever so slightly when he moves.

"It's really . . . nice."

"Nice? That's it?"

"No, really. It's just not something I'd expect from you."

"How so?"

"Like, the design. It's fancy. Your other jacket was more . . . simple. It's not something I'd expect of you."

"Unexpected is my favorite thing to be," he says, grinning. He goes up the stairs and slams the garage door behind him. *That guy.*

It takes an annoyingly long time for my heart rate to go down.

I distract myself by calling home. Mom doesn't answer— and I'm relieved she doesn't. I leave a message.

"Hey, Mom. It's me. Just checking in. I'm okay. I hope things are going okay. I know Dad's there now. Tell him I say hi. I love you. I'll call again soon. Bye."

I hang up with a sigh. A short, uninspired message some-how seems worse than forgetting to call.

A moment later, Mako opens the upstairs door and peeks down. "Hey, Val? I think something's burning."

"Shit!" I sprint back up the stairs, but I'm too late. The bot-toms are definitely burned. *Where did Kate go?* Mako helps me dump the burnt ones in the garbage as I pull the second half of the dough from the fridge.

"Redemption round," he says, smiling, as I roll the fresh dough into balls and place them on the tray.

"Here's hoping," I reply. I reset the timer as we wait. Mako grabs a frozen burrito from the fridge and sets it in the micro-wave, crossing his arms and leaning against the counter as he waits. Nothing ever seems to really bother Mako, which I like—and admire. If only I had his easygoing nature, I wouldn't still be thinking about what happened downstairs with Jax. Inhaling and exhaling carefully to fight the blush I'm sure is still evident on my face, I clear my throat.

"Hey, Mako?" I say quietly. "Can I ask you something?"

He nods. "Shoot."

"Do you . . ." I start. "Do you trust Jax?"

"Yeah."

"That was quick."

He bobs his head from side to side, weighing his thoughts in his mind. "When it comes to Stags, yes. This is his life."

"Yeah, I guess. But he's so . . ."

"I know." Mako laughs. "But he doesn't mess around on Stag business. At least he hasn't before. Why do you ask? Did something happen?"

"Just curious." I shrug. "Thanks."

Minutes later, Mako's burning his tongue on the burrito as I'm eyeing the bottoms of the second batch of cookies. Golden brown—perfect.

Mako takes a cookie from the tray and I barely have time to say "They're still hot" before he pops the whole thing in his mouth.

"Ow," he says, exhaling and cupping his hand in front of his mouth. "Too hot."

"I told you!" I reply, laughing. "Good though?"

"Soooo good." He gets up and dumps his plate in the sink. Once all the cookies are off the tray, he takes that too and starts scrubbing. "Almost showtime. Go get dressed."

"Okay," I reply. "Thanks, dude."

"No problemo."

Back downstairs, I find a long-sleeved black shirt and pull on my fleece-lined running jacket over it. I pull my hair into a French braid and slip on a pair of boots.

First time meeting a new gang. If all goes like Jax and Mako say it will, then it should be pretty calm. Still, from the way Nianna reacted, I know it's not common for these meetings to happen. Taking my knife from under the bed, I clip it to my jeans and hide it under my shirt. *Better safe than sorry.*

The upstairs door opens and Mako leans down. "First, these cookies are insane and I might eat them all."

"And second?" I ask, hopping onto the stairs myself.

"Second is we're about ready to go."

I rejoin the others in the kitchen. Jax is on the couch lacing up a pair of black combat boots, and waves me over when he sees me.

"I had a weird dream last night," he says, voice hushed. Reverent.

"What was the dream?"

He tilts his chin toward the others. "We were all on a beach. It was dark, no stars. No moon. Then these two fires started burning—your eyes—and you were walking into the water. Those guys followed you."

"You didn't?"

"Nah, I wanted to turn the other way. I screamed and screamed at you. All of you. Then the lights went out, and I woke up. What do you think it means?"

"I don't know." It's a weird thing to share—dreams rarely make sense even to the dreamer. Jax doesn't respond right away. He takes my hand and stands, pulling me with him as Nianna strides in from the kitchen.

"Let's go," she says.

Nianna opens the front door. A gush of chilly night air slides in, graceful and dark as a panther. The van is parked in the driveway. Jaws waits for us behind the wheel. As I pass the wilting hydrangeas and take a seat in the van, I find myself smiling. I feel like a part of something. We have a purpose. A name to protect. Allegiance runs like a magnetic pull between the Stags and me. I'm scared. I miss home and Matthew. But I am also free. I am free and ready to atone for what I did.

This is for you, Leo.

We are wild, neon-blooded devils as we go into the night.

We get to the rendezvous point just before midnight. The air is laden with hushed reverence and the itch for bloodshed.

Mission Dolores isn't even "Mission Dolores." It's Mission San Francisco de Asís. There are two buildings, the original mission and the basilica. The former is made of four-foot-thick adobe and it's a survivor of some of the city's worst earthquakes, including the one in 1906 and Loma Prieta in 1989.

I came here a long time ago on a class field trip. The air inside the mission was calm. It *felt* like a church.

The basilica, on the other hand, took me somewhere I don't even know. I remember the shining mosaics that race up the

walls and along the arching ribs of the ceiling. The fiery glow
from the honeycombs of orange stained glass. Mom chaper-
oned that day. I remember her saying that being inside the
basilica is the closest you can get to Heaven while still alive.

But that was before Leo. I'm not sure what she believes
now. I'm even less sure of what I believe.

There isn't much cover for us to take. Jaws stays in the car,
which is odd, given his intimidating presence—but I don't
question it. Jax assigns Mako and me a place behind a mailbox and a recycling bin on the opposite street.

Before we separate, Kate and Mako kiss each other once
on the cheek, in what must be some ritual of theirs. She and
Nianna are stationed a bit farther down Dolores Street, where
the adobe wall turns toward the cemetery. I bet Mako would
rather be stationed with his girlfriend, but I can't help but be
grateful for his bulk.

Micah is the most exposed. Peering around the mailbox, I
can see him leaning against the dark wood of a palm tree across
from where Jax sits on the steps of the mission.

We wait.

I bury my hands in my pockets. I should have brought
gloves. My mind wanders as the seconds tick closer to the
Boars' arrival.

Back in the van, Kate assured me that unless something
goes really, really wrong, this'll be an easy encounter.

"Ty wants to talk. That's all the IRIS said," she whispered.
"To make this a fight would be a breach of the rules. It'd be
seriously frowned upon."

Mako nudges my shoulder, and I'm pulled back to attention. "They're here."

Ghosts materialize out of the fog. The Boars huddle
together as they approach from both Sixteenth Street and
Dolores. With their gray hoods up, they are every bit an army.

Some are whispering to each other, others laughing like jack-als. Someone snaps for them to shut up. My eyes dart from face to face as I try to identify at least one of them.

I get my one.

A tall, lanky guy walks ahead of the others—Ty Boreas, the Boar leader. His gaze is trained forward. Unlike the other Boars, his sleeves are rolled up. The painterly slashes that compose the Boars' insignia are displayed proudly on his right forearm.

Since Leo died, I've imagined the leader of the killers who shot my brother to be grimy, ugly, and radiating with malice.

But from what I can tell, this guy is like any other SF na-tive. He moves with the laid-back gait of someone who's grown up walking these streets, breathing this air. Between bay windows and white-trimmed houses, he knows exactly where he is.

With a quick raise of his hand, the Boars halt. Jax gives Ty a nod as he comes up the steps.

"How do we know the Boars will cooperate with our terms?" I ask.

"It's part of the rules. The leaders agreed to it through IRIS, so it's legit."

"Who thinks of these rules?"

"The leaders did, early on, after too many people died in the first couple of years and the cops nearly got the survi-vors. It's a way to control it—keep the anger and the fight, but without destroying the city or bringing the law down on us."

I keep a wary eye on the line of Boars. Kate was right—to fight would go against what this meeting is about. The knot in my stomach unclenches, but only just.

I wonder if the Boars know why this meeting is happen-ing. Maybe Ty is more transparent with his crew than Jax is.

Just then, Ty and Jax shake hands. Ty half jogs back to his crew. He gives a single wave of his hand and the Boars move out.

A gunshot sounds.

The once orderly group of Boars scatter, transforming into a frenzy of panicked animals. Mako shoves me behind him and puts his hand on the back of my head like a protective parent.

"Fucking Boars!" he shouts.

Jax yells at Ty, cursing the day he was born and calling him every name under the sun. Somewhere beyond me, the din calms, enough for me to hear Ty's voice shouting back.

A tightrope silence follows, thin and tense.

"Oh, fuck," Mako says. The tone in his voice has changed. "It's some newbie. Get up, Val."

Legs trembling, I stand. Over at the church, Jax walks toward Ty. There's a third guy on the ground trying to get up, but Ty kicks him in the side—hard—and the guy doubles over again. Jax turns toward Mako and me, waving us over.

"It's cool," says Mako. "Come on."

We cross Dolores Street together, but Jax shakes his head. "Just Valentine."

I freeze. Mako turns to me and shrugs. "You heard the man."

I feel the Boars' eyes on me as my breath curls into the cold air like smoke. Any one of them could shoot me. *One step at a time,* I think. *Keep moving.* After what feels like a decade, I take a place next to Jax.

"This is Valerie Simons," says Jax. "My recruit."

"Valerie." Ty says my name like it's a question he already knows the answer to.

Jax points toward the guy on the ground. "Valentine, this

is Michael Hennessy. Now, Michael has been very bad. Do you know why?"

I should answer. I should answer so I look brave and tough, but I don't trust the right words to come to my mind. I shake my head.

"Michael fired his gun at me during a meeting where Ty and I had agreed on no violence. On neutral territory. At Mission fucking Dolores."

Each word is a drill into Michael Hennessy's head. He whimpers—actually *whimpers*—as Jax goes on.

"He's a new recruit, like you. But you know the rules, don't you, Valentine?"

That I do know how to answer: "Yes."

"And you would never break a truce that's been agreed upon by your leader."

"No."

"Good."

I only have a second to look at Ty. His hazel eyes are filled with something, but I don't know what. He takes a deep breath, then nods at Jax.

"Do what you will."

"Ty! Ty!" Michael howls, but his leader has already turned his back and started to vanish into the mist. Jax grabs Michael by the collar and drags him into the street. Following Jax, I look over my shoulder once—and see Ty staring back, too. Not at Nianna or Micah, but just at me. Our gazes meet, and he turns away, shaking his head. *What was that?*

I fall quiet behind Nianna and Micah. The way Ty looked at me—it was like he saw something else. Someone else. His expression had been sheepish, almost guilty. Trouble is, I don't know what a person as heartless as he is could ever feel guilty for.

Michael keeps screaming. He's done asking for Ty. Now he's just calling for help.

But the people in the Mission know this game. They know the nights belong to the Wars.

Mako grabs a fistful of Michael Hennessy's sweatshirt and tells him to shut the fuck up. The Stags form a kind of battle formation around the Boar. My hands shake, partly because I think I know what's about to happen and partly because I'm not sure if I want it to. *This is a Boar.* They're thugs, criminals, all of them. *They killed your brother.*

Mako and Jax drag Michael until we've reached the embankment in the middle of the street.

Mako looks back to the church, as if checking whether we are still in sight of the saints. At the same time, Nianna holds her arm out in front of my stomach and pushes me back. Words bubble up in my throat. *No. Stop. Wait.* I can't get a sound out.

Jax faces the Boar. Illuminated by the streetlights, he is menacing—dark and fuming and singular in his command.

"Please," Michael whispers. Snot and tears pour down his cheeks. "I'll do anything, Jax. I was just doing what the guys wanted me to."

"Ty told you?"

"No, some other guys."

"Who? Why?" Jax demands.

Michael inhales, leaning forward eagerly. "Because you betrayed us. They said Ty wanted you dead but couldn't do it himse—"

Jax lifts his gun and shoots Michael Hennessy in the leg.

8

Blood doesn't look like it does in the movies.

My ears are still ringing as Micah guides me into the middle row of the van. My arms and legs tremble, and I hope he can't feel it. Fumbling into the backseat, I find his seat belt and pass it to him. The van lurches to life, and soon we're far from the scene.

On the surface, we could be anyone—a bunch of college kids on their way to the bars, or a rock band, breathless and high as we leave a gig where the crowd was screaming our names. But we're not. We are the Stags, and we just shot a guy on the steps of Mission Dolores.

"What are you gonna do?" Micah asks Jax.

"What do you think I should do?" our leader replies.

Micah is steady. "We should find out who he talked to. If he's right, then working with the Boars is gonna get you killed."

Jax ponders this a while, the only sound in the van that of raindrops starting to hit the windshield. "I need to think on this," he says finally. "But until I say otherwise, the Boars are our allies."

Micah sits back in his seat. "To go against the Herons?"

"Bingo."

"It's a good idea," Nianna says coolly from Micah's right.

"The Herons are getting too cocky, capitalizing on the Silicon Valley bimbos and their money."

"Ty's heard more, too," Jax replies. "The new police chief they hired last year—Ty thinks he and the Herons are going to try and oust us."

"How?" Micah asks.

"Some program to make it seem like they're fixing us evil, evil gangs. We're gonna find out."

The road turns sharply, and I fall into Micah's shoulder—I remembered his seat belt and forgot my own. I take a breath and clip myself in, fingers shaky.

I witnessed a shooting tonight. The gang I'm sworn to has teamed up with the one I hate to take down the group that the guy I'm in love with belongs to. *Sounds like a movie trailer,* I think bitterly. Only this isn't a movie, it's my real fucking life and I don't know what I can do. Worst of all, I signed up for this. *Still . . .*

I am part of Jax's game, or whatever this is. I've met a gang leader and did my part in participating in—or, at least, consenting to—what happened to Michael Hennessy. I'm one night closer to earning his trust and finding out who it was that shot Leo, and that's what I've wanted all along.

We get home and Jax starts drinking. We all do. I down my first beer quickly and a second just as fast. All I want is for the image—the sound of Michael shrieking, the smell of blood—to go away. Mako fires up the PlayStation, and soon the boys are lost to their games.

The alcohol hits me. My mind switches off. Something else switches on.

"S'cuse me," I say, scooting past Kate and into the kitchen. I open drawers one by one until I find what I need.

I shouldn't do this. Everyone says it's bad. Lyla made me swear to call her—anytime, any day—instead of doing it.

But it's not a problem. I don't do it all the time. It's not a problem. It's a last resort.

I head for the bathroom and shut the door firmly behind me. The scissors smile in my hand. No one saw me take them, right?

I unbutton my jeans and tug them down. My right side, always the right side. I don't know why. I bring the blade down, press it onto my skin—then jerk my arm back. Slow then fast. Slow then fast. Breathe. Breathe. Tell no one.

I exhale, nearly sobbing in relief. It works every fucking time.

Two more cuts. Always three. One for each letter.

L-E-O.

When I'm done, I tug my pants up and wash the scissors with soap and water.

Someone knocks on the door. "You okay?"

"Yeah!" I shout back. *Clearly I'm fine.*

The cuts are not the worst I've ever done—two or so inches, wider in the middle. Blood beads along the edge but doesn't drip down. Plenty of people cut way worse than me. I'm not even cutting, really, just scraping.

I turn and stare down my own reflection in the mirror, like I've done a million times before. "You were his big sister," I whisper. "It was your job to be there. You should have protected him." My voice cracks. "You can't now, but you can protect other people. You can stop the Boars from killing any more innocent people." Michael Hennessy wasn't innocent. He chose this, just like I did.

I slip back into the kitchen and tuck the friendly scissors in their place.

Kate's leaning into the fridge, one arm draped over the open door. She twirls the end of her braid around her pointer finger, then lets it go and grabs a can of beer.

"You want one?"

I wave her off and motion to her hair. "I don't know how you keep it so long." *She didn't see me put the scissors back. She'd have said something if she did.* "This is about as long as I get before I go crazy."

"I love having long hair." She teeters on her feet even though she's still holding the door. "My mom had long hair like mine, then she got cancer and *poof!* It all fell out. I asked her if she wanted me to cut mine—like, was it painful for her to look at, you know? But Mom said no, because when she looked at me she could see something beautiful. Then we weren't able to afford her chemo and she died and I had to go live with my shitbag of a dad."

There's so much in that one breathless confession and each part splinters my heart in a different way. "Oh my god, Kate. I'm so sorry."

The corner of Kate's lip twitches. Her hand goes to her back pocket, and she pulls out a square of neon paper. She pinches the corner, and I want to say something—anything—but Mako cuts me off.

"Kate, stop hogging Valentine and get over here. We're taking shots."

"Okay," is her reply. I catch her eye and she gives me a weak smile. "Go."

I pretend to take the shot, but leave half of it in the glass. This doesn't feel good. For the next ten minutes or so, I think I've gotten away scot-free, that I'd stopped drinking in time. Then, slowly, I begin to slide away. I'm lifting. I'm a thousand helium balloons, light and free in a blue sky. I feel blizzardy. *Blizzardy.* Is that even a word? I don't know. I don't care. Blizzardy blizzardy!

Everything is hilarious. Everyone around me is radiant and perfect—and I want to tell them. I am *going* to tell them.

Music booms from the speakers as I dart from Stag to Stag. I kiss Kate on the cheek, and when Mako protests I kiss his cheek, too. Nianna, Jax, and Micah are trying to set up some drinking game, but I ignore their process and flit to each of them. Micah is welcoming and gentle. Nianna is beautiful and strange.

My mind is a tangle of downed wires on the side of the freeway. Downed by a blizzardy blizzard. Little sparks.

But I'm in control enough to know that when I reach Jax, he puts his arm around me first, and kisses the top of my head like I'm precious, like I'm special.

Like I'm his.

9

The next night, after a long day of being hungover and trying to get my mind off the previous night by watching baking shows on Netflix, Jax calls all the active Stags together. "Time to show the Herons their reign is over," he says. He takes a sip of his beer and gives me a wink. "Plus it's time you met everyone else."

After last night, I'm not really ready for any more Stag business, but this is what I signed up for, so I man up and am in the kitchen at the appointed time.

Kurt arrives first with two more Stags, Juliet and Cameron. Juliet is heavyset with a long braid of black hair; she keeps her arms folded as she leans against the wall. "Half Filipino, half Chinese," she tells me when I ask. Her eyes smile from beneath long, thick lines of eyeliner. She throws some punches into the air with practiced motions and says, "Fighter on both sides."

"Me, too," I reply, relieved to have something in common. "Well, half Filipino."

She cocks her head to the side. "Really? You don't look it."

"Yeah," I say. "My mom's side is pretty light skinned for Filipinos as is. And since my other half is white, it's super hard to tell."

"Gotcha." She puts her arm around my shoulder. "I'm just

glad there's going to be someone else to back me up when I argue *halo halo* is the best dessert of all time."

"Ooh," I reply, salivating at the thought of the red bean, shaved ice, and purple *ube* ice cream concoction that is *halo halo*. "A hundred percent will back you up. Have you ever been there? To the Philippines?"

"Yeah, a few times. My grandma and cousins are there."

"Wow," I say. "I've always wanted to go."

"Why haven't you?"

I hesitate. "Just never got around to it, I guess. My mom hasn't been since she came to the U.S., and it's not a big deal to her. So we never did."

"Dude, you should go, at least once," Juliet replies. "It's pretty cool."

Cameron shakes my hand when I offer it, but doesn't say anything else. He lives and breathes monotone—gray hat with black pants and shoes. The side of his head and face is tattooed with a series of interlocking gears. A dagger entangled in barbed wire rides up his forearm.

"Where's your Stag tattoo?" I ask, going with the safest bit of small talk I have.

"My back," he replies flatly. Then he turns and greets Jax, who'd just stomped down the stairs. An amused laugh sounds from behind me.

"Don't worry about Cameron," Nianna says. "He tries to look all tough, but he's scared shitless around girls."

The three of them stay and we have a feast of enchiladas, rice, beans, and everything in between. Juliet tells a story about a guy who tried to hit on her by talking about bird hunting, which makes Nianna laugh so hard she cries.

Once we've all eaten, Jax tells us to leave the plates and gather in the living room.

"As you all know," he says, "we're partnering with the

Boars to take on the Herons once and for all. And thanks to Theresa, I know exactly where we're going to hit 'em."

I frown and sip my water. I always found it bizarre when people refer to their parents by their first names.

"There's a corner store in the Lower Haight that's been owned by the same family for three generations. The Herons want to tear it down as part of a redevelopment plan. This store is the last holdout on the block. Now there are plans to build an apartment complex there."

"Of course," Juliet mutters.

"The company building the complex isn't publicly associated with her Herons. Theresa says the Herons are trying to fund the building through a San Francisco-based company to avoid backlash. They won't reveal they're with the Herons until after everything's done."

"Sneaky," Kate murmurs.

Jax continues. "Anyway, demolition is scheduled for next week. Media will be there, and probably some city officials keeping people away from the area. We're going to make sure that the building remains standing by flooding the streets with people protesting."

"What do the Boars need us for?" Nianna asks, swirling the last of her beer.

"To make it two against one. I agree with the move. Everyone's going to pitch in getting the word out, and getting people there," Jax replies. Taking a hair tie from his wrist, he pulls his hair back into a man bun. *It's like freakin' Thor is in our living room,* I think, laughing inwardly.

"Jules and I will hit up bars in the area and feel out people's moods," Jax continues. "Nianna and Micah, I'll need you to use your Oakland connections to see if we can get support from the other side of the bay."

"Done," she replies. Micah nods.

"Kate and Val, you're on social. Micah will draw a logo for you to use and give you the logins for the accounts we have already. You'll use burner phones to call media to draw attention to our cause, emphasizing that it's now two against one. With us united with the Boars, the Herons look like the big bad wolf."

Make calls and organize a protest. I think I can handle that. "Okay," I say affirmatively. I nudge Kate's shoulder. "We got it."

She flinches, like she's suddenly paying attention. "Oh. Definitely."

Jax runs through the rest of the roles—Mako and Kurt are on recon about the demolition itself. Cameron will dig into the right forums on Reddit and other sites to get people to the rally.

"Remember the cause," says Jax. "But be smart about it. If we all go in guns blazing, saying how this is all part of a plan, then no one will come. We have to make them care. Make them feel like this is their chance to have their voices heard. This is the march for our city, to protect the San Francisco that people know and love. Make them remember the decisions they disagreed with, the places they miss—"

"And streets without all those fucking scooters laying around," says Mako, getting all of us to laugh.

Jax raises his beer. "Appeal to their hearts. Injustice is a rallying cry."

"Amen," says Nianna, and we all raise a glass. Over in the papasan, Micah lifts his cup, too, but later than the rest of us. While the others kick off a round of Call of Duty, I catch Micah's eye and motion back over to the kitchen. I wait until the noise from the TV is loud enough to say anything.

"You okay?" I ask.

He tucks his hand into his sweatshirt. "Yeah, sure."

"You don't look it."

"I'm nervous about working with the Boars. It's been a while, but even the newbies would know that Jax left them. They might want to get back at him."

The plate I'm holding slips out of my grasp and clangs around the sink. "You think?"

"Maybe. The Boars are unpredictable. Always have been."

"Are you gonna tell Jax?"

He shrugs. "He knows how I feel." Micah grabs another pair of plates from the table and scoots me out of the way. I relinquish the sink but hop up on the counter. I'm not sure what else to say, so I just hang out as he finishes up the dishes, then starts the washer.

"You wanna split a beer?" he asks me, and I nod. He goes and grabs it, then sits up on the counter next to me.

"Don't tell Jax what I said, okay?" he says quietly, handing me the beer.

I take it. "I thought you said he knew how you felt."

"He does. But he probably doesn't want me corrupting your opinions."

I think, take a sip, and hold out the bottle for him to take back. "I don't exactly disagree though."

He sighs. "Best not tell Jax that either."

The next morning, I trudge upstairs and head straight for the kitchen. After staying up late last night, I'm desperate for coffee. Nianna's at the table reading the newspaper.

"Good morning," I say. "Anything interesting in there?"

"Morning," she replies. "And kinda, yeah. Says here that the San Francisco police chief John Kilmer is in talks with private security companies about getting help on a new public safety campaign."

Kilmer. That name. Nianna has her eyes back on the page— she doesn't see my shock. *It can't be the same person.*

She takes a sip of her coffee. "Kilmer's plans appear effective. There have been just two gang-related murders since December of last year and over a dozen arrests." Her voice rises at the last part, like she's asking a question. "Do you think that's true?"

"What? Sorry."

"The arrests. Do you think that's true?"

"Oh. Um, Jax would've said something if it was," I say. "Isn't that what he's working on with Ty, or part of it at least?"

"Yeah, maybe," she replies. "Still . . ."

"Yeah."

I grab a pan to fry up an egg, praying food will distract me from my memories. I didn't know Deputy Kilmer had become chief of police, but I guess it has been two years since he worked on Leo's case. *Would he recognize me if he saw me now?*

I push the thought out of my mind, finish cooking, then sit down at the table to eat. *One thing at a time, Valerie.* And right now that thing is planning a damn protest.

Kate's never used Twitter, and I have an account that I barely use, so that makes me the Twitter expert. She and I sit next to each other at the table, laptops side by side.

"Okay, so the Stags have an account already, right?" I say. Before the Wars, I would read it from time to time, but they barely posted. "What's the login?"

She doesn't know, so I ask Micah. After digging around, he finds a crumpled piece of paper with some passwords, one

of which works. There's a meager following of eight hundred
or so people, but it's something, at least. We start with the
basics—when and where, what we're protesting, and how to
help.

"*Nonviolent* protest," I say as we read through our copy.

"Nonviolent, peaceful protest," echoes Kate as she types.
"Should people wear any particular thing? Like the pink hats
for the Women's March."

"Hmm," I respond. "It's kinda short notice for anyone to
get anything."

"I dunno. People are really resourceful. Maybe red hats?
For the Red Bridge Wars."

"Oh, maybe," I reply. "Let's come back to that. We need a
hashtag."

"Oooh, yes."

As Kate and I bounce ideas around, I fight the urge to ask
if she feels like Micah and I feel—that the Boars are dangerous, and we shouldn't be working with them. They could have
planned a protest on their own—is it really that much of a
benefit to work together?

"Well?" says Kate.

"Sorry, kinda spaced. What did you say?"

"I said what about 'Halt the Herons'? As a tagline?"

"Oh! Yeah, that's perfect."

She beams and gets back to typing the copy for the event
website. She's in a good mood today, which I'm glad about.
Kate's moods remind me of a girl in my class at school, Ella.
She sat next to Lyla in history and would hang out with our
group here and there. She was friendly but reserved. Some
days she'd be silent, and other days she'd hop into the conversation like she was born ready.

When she stopped showing up to lunches, Lyla told me in
confidence that Ella was seeing the school counselor during

that time. "Her parents are getting divorced and putting her in the middle of everything," Lyla had said. "It's super fucked up. I told her she should talk to someone about it. I miss eating lunch with her, but I'm glad she's getting help."

If only Kate could get help. I don't know her well enough to say anything to her face, but I decide then to talk to Mako about it, no matter how awkward that convo might be.

I switch gears back to my role—spreading the word on Twitter. Tweeting out pieces of Kate's website copy, I start tacking on all the hashtags I can think of, including #HaltThe-Herons. Next, I click around until I find the accounts of groups already fighting the gang violence. After I message them in private, I start commenting on their posts. My notifications tick up and up. For good measure, I do a quick search for "top Twitter tips for hosting an event" just to make sure I'm not forgetting anything.

"You should tweet a picture of the corner store," says Kate. "Here, this one has the owner right in front. He's such a sweet old guy."

She sends me the picture, and a few tweets later, I shut the laptop. "God I hope this works."

Kate shrugs. "Well, we did what Jax wanted us to."

"What if it's not enough?"

"Then you figure out ways to make it enough," Jax says from behind us. Kate and I both turn and see him leaning against the post in the foyer.

"You two keep working. I'll be back after last call."

When the door shuts behind them, Kate huffs. "Some work he and Jules have to do. Drink and schmooze with people while asking them about our protest."

"Hopefully it gains some traction by the time bars start getting busy," I say, glancing at the microwave clock. It's 4:14 P.M. "Let's keep working."

"Fine," she replies, reopening her laptop. "You want to email KTVU, and I'll take KPIX 5?"

We divide up the news stations, and then email a few smaller outlets like the Wars fansite I know. I answer the hits we get off Twitter—what we need, how they can help. I email the fair housing and activist sites, explaining what we're trying to do with our protest and asking that they sound the rallying cry, too.

We're up against the clock, but with everyone on board, I start to have hope that we can really pull this off. It'd be one step closer to showing Jax I'm loyal to the Stags, and therefore one step closer to finding out who Leo's killer is.

Besides, despite my intentions or even the Stags', I believe in this. We truly are giving people a platform. And that's all a person needs—someplace to spark the tinder of change, and an audience to watch the flames.

10

The day of the protest arrives.

We get off the bus to the sound of chants in the distance. I spot a fellow protester carrying a sign—SAVE OUR CITY. The man spots me, too, giving me a nod from a bandana-clad face. Tugging up my own mask, I nod back and keep following the others toward the store.

I'm in jeans and a dark jacket, nothing too ostentatious. Even though we're technically hosting this, Jax wants us all to blend in.

From the storefronts, shop owners and patrons watch us with wide eyes. Whether they're supporting us or wishing we'd go home, I can't tell. We round the corner and I almost *whoop* with joy. "Holy shit."

San Francisco came out. Sure, it's not like the Women's March or protests after the election, but it's a goddamn *rally* if I've ever seen one. Marchers carry handmade signs and sport bright red hats—just as the campaign told them to. Men and women march side by side—I even spot one little girl among the crowd, carrying a sign that says NO MORE BIG BUSINESS. With all the people gathered, I can hardly see the other side of the street where the demolition was supposed to take place.

The Stags got here in waves—Juliet, Cameron, and Mako

came early. Kate, Micah, and Nianna are on the other street corner. Kurt is somewhere in one of the buildings above, keeping an eye out for us. Why Jax wanted me with him and Jaws, I'm not sure. The three of us were quiet on the MUNI ride over—Jaws a boundless depth and Jax an arrow, notched and ready to be loosed.

Beside me, Jax comes to a stop, his breath rising in the chilly air. "Wait here a sec," he says, indicating a spot between a pair of parked cars. "You got everything you need?"

He's asking if I have the means to protect myself if needed. "Yes."

"Keep your mask up. Don't let them take it off you."

"Okay."

He nods, then turns to go. "I'll be right back. Jaws, with me."

I watch them melt into the crowd. *Jax is so different today,* I think. I wonder if he's thinking of what happened at Missions Dolores. Would the Boars try to take him out here? I shiver, and look around at the growing group of people around me. The Boars have blended in seamlessly with the civilians—peaceful for now, but even the tiniest spark will ignite their fury, and all bets about this being a nonviolent protest will be off.

Keeping close to the left side of the crowd between a building and a bus stop, I find a perch on a set of stairs. My phone buzzes—Jax telling me to hang tight. Scanning the throng for the other Stags in their positions, something else catches my eye. I gasp, hands flying to my face.

"Oh my god."

I see her backpack first—a ratty, aqua-colored JanSport she's had since freshman year. There's a BLACK LIVES MATTER pin next to a rainbow heart pin under a Sharpie drawing of a cat that I had done one day when we were bored during pre-calc. I'd recognize the backpack anywhere, and when the girl wearing it turns and tucks a lock of lilac-dyed hair out of her face, I can't help but call her name.

"Lyla!" I scream. My best friend turns, shrieks, and opens her arms in time for me to run into her.

"Oh my god, oh my god," she whispers into my ear. "Valerie. Oh my god. Holy shit."

"I can't believe you're here," I say, my face squished against her shoulder.

"Me either," she replies. "How are you? What are you doing here?"

"Um, protesting," I reply. "Are you here for the rally? Are you with people?"

"No," she replies. "I Lyfted over. I'm supposed to meet up with Michelle and Nerrisa, but I don't know how the hell I'm going to find them . . ." I nod—those girls are from theater club. She waves herself off, like *never mind*. "Anyway. You. How are you? I was so confused when you didn't show up that night. I kept calling and calling, then eventually called Matthew. When he didn't answer either, I knew something was up. I can't believe you said yes." She shakes her head. "What about graduating? What about college?"

"I don't know," I reply. "I really don't. But I had to join. The Stags are going to help me find the person who killed Leo."

Her expression changes at the sound of his name. "Do you really think they'll help you?"

"Yes."

"I'm just scared for you." Her voice lowers. "Like, are you safe?"

"The Stags aren't like that. It's totally different, but in a good way."

I don't know how I'm going to cover everything in whatever time we have, but I try. I assure her I'm fine over and over. I tell her what the Stags are really about—stopping the Herons from advancing, and their monthly call for peace. How Jax handles all the dirty work himself, to keep blood off the hands of those in his charge. How we built this rally from the ground up.

Her eyes get wider and wider, until finally she puts her hands up like *stop*.

"Time-out. You did this?" she says, motioning to the rally. "No one knows the Stags want peace. You'd get so much more support if people knew."

They still shoot people, I want to say, but I bite my tongue. "It's not that simple. For now, I'm just doing as I'm told. I have to stay in until I find the guy who killed Leo."

She shakes her head. "A year is such a long time."

"I know," I reply. "And I barely know what I'm doing, but we're both here. Protesting for what we believe in. I'm in the Stags, yeah, but that doesn't mean I'm no longer me. I'm still the same Valerie, but now I have a chance at getting the one thing I want more than anything *and* standing up for something more important. I get to do both."

Her eyes look to the ground as she thinks. For a moment, I think she's going to run for the hills. Instead, she pulls me into a hug.

"I don't exactly agree," she says into my ear. "But I love you. You're my best friend. And you're talking like the Val I like best."

"What do you mean?"

"You're talking like you give a shit," she replies. "Like, you're alive again instead of sleepwalking, and this is what you want to do. And you're doing it. And that's good."

"Thank you. Lyla, I mean it. God, I'm so glad I found you."

"Valentine!"

I turn and see Jax sauntering toward me, a scowl on his face but his expression curious.

"Is that guy with you?" Lyla whispers, gripping my shoulder. "Is he a Stag?"

"Technically, I'm with him. I gotta go," I say, giving her hand a squeeze. "You're the best, Lyla."

"Stay safe!" she says. Then louder, she says, "You better take care of her, okay?"

My best friend is yelling at the leader of a gang—a guy who has killed people, no less. It's the most on-brand thing Lyla's ever done.

Jax gives her a salute but pulls me toward him forcefully. "Don't wander off," he says. "We have a job to do."

"I know." Avoiding his gaze, I smile. Lyla's words seem to wrap around my limbs, giving me strength. I can do this.

The crowd around the site has doubled in the few minutes I was with Lyla. Catching a glimpse of a girl's cell phone, I see Twitter opened on it. #HaltTheHerons is trending.

"The people were already mad," Jax says, nodding toward the girl with the phone. I guess he saw, too. "All you have to do is give them a voice. The Herons think they can get people to love them. That's their mistake. They forget how much easier it is to motivate around hate."

I follow closely behind Jax as he shoulders his way through the crowd. Bodies rock into mine but I keep my head high.

A girl on a megaphone stands on the top of a newspaper stand, her fist raised. She stamps her black combat boots. "Whose city? Our city!"

She lowers the megaphone, and as a roar of assent follows, I realize it's Juliet smiling at me from that newspaper stand. *Fighter.*

I catch Jax grinning before joining the chant himself.

Across the street, the police have set up a barrier and are

holding firm. A cop blares on his own megaphone, telling us to disperse—but our chants are louder. Out of nowhere, a black object goes whizzing from our side to the police, followed by a pop.

Shouts turn to screams as the flare explodes. It's all the crowd needs.

People scatter—or try to—some toward the cops and others anywhere but. Someone slams into me and I'm knocked back just as the smoke from a tear-gas canister begins wafting over to me.

Jax warned us about them, and I do my best to follow his training. *Don't take big breaths,* I remember. Cupping my hand over my bandana, I keep to the edge of the chaos as best I can, but fear tugs at my heart. Lyla.

Desperate, I search the people ahead of me and those already fleeing down the street for a glimpse of lilac hair. I can feel my phone buzzing in my hand—probably Jax telling us to get the fuck out—but I can't go unless I know Lyla's okay.

Wind cuts through the smoke of the tear gas, and I see her. She's bent over on the ground with someone else who's trying to tug her out of the way as a Boar rushes forward and slams into the riot gear of a cop who's materialized from the crowd.

I run straight toward her.

Battling through the crush of bodies, I snap my goggles over my eyes. Another Boar—his tattoo proudly showing from his shoulder despite the December chill—sprints up from behind me, drops to his knees, and slides a flare or a bomb or something glowing with the telltale light of a fuse. I reach Lyla and yank her up by the shoulders, her red and tearstained eyes meeting mine just as the explosion goes off.

If my friend screams, I don't hear her. Debris from the street and branches from the tree above rain down on us, and I squeeze my mouth shut to keep the dust out. Lyla and I make it a few strides when suddenly a firm hand grips down on my arm, yanking me back. I turn and see unnerving, blank eyes and midnight-black riot gear. SFPD. I scream again, shoving Lyla in the other direction and begging the universe for her to get away. The policeman drags me down, shoving my cheek into the concrete sidewalk of San Francisco.

I'm coughing, crying, and choking for air as the cold metal of handcuffs snaps cruelly over my wrists. If any of the Stags are near, they're not coming for me now. I'm dizzy and defeated as the officer recites my rights, and I'm hauled away.

11

Getting arrested feels exactly how I always imagined it'd feel: shitty.

"Name?"

"Valerie Simons."

"Age?"

"Eighteen."

The officer types in my information with an alarming speed, her fingers hammering at the keys like she has seen my kind before, and she's sick of it. I answer each of her questions calmly but respectfully. I can hear Jax's voice telling me to play the good girl and I have no problems whatsoever doing so. *Act scared, act clueless.*

"No criminal record," the officer says as she reviews my information. Her eyes stay on the computer screen, barely acknowledging my presence. "What were you doing at the rally?"

"Just showing my support," I respond. "I was really sad to hear they were going to tear down that corner store."

"How'd you hear about it? The protest."

"Twitter."

"Twitter?"

"Yes, ma'am."

She makes a note of this. While she types, I can feel sweat

beading at the back of my neck underneath my jacket. So far, no one has seen my tattoo.

"Have you attended an event like this before, and are you affiliated with any of the local groups who supposedly hosted said rally?"

"No, ma'am," I answer, feigning shock. "My mom would kill me if I joined any of the gangs, or whatever. Hell, she's going to kill me if she ever finds out about *this*."

The officer doesn't give any hint that she cares, and instead stays all business. "Officer Ramirez will take you to booking. Next."

The whole process feels almost made up, like I'm an extra on *CSI*. I hand over my phone and everything else in my pockets. They pat me down again, this second time just as thoroughly as when the officer pinned me to the sidewalk.

After the pat down is fingerprinting. The officer has to shove my shaking hand to the paper. The black ink seals itself to the paper as surely as one thought has sealed itself in my mind over and over again—*I am so fucked.*

Finally, the grand finale—the photograph. The camera flashes before I have a chance to sit up straight, but they don't care about the formalities. I can still see the afterimage of the flash as I'm shoved into the holding cell.

There are six other women here. Immediately, I spot Juliet. Her head tilts back, propped against the concrete wall. A trail of dried blood runs from her bottom lip down to her chin.

Taking the seat next to her, she almost imperceptibly touches her knee to mine. Then she pulls it away. I try to understand her signal—*I'm here for you, but we should act like we don't know each other.*

Jax will get me out. Someone will post my bail. I'm shivering, scared, and feeling absolutely stupid for getting caught. *Well, at least I'm not alone.*

"Some fucker grabbed my leg and my knee buckled," Juliet whispers out of nowhere. "Once I was on the ground, I clocked him pretty hard, but here we are."

"What do we do now?" I whisper.

"Wait," Juliet replies.

I huddle down as best I can, wishing my jacket hadn't been among the items confiscated. Goose bumps creep along my arms, and I draw my knees to my chest to try and keep warm.

Hours tick by. Outside, daytime fades to an unforgiving night. A door opens, and an officer walks in front of the cell, eyes low on a clipboard. "Flora Santos?" she asks.

One of the women on the opposite side of the cell sits up and shuffles over to the door. The officer tells us all to keep back as the metal bars slide open, and Flora goes. My heart sinks, and I shift on the metal bench just as the officer comes back around.

"Valerie Simons?"

Jumping up, I look back at Juliet, who gives me a look that says: *Go on, get outta here.*

I follow behind the officer as another attendant hands her a plastic tub with my stuff—jacket, phone, wallet.

"Your charges have been formally dropped," the female officer says to me. "And you're free to go. But I'd advise you not to participate in such protests again. They've been known to get pretty violent."

With that, she pushes open a side door leading into what I imagine is the rest of the police station. I tug on my jacket, my heart pounding, as if someone might try to stop me from leaving.

But no one does, and I step outside to get my bearings. A rush of cold wind greets me, and after spotting a sign for Fillmore Street, I walk a block or so on Turk, which I know will eventually get me back toward Civic Center and a BART

station. Pressing the power button on my phone, I wait for it
to turn on. A whistle sounds from my right. I turn.

"Mako!"

"What up, V?" he responds, opening his arms for a hug.
His muscular arms give me a tight squeeze. "You okay? What'd
they say?"

"No charges," I respond. "I didn't have a weapon on me."

"Atta girl," he replies. "Where'd you drop it?"

I cringe, guiltily. "I didn't bring one. I know Jax said to in
case we needed it. But I was really hoping I wouldn't need it."

"Damn, okay," he replies, putting an arm around me and
steering me in the opposite direction of where I was going.
"My phone's dead. Can you text Jaws you're out? He's somewhere around here with the car."

After a few minutes of waiting, the man in question pulls
up and we climb in. When we get back to Holloway, everyone's in the kitchen. Their faces light up when they see
me—but my eyes are only on Jax. Which Jax am I going to
get—pissed or concerned?

My leader gets up and saunters over to me—and immediately pulls me into a hug.

"Sorry I lost track of you," he says. "You okay?" I nod
into his chest, taken aback by the gesture. *Shit, he smells good.*

Jax guides me over to the others, and I get hugs from each
of them. When I finally sit, Nianna slides me a glass of water
and I drink heartily.

"How's Jules?" she asks, tugging at the end of her sleeves
and bundling herself in her sweater.

"Okay," I reply. "Her lip was cut pretty badly. How come
she didn't get released, too?"

"Not her first offense," Jax answers. "We'll get her out on
bail, but she'll probably be arraigned and everything."

"Shit."

"Jules will be okay," he responds pointedly. There's something else implied there.

"I'm okay, too," I say, shrugging. "I didn't even get charged."

"Good to hear." He smiles, but not all the way. Something's up.

"Tell her, Jax," says Micah. I swivel so I can see him. He shifts his beanie around his black hair and sighs. "She's gonna find out anyway."

"Find out what?" I ask.

Jax scratches his head. "You were doxxed. Everyone who was arrested was."

I know the word, but barely. "What does that mean?"

"SFPD put out your photo and name on their social media accounts. It's a deterrent, so that others don't join the next protest for fear of being outed, too."

Oh. My. God. "They put my fucking mug shot online?"

"Yeah."

"*What?*" I am going to throw up. "Can they do that? Is that legal?" Daughter of a lawyer, my first thought is always going to be whether it's legal.

"Kinda," Jax replies. "Bit of a gray area, but it's already done."

"It's not a new tactic. Berkeley police have done it before," Micah chimes in. He scoots around Mako so that he can take the seat next to mine. "We've already started the rallying cry for them to be taken down."

"My parents. All my friends . . . they're gonna see me on the news." My voices rises in disbelief and horror. Mom always watches the eleven o'clock news. I could tell her not to watch, but that might only make her want to watch more. *I'll call,* I decide. *If they're gonna hear it, I want it to be from me.*

"It's gonna be okay," Micah says, and Nianna nods her assent. "We've dealt with worse."

"Until then, you stay here," says Jax. "I want you—and Jules, once we get her out—to lie low for a few weeks unless I say otherwise."

"Okay," I say. My head is still swimming, the pit in my stomach getting worse and worse.

"There's more," says Jax. The rest of the Stags look at him, eyes curious.

Nianna frowns. "What do you mean, 'more'?"

"A message from the Herons." He shifts and takes out a piece of paper from his back pocket. He holds it out to me. Nianna pauses and, getting an affirmative nod from Jax, leans over my shoulder.

"The Herons want to meet with me?" I ask.

"The Herons," Jax repeats in a lilting voice. "You know who actually wants to meet with you."

Matthew. "It . . . it doesn't say who."

"It doesn't have to."

"Are you going to let me go?" I ask. "You literally just said to lie low."

"Unless I say so. So yes, you're going to this. You're gonna be my mole. You can find out what the Herons thought about today, as well as what their next move will be."

I open my mouth, ready to fire back that I would never spy on Matthew, but I hold my tongue. The tattoo on my neck prickles. "Okay."

He eyes me for a moment, then nods. "I'll send out the message. Camille will insist on no weapons, but that's fine. I'll insist on our turf, which she'll accept. Somewhere that's clearly ours and public. You'll be safe."

"Okay."

"All right." Jax goes back to his room, and I make a beeline for the basement.

I kick off my shoes and dive onto my bed. In the safety of solitude, I read the fragile gray print over and over. Matthew. My Matthew.

I'll see him, and everything is going to be better. Right now, I have to catch my parents before the eleven o'clock broadcast.

Mom picks up first ring. "Val? Peter! It's Val!"

There's the sound of a door quickly opening, followed by my dad's voice in the background.

"Valerie?"

"Hi, Mom. Hi, Dad."

"Oh my gosh, honey. Are you okay?" My parents always ask that first. I guess I would, too, if the situations were reversed. I answer all their questions slowly—yes, I'm totally fine. No, I won't come home.

"There's something I have to tell you," I say finally. "And I wanted you to hear it from me before you heard it from someone else." In any other universe, my parents might be worrying I'm pregnant or flunked out of school. Instead, I explain doxxing and what it means. Which also means admitting I was arrested.

"Oh, Valerie. Oh my god" is my mom's reply.

"I know," I say. Tears well up unexpectedly. I'm letting them down, in so many ways. "But the others are working on getting them taken down. I just didn't want you seeing it on the news."

Mom must have handed the phone over, because it's my dad who replies. "Honey, you did the right thing in telling us. But Valerie, this is getting out of hand. You could have gotten hurt, or worse. Just tell us where you are, and we'll come get you."

"Please," Mom echoes.

I've done this enough to know that this is the point where I have to be my strongest, even if it feels absolutely and un-equivocally wrong.

"I am not coming home. I'm doing this, and I'm making it right. I love you both so much. I'm sorry. I love you."

And then I hang up. Sobs rack my body and I fall back onto the bed. *What am I doing?* Turning onto my side, I roll over on the bed and something under my hip crunches. The IRIS.

I clutch the paper to my chest, aware of the girly cliché. But I don't care. For once it's for a good reason that I. Don't. Care. What I need now is something and someone familiar. Some-one who made the same choice as me, whose story is inter-twined with my own.

And Matthew Weston is the only person on the planet who fits the bill.

12

Stonestown Galleria is not the biggest or the best of San Francisco's shopping malls. It's swarmed with college students killing time between classes and drinking overpriced juices. There's a movie theater on one end and a gym on the other, but I've never known anyone to go to either. In short, it's not much.

But tonight, Stonestown is everything.

I'm bundled in my best coat, the glossy waves of my hair rising and falling with the wind. It feels strange to be so dressed up after days of wearing nothing but black sweats and workout gear, but I'm glad I am. Waiting here in the cold, I feel more like myself—more Valerie, less Valentine—than I have in weeks.

And after a week of not being allowed to leave Holloway, I'm just happy to be anywhere but there.

Kate has her arm looped through mine. We huddle together outside the Peet's Coffee by the parking lot.

"He's cute," she whispers.

"What?"

"Matthew Weston," she says. "Jax had me scout him soon after I joined. I guess I was scouting you, too. I remember he was hot." Then she makes a face. "Don't tell Jax I said that.

You just look so excited." Kate nudges my side. "You think he is, too, yeah?"

"Matthew's the best." *And he is.*

Kate's phone buzzes. She unhooks her arm from mine and I catch the time on its glowing screen: 6:44 P.M. One minute before the appointed rendezvous.

"It's Jax." She types a reply and slips the phone back in her pocket. "Damn, I should have brought gloves."

"Oh, I've got you." I reach into my bag and hand her a pair. "Figured you might want some."

"Seriously? You're a goddess." She claps her now gloved hands together. "Much better."

A gaggle of girls pass by. One of them bumps me and mutters a quick sorry.

"It's fine," I say. Almost immediately, another shoulder bumps into mine, this time moving in the opposite direction. I'm peeved until I catch a wave of cologne. Sexy, boyish, and expensive. Summer days and starlight.

Matthew pulls me with him. Kate yells my name as three enormous guys surround her, the Heron emblem on their jacket lapels.

"Matthew?" I say. "What the hell?"

"Don't talk. Not yet." He loosens his grip enough for me to turn and walk properly.

We go inside, hustling past the stores and shoppers. He turns into a hallway toward the bathrooms. A side door opens, and there's another Heron waiting.

"Followed?" the girl asks Matthew.

"No." Matthew puts his hand at the small of my back, pushing me forward into the dark. "Go on. Follow Aure."

I repeat the sound of her name in my head—*R-E,* like the letters—and trail behind her through the concrete maze. Aurelia. Aurelia Saint-Helene. I remember her from the binders . . .

and from before. She looks so different now. Only her gray eyes are as I remember them—bright and determined. She glances at me once then focuses on moving us forward, winging us into the dark.

We pass doors labeled as storage units and pipelines. Matthew keeps close behind me.

"You're safe," he says again, as if I don't believe him. But I do. I believe him in a way I'll never believe Jax or even Micah.

A set of double doors opens. Night air rushes in. Orange light illuminates an alley and a trio of limos parked all in a line, their engines already on.

"Val?" says Matthew. I turn.

My stalwart trust fades as fast as a falling star. It only takes me a moment to see the regret in his eyes as he presses a damp cloth over my nose and face.

Last thing I remember is Matthew telling me he's sorry.

He's sorry, and I'm safe.

When I come to, I'm lying on a soft couch and covered with a blanket. *Goddammit, how many times am I going to be knocked out?* Whatever it is that I'm breathing in, it can't be good for me.

I sit up and cough repeatedly, lungs wheezing. My windpipe and lungs are paper-dry, and my mind flashes back to when I woke up at Holloway for the first time. The rooms couldn't be more different.

The air here has the light perfume of fresh flowers, courtesy of a bouquet just behind my head. The fabric of the couch is uncomfortably soft, the blanket heavy velvet. Light fills the room from dimmed chandeliers overhead.

Across the room, Matthew, Aure, and three other Herons are seated around a table, eating. Aure and another girl look as if they could be cousins, the latter having shorter, curly hair but the same stern expression. The others have their backs to me.

I listen for a moment as silverware clinks against plates. Low ripples of laughter carry from Aure to the three others then to Matthew. She must have told a joke.

Camille isn't there, but that doesn't mean she's not watching. I check the corners of the room for cameras.

I choke-cough a few more times, and the group turns. Aure tucks her brown hair behind her ear, frowning. I don't know why I looked at her and not at Matthew.

"Val." Matthew sets his fork down, and the whole group stands as he walks over to me. "Feel okay?"

"Yes."

"Check her," Aure says.

When Matthew doesn't move, another Heron—an African American guy with muscles that could rip off limbs—steps forward. Heat rises to my cheeks as he takes his time patting me down. I stare at Matthew and blink carefully to keep the tears from slipping out.

How many times has Matthew himself flipped me upside-down as a prank, or poked my sides because he knows how ticklish I am? We've known each other our whole lives. Seen each other naked, for Christ's sake. We're *us*. Does he really think I'd come here armed?

Matthew frowns at me, apologetic but unmoving.

"Clean," the guy says.

"Of course I am," I snap back.

Aure folds her arms across her chest. As she does, I see the bold feathers of the Heron emblem on the inside of her wrist. One wing curls around and extends farther to encircle her left ring finger, like a wedding band.

It strikes me suddenly that she looks a lot like me, only

more polished. Same hair, same build, but with more refinement. She stands straighter and exhales grace. Like Valerie 2.0, the expensive version.

But there is something sad about her, too. She must be around my age, but her cheeks are etched with frown lines—as if she's seen too much, borne too much.

I'm too caught up in my thoughts to realize that the group of us have been standing in a tense, shivery—not to mention awkward—silence.

"Can I talk to her alone?" Matthew asks Aure.

"Camille said five minutes," she says. "No more."

"No more."

She leads the rest of the Herons out a side door, her hand brushing Matthew's shoulder as he goes. The door swings shut, and it's just me and Matthew, Matthew and me. The last time we saw each other, we said I love you. Now he's with the Herons, and I'm a Stag. I say the first thing that comes to mind.

"Where did you get your tattoo?"

Wordlessly, Matthew unbuttons his shirt, tugging down the powder-blue fabric and scrunching up an undershirt until I can see his arm: an arm that's wrapped me in a thousand hugs, reached for me across the hallways at school, pulled me close . . .

The heron takes up most of his shoulder. Its wings nearly touch his collarbone then wrap around to where I cannot see.

"You?" he asks.

I sweep my hair off my neck and turn around. After a few moments, I let my hair fall and face him. Heron. Stag. Matthew. Me.

We break.

Matthew rushes forward and pulls me into a hug. I press my face into his chest, almost struggling to breathe for how tightly he's holding me. My lips find the smooth skin of his neck, his cheek. He kisses me back, and the earthquake between us shakes the room. How could I ever have forgotten this? How have I not wanted it every moment of every day since our birthday? We part and lean our foreheads together.

"Are you okay?" he whispers.

"I'm fine, I'm fine." I put my hand on his arm, feeling the warmth of his skin beneath his shirt.

"I wanted to come for you right away," he says. "That night. You left for the airport. The Herons were at my house when I got back." Another nod. "You're okay, though? You sure?"

"Yes."

"Have you been cutting?"

I think for a moment. "No, actually. I haven't. Not a lot." His eyebrows rise in surprise—but it's as shocking to me as it is to him. "What about you? Are you okay?"

"Yeah. I'm bored, mostly. I've been cooped up here for weeks. I've only gone outside twice since I was recruited."

"*Twice?*" And I thought my cabin fever was bad.

"Twice."

"Why don't they let you out?"

"I don't know. Because they can, I guess. Camille says it's for my own protection. A lot of people hated Alex." He sits down on the sofa and puts his face in his hands. "The Wars isn't what I expected. I thought I'd know because of Alex and Aaron but . . . damn. Some of these people." He lowers his voice. "They don't care about anyone but themselves. I'm just pretending to go along with everything, at this point."

"Matthew," I say. "Why am I here? Like, didn't it get you in trouble?"

He runs his hand across his lips. "Camille knows Alex well enough. I kind of took advantage of that. I had to see if you were okay."

"That's all?"

"More or less."

"What's the more?"

Matthew fidgets and shakes his head. "Val, why did you say yes? When Jax recruited you—why did you say yes?" He shakes his head. "I thought since it wasn't the Herons, you'd say no."

"I had to accept," I reply. "For Leo."

"But I wanted you to be safe."

"I wouldn't have been safe even if the Herons *did* recruit me."

"No. But you would have been if you hadn't joined the Wars at all." He steps back from me. "I told you I'd take care of it, remember?"

I do remember. It was back at the end of spring, beginning of summer. Matthew and I were walking down on the Embarcadero by *Cupid's Span,* an enormous statue of a bow and arrow. It should have been a dream of an outing, but the air between us was jagged. That was the day I told Matthew I wanted to join the Wars.

"It's a bad idea," he had said. "I know how you feel . . . with Leo . . . but come on. Joining the Wars won't fix anything."

"I knew you'd be upset." Both of us had our arms folded across our chests. It's a funny mirroring thing I'd noticed we did early on. It didn't feel fun or cute that time.

"You could die," he said.

"Most people live through it. Alex did."

"Still." He stopped walking and I did, too. The yellow lights of the streetlamps looked like fidgety torches on the bay. "What if I do it for you?"

"What, join the Wars? I mean, I kind of assumed . . ."

"Yeah, well. I meant what if I find the guy? I can ask Alex to look into it. We can find him and you won't have to join."

Back in the present, I shake my head slowly as it dawns on

me. I can imagine the moment that the idea sparked in his mind. Matthew's always been the kind of guy who'd do the right thing, and keeping me out of the Wars counts. So he did what he could to stop me . . .

"You told the Herons not to recruit me," I whisper. "Didn't you?"

Matthew keeps his eyes on the ground, which is all the answer I need.

"You told the Herons not to recruit me," I repeat. "But you didn't think to keep the Stags from doing it. We could have done our year *together*."

"I didn't want you here at all! I thought maybe if we weren't dating . . . if I could put distance between you and me, and you and the Wars, that you wouldn't join. I was trying to protect you, Val."

"You swore you didn't know anything," I say. *Double pinky promise.* "You lied to me."

"I just wanted you safe and out of the Wars. If you weren't recruited I thought . . . I thought maybe you'd realize it's okay to move on."

"You joined," I fire back defensively.

"I had to," he says. "This is all my parents have cared about my whole life. All the trophies, all the titles I held at school— it never mattered. They would brush it off, like I hadn't worked for any of it. All they cared about was my maintaining our family's honor by getting revenge for what happened to Aaron."

I interrupt. "It's true, then."

He pauses. "What did they tell you?"

"That Annie died, and Ty Boreas's brother went berserk. Aaron soon after. That's why he never comes home, isn't it?"

Matthew nods solemnly. "Aaron doesn't just live in Tahoe.

My parents sent him there. He's not . . . all there, anymore. He's under psychiatric care twenty-four/seven."

I lift my hands like, *What?* "How come you never told me any of this? You should have been honest with me."

"Yeah," he says. "I see that now."

"So we're both here for our brothers," I say. "And the protests, the beatings, the *murder*—started over one poor dead girl, and now it's totally out of control? That's all this is?"

"Yes." He exhales heavily. "And that's the real reason why I joined. *That's* why I asked to see you." Matthew gets up and starts pacing like the walls are made of fire. "Alex is already out. Camille and Aure and the others are in too deep. But you . . . I need you to do something for me."

"What is it?" Two minutes ago, I would have agreed to anything, but right now I'm still so confused. I wonder what Matthew sees when he looks at me—his friend, the girl he says he loves, or an enemy. Maybe all three.

My curiosity ends with seven sharp words:

"I need you to leave the Stags."

13

He must be joking.

"No one leaves the Wars," I say, waving my hand up, like *duh*. "It's one of the rules. No one goes before their year is up."

"No one has *before*."

"No one who has left has lived before," I say. I think back to my first day, when Jax cornered me in the basement. "The gangs always find you. And if they don't find you, they'll go after your family. Don't desert. That's a rule."

"I know, I know. But I have a plan." He takes my hand and gently pulls me back to the couch. We both sit, and he puts a hand on my knee. "Look, *I'm* working with the police. Not the Herons. I have my own plans. Just me."

"What do you mean?"

There's no time for me to respond. Aure glides back into the room followed by the two guys from before.

"Time's up," she says.

"A few more minutes."

"Camille said five. You got five."

"Fine," he says. He gives me a look like *I will fix this*. "You can take Ms. Simons back to Stag territory."

"Wait," I say at the same moment Aure says, "Come on."

A Heron—Jacob Fisher, according to the binders—takes my wrists and deftly tightens a zip tie around them. When the other Herons have all turned their backs, Matthew mouths the words *I love you* and I die on the spot.

We exit the dining room and go into a long hallway, then out into an enormous foyer. A glittering, curling staircase winds past yet another sparkling chandelier. Roses burst from gilded vases in little alcoves. Affluence imbues every piece of décor.

Aure pushes me from behind. "Hurry up."

Just me. Not the Herons. What did Matthew mean by that? It's horrible to realize I don't know when I'll see him again— it might not be for the rest of our year. I can't go that long without knowing more, without understanding more. Because right now all I know is Matthew kept things from me when he said he loved me, and that doesn't sound very much like love.

Tears slip from my eyes. Aure stiffens and she gives me what must pass as a sympathetic look. "You cried a lot as a kid, too."

"You smiled more back then," I fire back. Aurelia Saint-Helene. Of course she'd become a Young Heron. Her family and Matthew's go way back. Even as a kid I remember her being prettier than I was, smiling and batting her eyes at the adults to get whatever she wanted.

But she was kind, too. One year when I was about six, Mom insisted on bringing a casserole to the Westons' Christmas party, despite the hosts insisting that guests bring nothing. "You always bring something," I remember my mom saying as her heels clacked on the sidewalk when we walked over. "It's polite."

I was ecstatic—her casserole was one of my favorite foods, and she rarely made it because it took so much prep. But the moment we stepped into the Westons' house, all eyes swerved to our small family: me in a dress Mom got at Macy's, my dad in a slightly wrinkled shirt he'd forgotten to steam, and Mom with her hands full of foil-covered casserole.

Our small Pyrex dish with burnt cheese at the edges stood out like a sore thumb on the table laden with luxurious delicacies—a huge roasted ham, miles of hors d'oeuvres, a triple-layer chocolate cake . . . and our casserole.

I was sent to eat and socialize with the other kids, who wasted no time in barraging me with questions.

"What *is* it?"

"No one else brought anything."

"It looks like vomit."

Seemingly above them all was Aure. When we were all allowed to grab food, she asked to be served the casserole and nothing else. We got back to the kids' table and she took a bite, her eyes going wide.

"This is the yummiest thing I have ever eaten." She smiled at me. A real smile. "Do you get to eat this every day?"

It's one of those moments that comes back even when you don't mean to think about it, like the time I called my fifth-grade teacher by her first name in front of the whole class or when I was learning to drive and backed into the neighbor's fence by accident. Kindness was an emotion just as powerful as embarrassment or guilt, perhaps even more so.

Kindness, evidently, is also not a virtue afforded to the Young Herons, at least not to anyone who isn't their own kind.

Back in the present, Aure exhales through her nose, scowling, and I brace for a slap or a punch, but her Heron restraint wins out. "You're lucky you have somewhere to be or I'd teach you to keep your fucking mouth shut." Then, her voice barely a whisper, "Maybe I'll just stop by your house later. Right down the street from the Westons', right?"

Mom and Dad. "No!" I shout, but Aure is done with me. She hands me back to Jacob and I swear his grip is tighter this time. I don't stop pulling at the zip tie. "Aure, don't. Please."

"Be quiet."

I should have kept out of this. No matter how much I try, I just make it worse. *Leo, if you're up there, look out for them, please. Please.*

I'm led out onto the street. Instead of a limo, I'm to travel in a nondescript sedan. From the height of the buildings I can tell we're somewhere between North Beach and the Financial District. Aure pushes a blindfold over my eyes before I can get a better look. I'm shoved into a car. Moments later, the front passenger side opens as she gets in.

"Take us to the drop-off point."

Jax is going to be livid. Not only did the Herons take me—breaking the all-important rules—but also I gained nothing of use to him. I can't tell him what Matthew said, can I? But Jax is my leader.

And I can't be loyal to both of them at the same time.

The car rolls up and down the city's famous hills until I know we're way past downtown. We stop suddenly, and someone else gets in the backseat with me. Holy shit. Horrible images flash in my mind—Aure said I had somewhere to be. Who got in the car? I'm as helpless as I was the night I was recruited. They're gonna knock me out, or worse . . .

"What's going on?" I say, plastering myself to the door behind me. "Who are you? Someone answer me!"

"Calm down, Stag," says a new voice.

The blindfold is lifted off my eyes and I'm face-to-face with Camille Sakurai. She holds a gun idly in her hands.

"What the fuck—" I say, jerking back as far as I can.

I struggle to breathe as my brain takes in the most absurd details—her perfect manicure, the jasmine of her perfume, and her painstakingly curled hair.

"I don't have a lot of time for you, so I'll cut to the chase. I know you and Weston are, like, close, but I don't want him forgetting what side he's on," she says. "I let him see you to-night because Alex has literally saved my life at least twice and I owed him. But this is it." She sets the gun down in her lap, but keeps it pointed in my direction. "I don't know what Jax has said to you, but the Stags are nothing. He made them up. So stop thinking you are a part of anything bigger. You are nothing."

She yanks the blindfold down again, nails scraping my forehead.

I swallow. If we were truly nothing, the Young Heron leader wouldn't have bothered to pull some shit like this herself. *They're scared.* My heart soars so high I almost laugh—I have something to tell Jax after all.

Sometime later, we come to a stop. The door beside me opens and I'm pulled out. Wherever I am, it's quiet. And cold. The sound of a crosswalk speaker echoes from somewhere nearby. The zip tie is snipped, but awkwardly so that the scissors catch my skin, too.

"Ow!" I say, covering the cut with my other hand, but I don't have more than a second to get my bearings before Aure slams the door and the car speeds off.

I pull the blindfold off. I'm in a neighborhood on a hill—which doesn't narrow it down very much, because hello, San Francisco—and all is still, save for a gray sedan working its way up the street toward me. The driver stares at me, as if trying to decide my purpose for being there. *If only you knew, pal.* Walking toward a nearby crosswalk, I pass the Parkmerced library branch.

I'm back at Stonestown.

Reaching into my pocket, I grab my phone and turn it back on. Someone must have turned it off during the ride there. I text Jax.

Safe. Headed back.

He replies immediately.

See you here.

See you here?

Well, fuck you, too, Jax. I wonder if he was even worried.

It's not that far of a walk—just a cold one—back to Holloway House. Besides, at this point I'm craving the solitude so that I can think. My once-perfect hair is ruined by the wind and misty air, and I don't care.

"Stupid, Valerie," I mutter to myself. "What an idiot, getting dressed up."

Matthew wants me out of the gangs. Safe. A part of me knows I should be worried about his safety just as much, but I can't muster the feeling. He hasn't left the Heron headquarters—he's safer than anyone else in the Wars. I bury my face into my coat and exhale, trying to get warm.

At least I'm not going back empty-handed. Our protest worked—at least enough that Camille is giving the Stags more than a passing glance.

I trudge past a burnt-out house. An old teddy bear stares up at me from the pile of sooty debris in the driveway. It looks like one that Leo had.

Classic Matthew, taking care of others without being asked. I check my wrist where the scissors sliced my skin. A well of dark blood runs down the side of my hand, and I lick my finger to try and clean the wound. It stings, but not any more than how passive Matthew was in front of Aure. *But he had to play a part for the other Herons, otherwise they'd know something bigger was up, right?*

It sucks to doubt. It sucks not to be able to remember every detail of what happened and what he said. Instead all I see is Aure touching his shoulder as she left the room.

Shivering, bewildered, and exhausted, I round the last corner to the house. This time I know to look for Jaws—arms folded and dressed in all black—in the shadows of the porch. I give him a nod. He returns it.

I open the door, and Kate flies off the couch. "Oh, thank God!" In a blink, she's wrapped me in a hug. "Fucking Herons. You okay?"

"I'm fine. They just wanted to talk."

"Still," she says. "Takes balls to break the rules like that. Jax!"

Our leader joins us in the living room, Micah right on his heels.

"What'd they want?" Micah asks.

"To talk," I reply. *He didn't ask if I was all right.*

Jax, apparently satisfied with my being alive, gets a beer from the fridge. "What did Weston say?"

I straighten up. "Nothing that matters. But I think I figured out Camille's second. It's Aurelia Saint-Helene."

Jax shrugs. "We knew that. Next."

Shit. "Camille talked to me."

That gets him, and he cocks his head to the side. "About what?"

"She told me the Stags should keep out of Heron business. That we're nothing."

Micah glances at Jax, his expression a mix of confusion and awe. "If Camille truly thought we were nothing, she wouldn't have bothered to tell you."

"The protest must have caught their attention," says Jax. "Rather, the attention of their fat-cat parents whose business partners weren't able to get in." He nods to himself, thinking.

That has to be a good thing, right? For a beat I'm hopeful, then Jax asks, "What about Weston? You talk to him?"

I swallow. "He was worried about me."

"And?"

"And what?"

"What did you talk about?"

It's as if there's no one in the room but Jax and me. His eyes stay trained on me, like they were the night we met, or like an animal watching its prey. Without warning Jax throws his beer to the side, the can clanging against the hardwood floor as Kate yelps, then turns and dives into Mako's waiting arms.

"You tell me what he said, Valentine," Jax roars. "Right now."

I lift my face. *I'm not prey. I'm a Stag, too. I can look bold, even if I'm freaking out inside.* "He wanted me to leave the Stags."

"What?"

"He wanted me to leave the Stags. That's what we talked about. Then Aure came in, pushed me around, and put me in the car again."

There's a moment of calm before Jax loses it. "Are you fucking serious?" He laughs. "Shit. What an idiot. You can't join the Herons. Not now."

"I know," I say quietly. Maybe I should look at him, but I can't take my eyes off the dented can on the ground.

"For fuck's sake, Valentine," Jax says as he settles down. "You didn't get anything, did you? This could have been your big shot."

"We know Camille got shit for the protest," Mako chimes in, his arm still around Kate's shoulders.

"Still," our leader replies. "She was in a Heron safe house and only confirmed something we could have already assumed."

This is worse than being yelled at. He's right, I should have used this to my advantage. Instead I was too excited to see Matthew that I forgot what really mattered, at least in Jax's eyes. My heart and head can only be pulled in so many directions.

Right now, that direction is straight down.

Jax goes back to his room without a word, leaving the rest of us standing around awkwardly. Micah puts his hand on my shoulder but I shake him off, fighting the tears gathering in my eyes.

"I'm going to bed," I say.

I slam the door behind me, tears streaming down my cheeks. As I stomp down the stairs, I'm surprised to hear it open up again behind me. Nianna follows me down.

"What do you want?" I say.

"I saw the way your eyes lit up when you first got that message." She pauses. "And now you're acting all defensive. You still care about Weston, don't you?"

"Yes? Maybe." I shrug. "Honestly I don't know. And what does it matter?"

"It *matters* because I'm still not sure you should have been recruited." Her nails dig into her arms. "If what you feel about Weston is true . . . I mean, would you kill him?"

"What—"

"If Jax ordered you to kill Matthew Weston—if he gave you the *order,* the opportunity. Gave you the gun. Would. You. Kill. Him?"

"That'd never happen."

"There," she says. "That's answer enough." She turns to go.

"What? Nianna, wait. What the hell is wrong with you?"

"You're what's wrong," she says. "You're still loyal to them. To Weston. You joined the Stags—the *Stags*—not some half-way bullshit where you get to decide which gang suits you best that day."

"I don't do that," I say. "I'm a Stag. I know that. It's what I wanted. And if you must know I'm pretty fucking pissed at Matthew right now, so it's not like I'm going to change my mind at any point."

"I don't believe you. You wanted to be a Heron. And you

know what? I bet you'd have fit right in with all their nice things, all their fancy parties. You've never wanted for anything, have you? Not like the rest of us. Never had to sleep in a shelter, never wondered if you're gonna get kicked out of your house. Never *been* kicked out of your house. Always had two parents who loved you."

"I can't help what I was born into," I say. "Neither can you, neither can Jax. Neither can anyone. So what?"

"So, at the end of the day you still want your nice cushy life with Matthew," she fires back.

"Things are different now," I say. "I've changed. I don't want that anymore."

Nianna rolls her eyes. "Sure you don't."

"Look, I want to make things right. I want to find the guy who killed my brother. And now that I know how the Herons are screwing people over, yeah, I want what's fair for everyone."

"I'll believe it when I see it. You need to fucking decide— are you in or out?" She shakes her head, arms crossed and tight like a coiled snake before it strikes. "Because right now you're not a Stag," she snaps. "You're a Heron with the wrong fucking tattoo."

She storms away and slams the garage door shut.

"Oh, come on," I shout.

Nianna answers my shouting with silence. I stagger into my space, taking stock of what's just happened. If Matthew were on his knees in front of me, and the gun was in my hand, I couldn't shoot. I absolutely would not, could not. Bitter and broken as I am, my answer would still be no.

Every bone in my body is desperate for rest, but I can't bring myself to sit still. Part of me wants to cut, but the other clings fast to the advice Lyla always gave me: to reach out, instead. But who do I reach out to? A pang of *aloneness* strikes me like lightning—a blinding pain of not knowing what to do, or who I can turn to . . . but I know who I'd want to turn to.

So I make up my mind. I grab my cash and my phone and order a cab. And I keep moving. Keep going, don't stop until I'm in the taxi and it's whirling north and I know that when Jax finds out he may, actually, kill me.

But I don't care.

I'm going home.

14

One summer I went to a camp in the Santa Cruz Mountains. It was just a week long, but I remember coming back and feeling foreign in my own home—it was too clean, too organized, and too different from what I'd just gotten used to.

Tonight feels a lot like that.

I unhook the gate to the backyard and retrieve the spare key from its hiding place beneath the clay pot that I painted in the second grade. The garage door is rusty, but after rattling the handle a bit, it comes dislodged.

Our alarm is on a timer, and I rush over and punch the code before it starts blaring. I wait, heart thundering, to see if the sound was enough to wake my parents.

What am I going to say to them? I'm not even sure why I'm here. Pacing the kitchen, I stick my opposite thumb on the spot on my wrist where the Young Heron's scissors tore my skin. I just wanted a moment of peace and solitude, of something I know for sure. The house smells like *my house,* in the weird way you get to know by virtue of having lived there before. I'd know it blind.

Walking into the living room, I run my hand across the fabric of the couch. Fatigue tugs at my eyes, but it vanishes when I hear a telltale creak on the stairs, followed by the padding of slippered feet.

"Mom?"

"Valerie!" she yells, and a moment later I'm in her arms. Her cheek is warm, arms strong. We dissolve into sobs like waves into sea foam.

"Hi, Mom."

"Val, oh honey." She pushes the hair from my face, her thumb pressing into my hairline. "Are you okay?"

I nod. "I'm fine. Totally fine. Where's Dad?"

"In LA meeting with a— Oh my god, you're bleeding," Mom says, gripping my wrist so that I too can see the new, dark well of blood beading up. "What happened?"

"It's hard to explain," I tell her. "All of it is."

Something clicks in her, and she goes full Mom-mode. She makes me sit, grabs the first-aid kit from the bathroom, and starts diligently unpacking a Band-Aid. She lays it on gently, holding on to my hand as if letting go would make me disappear.

"Thank you," I say quietly. "How are you?"

She closes the kit. "Fine, baby."

"Mom."

Tears brim in her eyes. "What do you want me to say? I'm a failure as a mother. You hated me so much that you signed up for . . . for . . . well, you know. And Leo—" Her voice cracks. "My baby. My sweet baby boy."

"Oh, Mom."

"If your dad and I had been around more . . . I don't know. We did our best. But look at our family now. Your father isn't even here. Again. No wonder you resented us. I would, too." She dabs her eyes on the sleeve of her robe. "I'm so sorry, Valerie."

She cries, and I do, too. My emotions well up in my chest, beating so strong against my ribs that I wonder how I don't explode. Words fail me. So I scoot my chair next to

Mom's and put my arms around her. We huddle together, overwhelmed with the great weight of our collective sorrow. I never knew Mom carried that burden with her, dragging her down like a splintered wheel across a battered beach.

I find my courage. "I was never mad at you, Mom." She sniffs. "There's nothing that you need to be sorry for. I promise."

"Valerie."

"I promise," I say again, pushing my face into the perfect softness of her terry cloth robe as new tears slide from the corners of my eyes. "I love you, Mom."

"I love you, too. Every time you call I'm afraid it won't be you, and that it'll be someone else telling me you're dead."

"I'm sorry. But I had to join. I just had to."

I don't know how long we stay there. Tired and trembling, we both go upstairs. My room shudders with stillness—like a museum or time capsule of my own life. My backpack leans against my desk, full of textbooks I'll never read and homework assignments I'll never do. On the walls are photos of Lyla and me, postcards, and cutouts from magazines. I tug on some PJs then open the door for Mom. She settles down next to me on the bed, stroking my hair like she did when I was little. She reaches behind her and pulls a floppy stuffed lamb from the pillows behind my head. I half smile, half sob at the sight of it.

"Where did you find him?" I whisper.

"In your closet," she says. "Remember what you called him?"

"Poppy. Duh," I say.

"Poppy," she repeats, voice already fading into gentle sleep.

We bury ourselves into the blankets. I know I should be worried about Jax, but as sleep washes over my mind the only things I can think of are home, Mom, and Leo. For the first time in a long fucking time, I can feel him looking down on me and smiling.

We needed this. All three of us.

Dawn finds us too soon. Mom's fast asleep beside me—she's always been a heavy sleeper. Slowly as I dare, I slide out of the bed. She doesn't stir.

Leaving is harder the second time. I grab my bundle of discarded clothes and shoes, whisper *mahal kita* one more time, and then leave my room.

I change back into my street clothes, and then grab a granola bar from the pantry to stanch my hunger. I move manically—both wanting to stay and knowing I need to go, absolutely need to go as soon as possible. If I'm lucky, Jax may never know I was gone.

A glint of metal shines from the countertop as I click the light on. Taking the spare key from where I left it, I walk over to the dining room table where I know Mom can easily find it. The table itself is covered in a familiar chaos—a stack of mail, binders bursting with details on different venues around the city, invoices, receipts, and every other kind of paper paraphernalia lie scattered on its surface. We haven't eaten a proper meal here since I was maybe ten—instead, Mom commandeered it for her workstation. I'd do my homework at the head of the table, both of us working separately but together.

Pushing some mail aside, I place the key down. An open letter catches my eye—rather, the name at the end of it. My blood freezes.

Slowly, I reach forward and tug the letter from beneath the rest of the pile and start reading. It's on the official letterhead of the San Francisco Police Department. Blood pounds in my ears as I keep reading, glossing over the "I'm sorry" and "wish I could have done more." It's the end that gets me—an idea he's been wanting to pursue for years. A program, a stop to the rising tide of violence borne from the Wars. The letter is an invitation—"I wanted to reach out to your family personally before the program goes public. Enclosed is my business card . . ."

I find the card and fold it back into the letter. A shivering hope rises in my chest. I even smile.

Pissed as Jax may be about what happened with the Young Herons, and as livid as he'll be if he catches me gone, this letter might just spare me.

Because I've found it. What Matthew was talking about— he said he was working with the police.

Matthew is going to end the Wars. And he's going to do it with the help of the man who could never bring me the peace of a closed case—the new chief of police, one John Kilmer.

Jax stands in the front yard, arms crossed.

Outside, the gray morning is still, with the clouds overhead hinting of future rain. The silence is only broken by the sound of the morning news coming out of the taxi's radio.

"Here OK?" the driver asks.

"Uh, yeah. Here's fine." *But maybe please wait in case this guy murders me.*

I take my time paying the fare and making sure I have all my stuff. Finally, there's nothing left for me to do but get out.

Jax hasn't moved, just stands there as the car pulls away. My panic rises and I spit out: "I'm sorry."

"Where did you go?"

"Home."

"Why?"

"I . . . I got scared." I hold the letter out. "I'm sorry, I shouldn't have gone, but I think I found something—here, open this."

Jax takes the paper, keeping his eyes on me the whole time. "What is it?"

"It's a letter the chief of police sent my mom. Well, to all of us."

Jax says nothing, just tucks the paper into his back pocket. The wind blows his unruly golden hair across his face.

"Are you going to leave again, Valentine?"

"No," I say. "I promise."

"Your word doesn't mean a lot to me anymore."

"I swear," I say, like that's any better. "I'm sorry." I reflect on the night—fleeting and flawed as it was. "I needed to make things right with my mom. And I did." *I think.* "I'm here, Jax. I promise. I need you, and I know that. So, I'm here."

He nods slowly, hazel eyes looking at me but somehow, I feel, *through me,* too. Like he knows me down to my dreams.

"You won't disobey me again," he says.

"I won't. I swear."

"That wasn't a question." Then he turns, finally taking the damn paper out of his pocket. "Now get inside before anyone else figures out you were gone."

I practically fly to his side, eyes on the ground. We go into the kitchen. Floorboards creak in Nianna's room—she's still doing her morning yoga.

"How did you know I was gone?" I ask. "You're not usually up this early."

Jax avoids my gaze. "I checked on you last night. You weren't there, so I looked at the tracker in your phone."

"Then why'd you ask where I was?"

"To see if you'd lie."

"Oh."

He must read the letter four times, given how long he stares at it. "TRUCE," he says. "That's what they're calling their magic program."

"Trust, respect, unity," I reply, reciting the details of the letter. "I forget the others."

"Community. Engagement. Fucking Herons," he says. "They've finally done it."

"What?"

"Valentine, this is the ultimate PR move. Think of how highly people will sing the praises of the tech-heads who end the Wars by giving gang members a . . ." He pauses, rereading the letter. "A second chance at life."

That doesn't sound so bad, I think, but I'm not about to say that in front of Jax.

He stuffs the paper in his pocket, eyes clouded with disgust. "This shit's not new. Rehab programs, mental health services. If this happens, then the Herons win it all. The Boars and the Stags will be locked away, while the Young Herons are quietly shipped back to Orange County or Marin or whatever rich fucking place they came from. The Old Herons will continue to make the city a tech playground and push everyone else out. Here. Take it back."

I do, silently hoping for more. No "Thanks for the info" or "Good to get ahead of this"?

He yawns, stretching his arms high. He swoops them back down again and shakes his head. "Fucking Herons." Jax looks back at me, as if remembering I'm there. "Go . . . go do something, Valentine. I need to be alone."

I leave Jax to his storm, uncertainty welling up in my stomach. Stepping down the stairs, each one seems to creak louder than I remember, as if echoing the mess of thoughts in my head.

It's scary to have been spared any punishment. I don't know what I was expecting—some brutal hazing, another tattoo that said LIAR on my forehead . . . or any of the myriad other thoughts I've had about Jax and me. It's not like Jax to be alone. What is going through his mind? Would anyone know, maybe Micah? He said they're pacifists. I thought maybe the TRUCE program would be welcome news, a stepping stone to getting me to the Boar that killed Leo.

But Jax is Jax, and he wants to do this his way, and no other. *He wants to be remembered for what he does with his life,* I think, recalling what he told me that night we made the truce with the Boars. That must mean doing things his way.

I'm standing on the shore with forward as my only option, no ships to bring me home. I can't run again—Jax would find me—and I have to stay, really *stay* and be in this. That's the only choice. One step at a time.

Forward, into a black fate.

15

Jax gives everyone more cash except me. I keep my mouth shut, knowing it's because I snuck out.

Still, I already have more than enough to mail gifts home, but even then, not being with my parents at Christmastime is almost unbearable. It's always been my favorite holiday—not so much for the gifts but for the warm feelings, glittering light, and opportunities to bake. But the best part, hands down, is Filipino breakfast on Christmas morning. Even my eat-a-salad-every-day dad can't resist salty pork *longanisa,* sweet *tocino,* fluffy scrambled eggs, and fresh white rice.

I try not to think of my parents on Christmas morning: just the two of them, with no reasons to celebrate. Instead I get a gingerbread cookie dough going and set to work. While the cookies are in the oven, I string the Christmas lights from my bedroom around the kitchen, then go back to prepping the cookies. Nianna's steps sound on the creaky floorboards just as I finish the last one.

She rounds the corner and jumps back. "You scared the shit outta me."

"Merry Christmas?" I reply, and we both laugh. She spots the cookies.

"Is that . . . us?"

Seven gingerbread men lie on their plates. The icing is

melting a little since I didn't leave them long enough to cool, but Nianna still recognizes hers and picks it up. "My bandana," she says. Pointing to Micah's, she laughs. "Oh my god, you did all his tattoos."

"Yep. Oh, and I made coffee."

She takes the mug I offer her. "Kate's going to freak out," she says, which I know well enough now to mean, *Thank you, this is nice.*

Kate does, indeed, freak out.

"Oh. My. God. Look at my icing hair!" she brags once we're all awake, indicating the long yellow hair. "I have the most icing. Ha!"

"I don't know," Micah says. He's already eaten parts of his but motions to its arms. "I think I won."

"Glad you guys like 'em," I say, happily eating my own.

"How'd you get so good at this?" Kate asks.

"Um," I reply, thinking. "There was this one summer, I think after my freshman year, that my family didn't go on any vacations or anything. So I was bored and watched a ton of baking shows on Food Network, then started looking up recipes online." I shrug. "The rest is history."

Mako finishes his and beams. "Sweet, delicious history."

Jaws declines his—*surprise, surprise*—but I like to think he was touched, too. Jax and Micah try and make the cookies high-five, leaving the rest of us in hysterics and part of Micah's cookie on the floor after the arm snaps. As I try to keep coffee from coming out of my nose, I even catch Nianna taking a picture of hers on her phone before eating it.

I sip my coffee, heart high. Looking after the Stags makes me feel like a big sister again. I feel like me, like the old Valerie. It's enough to make me forget that I'm away from home on Christmas for the first time. Well, almost.

As the others break to find a cheesy movie on TV, I quickly get started on the dishes. Jax comes up to me and hugs me from behind. He kisses my cheek, fingers lingering on my shoulders as he pulls away.

"Merry Christmas, Valentine," he says. "Thank you."

"Sure," I say, swallowing quickly to hide my surprise. The spot on my cheek where his lips met my skin feels like a new tattoo radiating with heat. "You want to help me with the dishes?"

"What's that? Oh, Micah's calling me," he says, leaning back and motioning toward the living room.

"You suck."

"Kidding, Valentine. Here." He doesn't help with the washing, but he does help load the extra mugs into the dishwasher, and I consider that a victory.

We order Chinese food from Micah's favorite place down the street and watch *A Christmas Story* on TBS. By the afternoon, we're boozy and sleepy and full of chow mein. While Jax and Micah square off in beer pong against Kate and Mako, Nianna and I flip through channels.

I watch the group of them together. Nianna says Mako and Micah both admire Jax—Micah for his self-confidence and Mako for his recklessness. Given what Mako told me about living with his family, I can see why he'd admire Jax's wild, devil-may-care attitude. But Micah? He seems to be sure of himself in a way that I wish I was. Then again, Micah and Jax have been friends for ages—there must be something to their relationship that I can't pick up on yet.

I guess I can believe that—from appearances alone, Lyla and I seem like polar opposites, with her wardrobe of oversized tees and my simple but more polished style. But when your first interaction was standing in line next to each other on the first day of kindergarten (our moms have the pictures to prove it) and you haven't been separated since, you know a thing or two—or two thousand—about each other.

I wonder what Nianna sees in Jax. He's enigmatic, for sure. Proud, as if the universe tips and tilts with the angle of his hand. I guess there's a lot I can't figure out about Nianna yet either. *Which reminds me . . .*

"Hey, can I ask you something?" I say to Nianna. She and I have avoided each other since our fight, but she seems happy enough now. "Why were you such a bitch to me the first time we met?"

Her eyes go wide. "What are you talking about?"

"Seriously! The whole 'gut me like a fish' thing," I say. "What was that about?"

"Come on, Val. Can't I enjoy a little hazing?" she replies, sipping her wine. "If it helps, I said as much to Kate when she arrived."

"Why?"

"You know why," she replies. "Brianna. Don't want history to repeat itself."

I finish my wine. "Did she like him back?"

She shrugs. "Honestly? I don't know. The way Micah describes her, she doesn't exactly strike me as a stable person."

"Huh. I haven't talked to Micah about her."

"You should," she replies. "I'd talk to him over Jax. They both cared about her, in their own way."

In their own way. Jax is the type to burn hot or cold at the drop of a hat, but Micah's relationship with Jax tells me he knows how to endure.

I look over at the guys in question, all high fives and bro hugs each time one of them lands a Ping-Pong ball in a cup. Micah steps back as Jax takes his shot, looking as contented as I've ever seen a person. He rolls his eyes at Jax's preshot ritual of raising the ball, and Micah catches me staring. I give a little wave, which he returns. Jax sinks the shot, winning the game, and the solace is broken but I lean into it all. Leaning in means less missing home, less missing Matthew. It gets me closer to the guy who killed Leo.

I close my eyes and settle into this moment, like Micah did just now. *You're here, Valerie, and you're alive.*

And today, that's enough to get me through.

The next morning, I wake to a symphony of squeaks on the garage stairs, and the sound of Jax calling my name. "Valentine, wake up!"

"Whaaat?" I say, blinking out of sleep. "What's going on?"

"I'm having something delivered," he said. "We gotta move your bed, though."

"What?"

"You'll see."

I roll out of bed and immediately pull on socks and a sweatshirt to fight the cold. "This better be good."

A few hours and a quick rearranging of the garage later, I have my answer. They bought a pool table.

Micah and I stand outside by the hydrangeas as the workmen unload it. I'm still in my pajamas and socks, my second coffee in hand.

"Were you a part of this?" I ask as I sip.

"I wasn't *not* a part of it."

"You suck."

"Yeah, yeah."

The workers set up the table in the garage. Our leader gives them a generous tip and calls for Micah to play him. After watching for a few minutes and pretending I know anything about billiards, I head back upstairs, phone in hand. I couldn't bear calling my parents on Christmas, but the day after I can. Going through the living room, I slide open the door to Holloway's tiny backyard.

The plants are dewy from the night before and a soothing, earthy smell hangs over the garden like a canopy. Phone in one hand, I dial home while idly pinching the cool leaves of the fern next to me. Mom answers right away.

"Hi, sweetie," she says, her voice small. "Merry late Christmas."

"Merry late Christmas," I tell her. "How are you? Everything . . . good?" *Any suspicious sounds? Any Herons following you, who, I don't know, might be looking to hurt you?*

"Oh, we're fine. Had a quiet holiday. Oh, Peter. It's Val. Let me put it on speaker."

My dad jumps on, and I wish him Merry Christmas, too.

"Did you have any *tocino*?" I ask.

A pause. "Yes," he replies, and I get the sense he's smiling.

Mom jumps back on. "Your dad ate a lot of it. He always says he won't."

"And he always does," I reply. It's as much a tradition as getting a damn tree.

We make small talk, and I smile just listening.

"Well, I was just calling to say hi," I say, sniffling. "I love you guys."

"We love you, too," Mom replies. "Val, please come home."

"I can't." We have this conversation every call. "Not yet."

"I . . . Just keep calling, then. I need to know you're okay."

"Okay. I love you." Can't hurt to say it twice.

"Oh, wait. Before you go. Alex came by."

"Alex . . . Weston?"

"Of course Alex Weston, baby. Who else?"

"What did he want?"

"Oh, he's been stopping by every week or so. He and your

dad watch the Warriors games. He has a fiancée, did you know that? He showed me her picture on his phone. Pretty girl, works at the hospital."

"Mom."

"Sorry. He had a late birthday gift for you is all. He ordered it online and it took this long to get here. Anyway. I told him . . . well, I told him I'd hang on to it."

My mind spins. Alex Weston has a gift for me.

Matthew. Matthew sent him.

"Um, hey, Dad? Can you bring it to work with you, and leave it with the receptionist downstairs? That . . . should be allowed."

"I'm sure it's not important," he says.

Oh, and I'm quite sure it is. "Still, is that okay?"

He sighs. "Yes, honey. I'll bring it."

"Okay, thank you. *Mahal kita.*"

"*Mahal kita,*" Mom replies.

I hang up and take a breath of chilly morning air. Whatever Alex Weston has for me, it's not nothing, and that gut feeling tells me Nianna wasn't totally right when she yelled at me the other day. Because if I truly didn't understand that I was a Stag, I wouldn't be so nervous to find out what his gift is.

I wouldn't be so scared that I'm falling right into a Heron trap.

16

The New Year arrives, fresh and full of possibility. As planned, Jax sends a message to the Young Herons asking for peace. They don't send anything back.

Dad's offices, closed for the holidays, finally reopen on January third, and I convince Jax to let me go on a run. Or, at least that's where I say I'm going.

Instead, I take an early train into downtown, watching my phone's clock the whole way. I need to be back as soon as possible, before Jax gets suspicious and looks up where I am. Fortunately, he seemed pretty tired at breakfast, and I hope he went back to bed.

Weary-eyed people jostle into the train car, sending the temperature rising even in the winter mist. By the time we're approaching downtown, I'm sweating buckets under my layers.

Dad better have remembered the gift. Alex isn't an active Heron anymore, so he couldn't give me anything dangerous. I think. Before I joined, I thought past members couldn't interfere with Wars business at all. God, that was naive. I see now the gangs are larger than I'd thought, more far-reaching, and the old members must lend a hand.

Then again, this is the same Alex who used to play-shove Matthew during family barbecues and who more than once offered to buy us booze. He went through Mom, for crying out loud. That had to mean it was safe, right?

I reach Montgomery and slide into the exodus of commuters. I take an escalator to the street and my sweaty self is immediately met by cool air. *Ahh.* I practically raise my hands in joy. How people do that hellish ride every day, I have no idea.

Cars and buses power up Market as I walk toward Dad's office. I move through the crowd—a mixed bag of tech workers with badges bouncing at their hips, stockbroker-types yelling into their phones, and slow-walking tourists who are pretty sure they got off at the right BART stop. I break through and fall into stride with a pair of normal-looking natives like me, moving ahead of the rest. That's the way we roll in SF—look straight, move fast, and mind your own damn business.

The building is an imposing structure of dark stone and black windows; in my workout top, leggings, and hot pink shoes, I'm way underdressed, but Jax had to think I was going on a run.

A sweet-faced girl greets me as I walk in. "Welcome to Monarch and Abbot. Can I help you?"

"Hi." I brush my hair down to make sure my tattoo is hidden. "I'm here to pick up something. My dad was supposed to have left it. His name is Peter Simons."

The girl frowns and starts opening and closing drawers, and my panic spikes. Did Dad forget?

A second receptionist catches my eye. She moves the phone from her ear to her chest. "I have it here." She slides open a shallow drawer, and sure enough, there's a small box wrapped in purple paper. "He just came by."

Just came by. I've been worrying so much about Mom that I haven't taken a lot of time to think about Dad. It would have been so nice to see him, even from a distance . . .

She hands the box to me, and I immediately want to sob at the sight of my father's handwriting. *VALERIE.* Big letters. Lopsided heart.

"Thank you," I tell them and hustle out of the building. Finding a spot outside, I rip open the paper. My name is there again, but this time in the hard, black ink of a computer:

> Val,
> If Jax finds this, he'll kill you.
> —Alex

The box alone tells me what it is. I lift the lid and the phone's screen reflects my anxious face back to me.

Hands shaking, I press the power button and wait the fifteen or so seconds it takes to boot up. "Come on, come on."

The screensaver is generic, but that's not even close to what matters. Under Contacts is a single phone number. I hit dial.

Matthew picks up on the third ring.

"Happy belated birthday."

Matthew couldn't talk long—something about a meeting— but he told me to call again tonight. Hearing his voice again reminded me of how he worked to keep me out of the Young Herons. On the night we were recruited, he already knew I wasn't getting in but didn't tell me.

It's one thing to know he lied by not telling me, it's another that he broke a promise made in my brother's spirit. He loved Leo, too. He knew what a double pinky promise meant.

When I get back to Holloway, I rough up my hair and do my best to make it look like I at least went walking, if not running. First thing I've got to do is hide Matthew's phone. Everything else is second.

That plan changes once I walk in. Everyone, even Jaws, is gathered at the table. A newspaper is spread out in front of them.

"What's going on?" I ask.

"A Boar safe house got raided and a bunch of them were arrested," Kate says, a lock of hair wrapped tightly around her index finger. "Like, a lot."

"How many?" I ask.

"Twenty-two."

"Holy shit." I take a seat, keeping Matthew's phone safe and out of view. "What happened?"

"The Young Herons happened," Nianna says. "They're working with the cops."

No, I think. *Just Matthew. And he'll be able to tell me more if I manage to get this stupid phone hidden.*

"The Boars were in the Mission," Micah says. "The Herons want that ground, and it feels like they're getting it, given how the area is gentrifying. They want the locals out, the Boars out, and more hipster techies in."

"They'll recruit more," Nianna replies. "The Boars always recruit fast." She turns to Jax. "We should build our numbers, too."

"I agree," says Mako. "And I know Kate does." The girl in question nods.

Jax bobs his head from side to side. "The Boars got big, then they got lazy. We work fine how we are." He nudges Micah. "Get Kurt and scout the Mission. I'll have Jules and Cameron go downtown. See if the Herons have tagged it or anything yet."

I skim the rest of the article while the others disperse— Matthew's name is nowhere in it. Phew. *Phone,* I remind myself. *Hide the damn phone.*

I hurry into the garage and wait until the door shuts behind me. Taking the phone from my waistband, I toss it up and down like it's a bomb I need to defuse. Hiding it in my clothes seems too obvious—and I know Jax has gone through those at least once, I remember with a blush. One of the boxes might be good, but I've seen Kate and Mako sift through those now and again when we need a certain kitchen gadget. Up on a shelf? I eye the height. It would be awkward getting it from there. And one wrong—possibly drunken—bump and it might fall.

I survey the garage, growing more desperate by the second. The phone's off, of course, with no alarms, but I still want it hidden.

Bed. Boxes. Pool table. Shelves.

Pool table. *Yes.*

I grab a stray sock from the floor and dig around in the boxes until I find a roll of masking tape. Lying down on my back, I scoot underneath the table. With the only lights directly above it, the bottom is all shadow. I place my hand on dark wood. I can barely see it.

It's the best I can think of right now.

Ripping off a strand of tape, I position the sock and secure it with just enough slack. I repeat the process twice more. I slide the phone in and back out, tugging on the tape to test it. *It'll hold, Valerie. It'll hold and so can you.*

I take a shower to keep up my charade, though I don't think anyone's even remotely suspicious. Steaming water dribbles off my fingertips as my mind flies ahead to six thirty. That's when Matthew told me to call.

It feels so good just to know the phone is there, that the line is open. I wonder how long it took for Alex to agree to give me the phone. Would he want the future leader of the

Herons to be talking to a Stag? Or would he see it as a favor to his little brother?

The thought of it being a trap comes back, sinking its teeth into my hopes. I stick my face in the shower's spray as if hot water were the panacea for dark thoughts. *It'll be fine. It's Matthew. It has to be fine.*

The rest of the day drags. I knock on Kate's door and ask if she wants to try to fold paper butterflies, but she shakes her head.

"I don't really care about it anymore," she says, handing me a stack of square paper. "You can look up how to do it online."

"Oh, okay." I take the paper. "Are you okay?"

She shrugs. "I'm fine. Just have a headache."

"Okay," I say. "But if there's ever anything you want to talk about—"

"I'm *fine*," she says, shutting the door behind her. "Just leave me alone."

I go dejectedly back into the kitchen, chucking the paper on the table. Well, that was a bust. Now I'm worried on top of bored. I kill time watching reruns on Netflix, but the distraction barely takes.

By six o'clock, I can no longer sit still. I need privacy for Matthew's call and breathing room for me. I find a fresh set of workout gear and put it on. Wrapping and unwrapping my headphones around my fingers, I pace the cold basement. I check and make sure I have my Stag phone—no new messages—then grab Matthew's also and tuck the latter into my waistband. I'm halfway up the stairs when Jax opens the basement door.

He cocks his head to the side. "You already ran today."

"I did," I say. My pulse quickens. "I'm just antsy. Thought I'd do another quick one."

"No. We're still lying low. You most of all. I shouldn't have even let you go earlier."

Shit. "I wouldn't be gone long."

He shakes his head, stepping down the rest of the stairs. I pivot, keeping my right hip—and the square block of Matthew's phone—out of his sight. Jax doesn't say anything. He just surveys the room, glancing at the recycling bins, my bed, and my things.

What time is it? Did I already turn Matthew's phone on? No. Definitely not. But what if it turned on by itself? No, that doesn't happen. It's off. I'm sure.

"I'll just do stretches or something in the yard then," I say quickly.

Jax shrugs. "No, no, I've changed my mind. Let's go run."

"You want to go running with me?"

"Yeah." He comes closer and I lose myself in the scent of his aftershave. "I used to run track, back in high school. It'll be nice."

I try to think of something, anything. Some excuse to get Jax out of the room so I can stash the phone. *I can say I need to change into something warmer. Something lighter. I need water. I need my shoes.*

"You go on." Glancing quickly at his body—I mean, his *clothes*—I add, "Go change. I want to grab a sweatshirt."

"I'll wait."

Matthew's phone is a live grenade against my skin. I move gingerly to my set of drawers, pull out the first sweatshirt I see, and tug it on. Thankfully it's one of my larger ones. My hip and Matthew's phone are covered, but just barely.

"Ready."

We go upstairs, and he goes to his room. I contemplate chucking Matthew's phone in a bathroom cabinet or under the couch—but Kate and Mako are watching TV, so I just stand there. *Fuck.*

Jax comes back in a loose hoodie and basketball shorts. "Come on, Valentine."

I expect Jax to say something about where to turn, to speed up or slow down, or to grab me and ask me what's in my waistband.

Instead, he lets me lead. He keeps pace two steps behind me, his hair catching in the wind as he moves. My body warms and I almost relax—almost.

The sweatshirt plan has backfired. Sweat beads my skin—including down at my hip. I can feel the moisture start to dislodge Matthew's phone. Every step and it slides down a little farther. I keep my strides short, trying to move my legs only and my hips as little as possible. It feels awkward. It looks awkward.

All the while I keep looking back at Jax. My leader keeps his finely wrought features facing forward, the streetlamps catching the green in his hazel eyes.

We reach a corner, and I stop short. I'm going to miss my call. What's Matthew going to think if I ignore him?

"Valentine?" Jax puts his hand on the small of my back.

I jump away from him. "I can't . . ."

Then it happens. The phone slides out past my waistband into the loose stretchy fabric of my leggings. Jax gently puts his hand on my arm.

"Can't what?" he asks.

"I. Just . . . give me a sec."

I crouch to the ground and fiddle with my shoelace. Jax surveys the houses around us, probably bored. We're near the bus stop that took Micah and me to get my tattoo. I feel so much older now.

"Take your time," he says. "No rush."

Yes, rush. Seizing my moment, I push the phone back up and get it to an almost secure spot. I haven't felt so panicked since my birthday. The gunfire, the weird intimidation tactic from the Boars . . . come to think of it, it was all a little off.

"Jax, can I ask you something?" I say. "Kate said most of what happens between the gangs is retaliation. Like what happened at Mission Dolores. You don't kill unless someone crossed you first."

He nods. "That's right."

"But on the night I was recruited, the Boars were going to kill me over nothing. For them to threaten me . . . it doesn't make sense."

Jax smiles, cocking his head to the side. "What do you think that means?"

I shrug. "Maybe they thought I was someone else."

"Or *you* thought they were something else."

"What?" I say, repeating it in my head. "Wait . . . were those not Boars?"

"Nope."

"Who were they?"

"Some buddies of mine." He's grinning.

"You shot at them!"

"I'm sure it sounded that way. It was probably overkill, but I wanted to see if you were really committed."

"You're insane," I say. A flood of worry hits me and I tack on a "sorry."

There's a moment of stillness, and then Jax asks, "Do you hate me?"

"No." I swallow. "You . . . I just don't understand you."

"I'm not asking you to."

"I know. But I want to."

Stillness again. Only this time I'm aware of how easily it'd be to close the distance between us. This time I'm wanting . . .

The wind rises, and Jax brushes my hair from my face. "We should get back," he says quietly.

He turns abruptly, heading back the way we came, waving his hand to tell me I should follow. The wind picks back up, blowing against our bodies and pushing us back toward the house. I follow behind, thinking. Something has to make him tick, and I don't know what that thing is. But I want to.

Even with Matthew in my heart, I've got Jax on my mind.

Jax turns back, sees me still sulking, and smiles. "You're so fucking cute when you're mad."

I missed Matthew's call.

I'm waiting, alone, and in bed. I told the others I had a headache and wanted some quiet for a bit. Matthew's phone rests in my hand. I send him a trio of texts, trying to explain what happened. Finally, he replies:

`I'm calling you`

Seconds later, the phone buzzes and I answer immediately. "Hello?"

"Hi," Matthew replies. "Why didn't you pick up?"

"Sorry. Jax made me go running with him. Well, I offered. Kinda."

He clears his throat. "Have you thought any more about what I said? About leaving the Wars?"

"Yeah."

"And?"

"And what? Matthew, no one leaves."

"No one has before," he says. "But they can now. You can. That's what I've been working with John about."

"John Kilmer," I say. "The chief of police."

"Jax told you?"

"I read it somewhere." I exhale hard into the phone. "Do you remember him?"

A pause. "Yes."

Memories flash in my brain like a silent movie—lying in my bed after getting no sleep. Mom making me get dressed and come downstairs. Two police officers sitting on our couch. Nothing had ever looked so unnatural to me. Kilmer had a beard then.

"I didn't know he'd become chief." When Matthew doesn't say anything, I exhale a small *huh*. "I take it you did."

"I kept in touch with him on and off." Matthew's tone hardens. "Hey, Val, are you okay?"

"Yeah, I'm fine." *So fucking cute when you're mad*—why can't I get that out of my head? "I was just afraid the phone might go off or something."

"Okay. It's all right. Listen, I don't have much time, so I'll just say it. I want to end the Wars. It's horrible, what happened to Annie, but that was a long time ago. Everything now is just retaliation. Or insanity. Jesus, Val, you should hear some of the things the other Herons say."

"Like what?"

"It's like I told you. They keep expanding and partnering with businesses because they can. Because they don't like the Boars. And they talk about it so casually under this pretense of improving the city. I don't know how Alex did this. It freaks me out." He clears his throat. "That's why I want to end it. The program John and I've made—it'll keep you safe. I know it. I just need you to be the first."

"Why don't you be first?"

"I can't. It'd be too convenient for the son of the family bankrolling it to enroll."

"Meaning your parents don't want you going public as being part of the Young Herons," I shoot back. "How are they okay with this, anyway? I thought they wanted revenge."

"Ending the Wars this way still gives the Herons some control. There's no way around that." He exhales heavily. "Look, I just need someone else. Why won't you just say yes? Ending it is the right thing to do."

"I can't go. I have to stay for Leo. I *want* to stay for Leo. That's the whole reason I joined!"

"I know, I know. I haven't forgotten. I'll find a way to take care of it. Just promise me you'll join TRUCE. Join up, then people in the gangs will see it's legit. Then we'll run. Anywhere you want."

An idea strikes me. "Can't you get one of the Boars from the Mission to sign up?"

"Kilmer says they're not caving. They don't trust the cops. You're different, Val. Leave the Stags. You'll be safe."

"How can you be so sure?"

"Trust me."

"I don't know if I can."

I want to catch the words as soon as they're out, but I can't. I envision Matthew on the other end of the line, maybe sitting down in shock, or with his thumb across his lips like he does when he's frustrated. Whatever he's doing, he is doing it in silence.

"I'm sorry," I whisper. "I'm sorry, Matthew. Please. It's just a lot. What you're asking. I want to help. And I'm trying my best but . . . I'm scared, okay? One of the Boars will cave. They've got to. Until then, I'm safe here. The Stags aren't like the others."

"Yes, they are."

Well, that's what they said about you. "Look, Jax knows who killed Leo. And I'm getting closer to him telling me. Just give me time."

"You'd stay with Jax? Val, no."

"Jax might be the only person who knows," I say. "I can't lose that chance. Not now."

"And I can't have you getting hurt for those, what? Godless heathens?"

I hear the desperate laugh in his voice. He's trying to make a joke. *Godless heathens* is a nickname Lyla and the other theater kids gave to themselves—with pride, I might add. Matthew and I only ever used it with playful sarcasm.

I don't laugh, and instead we drift into a long silence. "What if they go after my parents?"

"They're safe. Alex and some of the Herons from his year have been keeping watch on them."

What? "My mom said he came over. You . . . did that?"

"Yeah."

"Thank you," I whisper.

"You're welcome. Now, please say you'll join TRUCE. I'll come get you. Right now. Wherever you are."

I weigh my choices, placing both options on a mental scale. The sides dip and sway as I try to keep track of the consequences of each choice. If I go, I'm with Matthew but I never get the Boar who killed Leo. I'm promised safety and Matthew's presence, but at the expense of my revenge—not to mention my name and privacy. Anyone who didn't see it when SFPD tweeted my face to the world would certainly see it this time. Mom and Dad will have to go through a new shade of the hell they've already been through.

If I stay, then I keep my growing hope for closure. I've already made it a few months. I bet I can make it a year. TRUCE will find someone else, I'm sure of it. Mom and Dad get their daughter back after her year away.

The scale clinks solidly. I stay.

"I can't go, Matthew," I say. "I won't put Mom and Dad through anything else. Not again. Besides, I think I'm close to finding the Boar."

"Val, you could save someone's life. A lot of lives, actually."

I'd been so wrapped up in my selfishness that I forgot the most obvious repercussion of my going—ending the Wars. How terrible of a person am I that I'd choose my own gain over other people's losses? My mental scale tips back again, uneven.

"I need time," I say, finally. "Let . . . let me think about it."

"Take all the time you need," he replies, though I suspect he doesn't mean it. "When you're ready, I'll come to you. I'll find a way out of here. What do you think?"

I think Jax may actually kill me if he finds out I've left again. "I'll think about it."

"Okay."

"Okay."

Matthew hangs up, and I feel his ghost instantly, like when you stare at something bright and see the spots after you close your eyes. A hollowness of something that is no longer there. I turn off Matthew's phone and put it back in its place. I trudge up the stairs to join the others. Nianna spots me first.

"How's the headache?"

"Better," I say, remembering my own excuse.

"There's aspirin in the bathroom," she says. She motions to Jax's room. "Micah's back from scouting. He and Jax are talking."

"Did he seem okay?" I ask.

"I think so," she replies. "But we'll see."

When the door finally opens, both Jax and Micah are smiling.

"Hey," I say. "So, what happened?"

Jax gives Micah a nod, and the latter clears his throat. "The Heron symbol was everywhere. Walls, telephone poles, café tables." I shiver—if the Herons take the Mission, it'll mean a lot of displaced families. Folks whose parents came here with nothing and who built their lives up around San Francisco.

"I wonder if people in the Mission want them there," Nianna says.

"Who wants what where?" asks Mako, coming in from the hall.

"Young Herons in the Mission," Nianna says again. "Money makes people feel safe. If you were a rich white twenty-whatever moving into an unfamiliar neighborhood, what would make you feel better?"

Mako frowns. "Other rich twenty-whatevers."

"Other *white* twenty-whatevers," Nianna corrects pointedly. "But yeah. More people like them with their own values."

"Let the people think what they think. Our next phase with the Boars will change their minds," says Jax. "Mako. Beers."

Mako dutifully gets the bottles. I wave mine off in favor of a glass of water. I need a clear head. Jax raises his drink. "To our comrade, Micah, who hath returned unscathed." Micah rolls his eyes, smiling, and raises his beer.

"And to Valentine," Jax finishes.

My head snaps up. "For what?"

"For being so damn pretty."

Mako chuckles. "And for letting us put the pool table in her bedroom."

All of them laugh and I smile, too, but I can feel Jax's gaze on me. I force a smile, focus on Micah, and raise my cup toward him.

The Stags do what they do best. Mako pours tequila shots. Someone knocks over the salt shaker and Jax freaks out at the possible bad omen, eliciting amused laughter from the rest of us. We make our way to the living room where Mako stretches his arm over the sofa. He laughs and reaches for Micah in the papasan across from him.

"Dude, you be Jesus, and I'll be God."

Micah reaches toward him with one finger extended with his mouth gaping, just like the painting. We explode into hysterics.

"It's not even Jesus in the painting," Nianna says, wiping a tear from her eye, and we laugh harder.

"Such a nerd," Mako retorts.

She shrugs. "You love me."

Jax, Mako, and Nianna take the couch. Kate joins later and sits on the ground, letting Nianna braid her hair. Nianna's fingers comb through the gold, working out the tangles. She turns to me. "Feeling better?"

I nod.

"Good."

"Yay," Kate murmurs. I sit down next to her as Mako gets a movie started.

The air is a shimmery haze. My breath is heavy and weightless at the same time. Godless heathens they may be, but they are mine. Like Matthew was mine—*is* mine?

The difference is that the Stags are here.

A couple days later, Jax rounds us all up to let us know our next plan of attack against the Herons. Mako calls Jules so she, Kurt, and Cameron can listen in from the Mission. They've been ordered to lie low and observe if the Young Herons are making a move without being too obvious.

"A propaganda campaign," Jax announces when we're all ready.

"Like, flyers?" says Juliet on speaker. "That's new."

"Think about it. We can't do anything violent or that would lend credibility to the Herons' claim that we're a violent bunch of uncontrollable idiots who need something like TRUCE," he says. "Instead, we're going to be smart about it. We're going to leverage the Boars' numbers and cover this town with evidence that the Young Herons have got to be stopped, plus ways they can help our cause."

"What kind of evidence?" I ask.

"Anything we can dig up," he replies. "Headlines about the businesses pushed out by tech, stats on the changing demographics of the city, costs of the Heron-owned housing. Numbers on how much these tech companies are making and how little they donate to the city. Even more—names of places where people can donate money and volunteer."

Over by the sink, Nianna hops down from her seat on the counter. "What's our endgame?"

"Turn the tide without shedding blood," Jax replies. "Anyone gets hurt, anything gets damaged—that's adding fuel to the Herons' fire. Instead, we're going to get citizens talking, get people to realize that the San Francisco they know now isn't the utopia the Young Herons have made them think it is. There's so much more we can do, but we have to loosen the Herons' grip first."

Micah clears his throat. "And the Boars are okay with this?"

"Ty said he had a few members resist, but any change brings resistance," Jax says. "Like I said, we're thinking like Stags and using the Boars for numbers. We'll hang up physical posters and run a social media campaign, since we got all those new followers after the protest." Jax pauses, reading the room. No one stirs. "I take it you all don't think it'll work."

More silence. Finally, Nianna caves. "I like the nonviolence, obviously. I just don't know if it'll have the splash you're looking for."

"It will when every single person going to work in FiDi and SoMa on Monday morning is swamped with these flyers. Trust me. It will work."

"All right," I say. "I'm in. What should we do first?"

Jax claps. "Thank you, Valentine. First, we all research. Put all your ideas, any headlines you find—anything that pops into your head goes into a document. Then I'll comb through it with Ty and combine the lists that the Boars make. Then we print. On Sunday night, we'll meet up with the Boars and divide the flyers and tape 'em up."

"I'll bring the Red Bull," Mako says, nodding approvingly.

We waste no time digging in. First on the list is the name of the corner store where we had the protest. Sharing the same doc, we add to the list all at once—recounting communities displaced by new Heron-affiliated housing, businesses like taxi services and restaurants that shuttered when tech offered their own free versions of the same services.

A new, ugly feeling blooms in my stomach. Dad works in the Mid-Market area, and his company is large enough that it offers its employees perks like that—perks that trickled down to me in some way, shape, or form. *Am I a hypocrite for helping put these companies on blast like this?* I sigh and hit enter to move myself to a new line. Even if I am a hypocrite, I do believe these companies can be doing more. *And now that I know the Young Herons purposely target vulnerable communities, I am fully in favor of stopping that.*

Down the hall, Jax is on the phone. The door's slightly ajar, and I can hear him talking slowly, purposefully. When he hangs up, I catch him saying, "Thanks, Theresa."

Jax comes into the living room where the group of us is

stationed, doing research. He hands me a paper with a couple of company names listed.

"What's this?" I ask.

"Gift from Theresa. More companies that the Herons are working with that aren't publicly affiliated with them yet."

"Got it," I reply. "So, dig in and find out what kind of work they have planned, because that's actually the Herons that have something planned."

"Bingo. More fuel for Sunday," he says.

"Awesome." I type the first name into Google and hand the paper to Mako on my left. "You take the second, and so on?"

We work until the evening. The next morning, Nianna and I weed through the document while Mako, Micah, and Kate map out the best routes for us and the Boars to take. Jax drifts in and out of his room, coordinating with Ty. The more I scroll, the more I can feel my disgust at the Herons rise. I sit back from my laptop and drain the rest of my coffee.

"There's so much here," I say quietly. "I didn't realize they were so involved in everything."

"The Herons are ruthless," Nianna replies. "I wasn't convinced this would work, but it's at least going to get folks talking."

"Like," I say, scrolling until I find the page I'm looking for, "there was a senior center that got ousted because of funding problems. They couldn't afford their rent. That's so sad."

"Yeah," Nianna replies. "I remember when that happened. That's why we gotta do our best to fight back now, for the ones who can't."

Sunday night rolls around, and we each pack a backpack with the flyers—thousands in all. Juliet, Cameron, and Kurt come by and grab their own backpacks.

"What do you think of this?" I ask Juliet as I tug on a black sweatshirt over my fleece sweater.

She shrugs. "Could go either way. Regardless, we're going to get shit for littering." She says the last bit with a smile. "Who knows? It's gonna make a hell of an impact."

Since we'll all be out with a handful of Boars, Jax has told us to stay wary, but welcoming. It is a partnership, after all.

Looping my hair into a ponytail, I tuck the length up and into a beanie. Zipping my sweatshirt all the way up, I go to the bathroom and check in the mirror that my tattoo is totally hidden. There's no telling what cameras may be on us as we canvass the streets.

Making sure the door is locked, I take out Matthew's phone, gripping it tight. I know we're going downtown. Will I have enough time to sneak away to see him? Sweat beads at the back of my neck as I open the phone and start typing. He's been texting every couple of days, asking me if I've come to a decision.

Truth is, no matter how much I seem to muddle it, I can't get myself to go into TRUCE—I couldn't do that to my parents, nor am I really confident I could bear being in the spotlight like that again.

The memories of the days following Leo's death are sharp as glass. Most people have no idea what it's like to lose someone so publicly. They don't know what it's like to have reporters show up on your doorstep asking for a statement. They don't know what it's like to watch the news and see your brother's face, in a photo that you'd be in too if you weren't cropped out of it.

My parents and I bore that both together and totally apart. They're already trying, already tired. I can't put them through the media circus again, not when staying with the Stags means I have the chance to make it right for all three of us. But that kind of an explanation isn't something for texting. And if I'm already going to be downtown, I might as well try to talk to him then.

I'll be downtown tonight. I don't know where yet. Can you meet me?

I take my time washing my hands, all the while keeping my eyes on my phone. My heart leaps in my throat as he answers:

I can try. When?

Late, I reply. We're leaving at midnight.

OK, he replies. Text me when and where.

Kate knocks at the door. "You ready, Val?"

"Yeah!" I join her and the others in the kitchen where, true to his word, Mako got us all Red Bulls. I'm hoping the nap I took earlier will help, but Jax wants us up most of the night. Lifting my can, I take a sip. *Not bad.* I drink the rest slowly as we all wait for Jax. Somehow he's always the last one ready.

We drive downtown to rendezvous with the Boars. It's a quiet night, with most of the city asleep and waiting to start their week. Would anyone bother to stop and read our signs at all? Or would they dismiss them as a nuisance and a waste of paper?

One thing's for sure, they're going to see them. Unzipping the backpack on my lap, I smile at the neon-colored paper inside. Neon—our signature's going to be all over downtown without one drop of paint.

"Ty wants each of you with some of his men. I'll be watching you guys on my phone the whole time," Jax says as we get close. "Anything goes off, you defend yourself and send the panic alert when you can."

"Wait, we're splitting up?" Micah asks.

Jax nods. "A sign of trust between us and Ty."

"And you're okay with it?"

"We do what we have to do. It's just for an hour, and Ty says he's picked his most loyal guys. It's us against the Herons. The Boars know that."

Micah sighs and sits back in his chair, defeated. I shoot him a look so he knows I'm not thrilled about the idea either. For good measure, I pull out my Stag phone and watch the blue light that represents me move across the screen. In the far right corner, a red bell symbol moves every few seconds. If I hit that, it sends an alert to the other Stags of where I am. *Hopefully I won't be dead in some alley by the time they come get me,* I think bitterly. *But if we're splitting up, there's a good chance I'll be able to meet Matthew.*

Jaws drops us off at the rendezvous spot. I climb out and stand beside Jax, watching as he scans the park. At first, I think Jaws got the spot wrong—then, slowly, the Boars start to come out from the dark. Even in the dim streetlight, I recognize Ty Boreas. His second, Adam Yglesias, follows right behind him, and groups of others trail behind.

"Right on time," says Ty.

Jax offers his hand. "Wouldn't want to be late to the party."

Ty shakes it, then turns and waves his hand to the figures behind him. "Three of my guys with each of yours," he says. "I've stationed others around the whole area, to keep watch."

"Roger that," Jax responds. He turns to us. "We do this as fast as we can, as much as we can. Don't make it perfect. One hour, then send your location to Jaws. He'll come get you."

"Okay," Nianna and I reply in unison. She gives me a look, but I ignore her. I'm thinking of the other phone in my pocket. I only have an hour, and I'm going to be with the Boars the whole time. My heart sinks. There's no way Matthew is going to be able to find me.

Ty turns to his men. "Go." It's a statement, not a question. *Ty is a leader, after all.*

All too soon, we divide up. I'm trying to be brave, but going solo with the Boars has me so on edge I could throw up. My adrenaline races, fueled by fear and Red Bull, as I look at the three Boars I'm with.

They introduce themselves one by one: Trey, TJ, and Red. I introduce myself as Valentine—why not, right? Trey shakes my hand first—though he looks like he resents the motion. TJ is next, his mess of long, stringy, dark hair falling in his face as he gives me an upward nod. Red shakes my hand last, keeping his hood up and head down the whole time.

"Here's our route," I say, and I lay the map down for all of them. "We take Battery to Jackson, then wind through the side streets and eventually end up on Kearny." The trio doesn't interrupt, so I keep going. "Remember what Jax said. We move fast. Our goal is coverage everywhere. Whatever's left over at the end, we'll just toss on the sidewalks. Got it?"

"Got it," TJ responds. He shifts so his own backpack is in front of him. "Load us up."

The four of us divide the papers, and each of the other groups does the same. As we head out, I look over my shoulder at Jax—and see Ty looking back, too. Not at his men, but just at me. Our gazes meet, and he turns away, shaking his head. *What was that?*

My nerves don't lessen as Trey, TJ, Red, and I start hanging up the Herons' "crimes." We use precut sticky foam—just peel, stick, move on. The Boars impress me with their efficiency, and after the first street I turn back, admiring the neon wake we're leaving. "Let's keep going," I say, shivering in the night's chill. "Next street."

I let them go ahead, getting my bearings as best I can. There won't be much time, and I'm not even sure if Matthew will find me, but I take out his phone anyway. Taking a deep breath, I switch it over to vibrate then go to Settings and activate Location. Then I send him where I am.

With Boars, I text quickly. Be careful.

"Hey, quit slacking!"

I look up, and Trey is looking at me, eyes wide like *What the fuck are you doing?* and I can't tell if he means it in jest or not.

"Sorry," I mutter, shoving Matthew's phone back in my pocket. "Just giving Jax an update."

I double my poster speed as we go. It doesn't take a lot of time to figure out it's easier in pairs, so Trey and I work in unison. He holds the poster, I do the foam stickers on the back, and he sets the poster up. The stack dwindles faster than I thought it would, and I keep checking Matthew's phone for an update. Maybe it's too difficult for him to sneak out after all—he did say they've been cooping him up. . . .

I send my location again.

"Jax again," I say apologetically as Trey tacks up another flyer on his own. "You guys go ahead, I'll catch up."

"Yes, ma'am," he replies.

I duck into an alley next to an Irish pub. I'm typing as fast as I can when—

"Val!"

Matthew's in a dark hoodie and sweats—he must have just rolled out of bed. We hesitate a moment, then hug. He kisses me, and for some reason I wasn't expecting it.

He takes my hand. "Let's go."

I tighten my hand around his. "Wait, what? Go where?"

"Back to the Herons," he says. He's breathless, but smiling. "I knew you'd understand."

"No, wait." *Shit.* "I didn't come here to join TRUCE. I'm sorry, but I just can't."

"Wait, what? Why not?"

Quickly and quietly, I recap my entire logic about my parents—sparing them any more hurt. And, frankly, I want revenge. Matthew listens, even leans in as I whisper but his face remains unchanged. "I just can't do that to them," I finish.

"Look, I get it. What you're saying makes sense. But in TRUCE, you'll be safe. Not out doing whatever it is you're doing here."

"I know, but Matthew," I say. "I joined the Wars for a reason, and that's to find the guy who killed Leo. I'm not going to abandon that. Not now."

"Fine," he says. "Well, if not you, then are there any other Stags that might?"

I let go of his hand. "That was fast."

"I know, but look. I know you; once you make up your mind you don't change it. I can't force you, and either way it'll look so much better if someone comes forward voluntarily."

My first thought is, of course, Kate. With the Herons' money and resources, she could get the help she needs—that is, if she's willing to take it. Besides, going into TRUCE would mean she'd be separated from Mako, who on most days I swear is what keeps her alive.

"There's one Stag I can try," I say. "But she's stubborn. I'll text you once I talk to her, but right now I gotta go."

"What?"

I try to hug him but since he doesn't lift his arms in time to return it, I mostly just succeed in pinning his arms to his sides. I duck back out the alley—and right into Red, TJ, and Trey. An empty backpack hangs at Red's side.

"Where did you—hey, what the fuck?" Red shoves me aside, and grabs at Matt's sweatshirt. The latter staggers back and tries to run, but soon all three of them are on him. "Who the fuck are you?"

Fuck fuck fuck. If they recognize Matt, they might very well kill him. So I say the exact opposite of what happened.

"He just came up and grabbed me!" I scream, real tears springing from my eyes because I don't just *know* what's going to happen next, I can *feel* it. "Holy shit, holy fucking shit."

I stagger back, the victim, as Red lands the first blow. If these are Ty's best men, they'll know what a truce between the Boars and Stags means. They may not protect me like Jax would, but they'll do enough.

Jax. I pull out my Stag phone and, with trembling fingers, push the alert button. The Boars take turns hitting Matthew as he staggers up from the ground. Blood, black as ink in the low light, litters the ground. I step between them, raising my hands. "That's enough! Let's go, let's just fucking go. Please."

Red spits and kicks Matthew hard in the ribs one last time. The sound of Matthew's wet coughs—spit, blood, who knows—rings in my ears worse than TJ saying "fucking bastard" as we leave.

The three surround me as we hustle back toward the rendezvous point. I text Jax:

Some guy tried to grab at me. I'm ok. With Boars heading back to rendezvous.

I hit send, but moments later a horn honks, and I spin. He got my alert. Jax practically launches himself out of the van door before Jaws pulls over, and he puts his arms around me so hard it nearly knocks me over.

"Where?" he says, voice ragged.

"A few streets back. I'm okay, I'm okay."

"I'll fucking kill them."

"The Boars got him," I reply. Jax loosens his grip, and I nod at the trio of them. "Thank you." *Please, for the love of God, none of you mention I was alone.*

"The Stags owe you guys one," Jax says. "I'll tell Ty, whatever you need."

"No problem," Trey replies, his glee evident.

"You have my word. You three good on your own?"

"Yes, sir."

"Good." He puts his arm around my shoulders. "Let's get the others."

I nod, and when we climb into the van I purposely take the farthest seat. Once we start moving, I pull out Matthew's phone and lower the brightness. *He literally just got beaten on the street, what the fuck can I say?* Stalling, I switch the Location setting back to off. After that, there's nothing else to keep me texting. Time is dwindling, so I just text what I thought in that one, impossible moment:

I'm sorry. If they recognized you, they would have killed you. Please say something.

I pause, breath tight in my throat when I see he's typing. Then:

Did you set me up?

Five words. Five words with the weight of worlds swallowed up inside of them, crashing into me. How could he think that? Does he really think I've changed so much? The Matthew I grew up with, the one who loved me, would never think that.

No. It just happened. I'm sorry, I type again, then shove the phone in my pocket just in time for us to come to a stop back at the rendezvous point as the van door slides open once more.

Micah sees me first, and climbs in next to me. "What happened?"

"Some guy jumped out of this alleyway," I say. "I'm fine, the Boars fought him off."

"What?" Kate says, and she immediately begs me for the details. I keep it simple and short, then switch gears.

"You guys do okay?"

Mako lifts off his cap and scratches under his hair. "Boars were pretty chill, though one of them did say they have never done shit like this before." He pauses, reading Jax's reaction from the front seat. "Direct quote."

Jax is quiet, only moving as the van bounces as we get onto the freeway. "We'll see what the city thinks in the morning. Tonight let's just get home."

Fine by me, I think, and I curl into a ball in the backseat. Blotting my eyes with my sweatshirt, I pray that when I get home I'll have a text from Matthew saying he understands, that he's okay.

We're nearly home when I remember I switched the phone to vibrate and never switched it back. Which means Matthew is silent as the distant stars, and I find myself repeating the same thought that circled the day my brother died: *What have I done?*

17

The next morning, I wake up, stumble up to the bathroom, and vomit.

In my dream, Leo and Matthew held hands on a mountaintop dusted with perfect, pure white snow. Leo looked at me like I'd hurt him. Matthew's face was bruised and bloodied.

Spitting the last bit of acid from my throat, I flush one more time for good measure and go to the kitchen. No one else is up yet. After swirling a cold glass of water around my mouth and teeth, I shuffle into the living room and switch on the TV, keeping the volume low.

Our flyers are the morning's big story. The news anchor switches over to a reporter on the street, a handful of the flyers in her grip.

"Police are investigating the pamphlets, which seem to have appeared overnight," the woman says. "We've reached out to a few of the companies mentioned here, but so far we've not received comment. We've also spoken to a few commuters here who, apart from being a little confused, are certainly talking about this morning's developments."

The report cuts away to a reel of people being interviewed. "You certainly can't ignore it," a guy says, chuckling for the camera. The reporter asks if he read the flyers. "I read part of it, yeah. I mean, I guess I knew this kind of thing was going on but it's pretty shocking to see it laid out in front of you."

The report ends, and I feel a little better after watching it. At least last night wasn't all for nothing—even if it meant Matthew getting so hurt in the process.

"Enough," I say to myself, and I head back downstairs. Finding my clothes from last night, I toss them into the washing machine. I top off the load with a few more things and start the cycle. *I'll erase the night, best I can.*

There's a knock from above my head.

"Valerie?" Micah comes down the stairs. "Are you okay?"

"Yeah."

"Were you throwing up earlier?"

I cringe. "You heard?"

"I was up and just messing around on my phone." He stares at me for a long while. "It's not for everybody."

"What?"

"This life. You can tell me if you're not okay. I won't tell Jax." I give him a disbelieving look, and he puts both his hands up in front of him. "I won't."

I sit down on my bed and start to bunch and unbunch the corner of my bedspread. How many weeks has it been since I joined the Wars? And how much have I seen since then? How much have I had to learn? Matthew's not the person I thought he was—and now he's mad at me for getting him hurt. I'm a marked criminal to everyone on Twitter. My poor parents are without their only child, and despite what I told Mom, I'd bet anything they're still thinking it's all their fault.

"It's just . . ." I start. "It's just a lot to take in. I barely know my own name at this point."

Micah walks over and takes my hand. "Come on. Let's get you some air."

"I'm not supposed to leave," I say. "I'm the idiot who got arrested and doxxed, remember?"

"I'll tell him we're going to the range or something. Put shoes on. I'll be right back."

Whatever Micah says to Jax, it works.

Micah drives west and onto the Great Highway. The Pacific stretches across the horizon in all of its gray and blue majesty. Fog banks swirled by the wind drift through the sky. Between the cypress trees, natives of the Outer Sunset are getting up and going to breakfast, or reading the paper in their tiny, pastel homes.

"Where are we going?" I ask as we pass the Murphy Windmill, one of two working windmills in Golden Gate Park.

"You'll see," says Micah.

We drive up a short ridge, past the rough waves of Ocean Beach and the historical Cliff House. We round a curve in the coastline, and it hits me.

I smile at Micah. "Lands End?"

He nods.

Lands End is exactly what it sounds like: where the top of the peninsula meets the water. Whitecaps dot the crashing green-blue water below us. Up ahead, hidden around the bluff, is the Golden Gate Bridge. Down below are the Sutro Baths.

The baths are a San Francisco landmark, albeit not one of her flashier attractions. Back in the 1900s, the area was home to a number of bathhouses owned by the Sutro family. Today, there's just ruins, but they're neat in their own way.

The moment Micah puts the car in park, I fling open the door and breathe in a full lungful of clean ocean air. "I haven't been here in years."

We take our time inching down a steep trail toward the sheltered cove. Below us, the old stones of the bathhouses stretch from either end of the cove like half-finished LEGOs.

Micah leaps up onto the nearest stone monument. We walk and trace the rectangular lines of the former bathhouse. I hold my hands out for balance—if you fall, you fall into an algae-ridden pool of seawater—but Micah walks as casually as ever.

Next, we go to the cave to the right of the ruins. It's pitch-black and nothing more than dirt and stone. But then . . . the sound.

A wave rushes into the caverns below us. All at once, the roar of the water swallows the tunnel. It feels too fake, too perfect, like the sound effects at a theme park. Only it's real. I close my eyes.

It's intoxicating and terrifying all at once. I could die in this sound. Die and be reborn.

The wave-thunder repeats itself again and again, crashing into me, and if I didn't know that Micah was waiting for me back outside, I'd have stayed there all day.

"Did you want to check it out?" I ask, indicating back to the cave as we wander back up the rocky path. "It's pretty cool."

"Nah, I don't like small places," he replies, shaking his head. "Never have."

We walk across to a bluff beneath a grove of trees. Micah plops down near one with a clear view of the sea. He pats the ground next to him, and I sit, huddling close so that the warmth of his body meets mine.

"So how are you, really?" he asks.

I shift my shoes in the dirt. "Not fine."

"Tell me."

I tug at my sweatshirt as if pulling the hood higher will help anything. "Joining the Wars was nothing like I thought it'd be," I say. "I'm glad I did, but . . . there's just a lot to adjust to."

"Like?"

I pick the obvious one. "Like being doxxed. Or being away

from my family." *And having my heart broken at the same time.* "Was it like this when you joined? Does it ever get easier?"

"Kinda. But it's also not great that it does."

"Yeah," I say. "But . . . it's so much to take in." I wipe the back of my sleeve against my snotty nose. Micah offers me his sleeve, too, and I laugh meekly.

"To answer your first question," Micah says, "I was a mess when I first joined."

"Did you know Brianna?" I ask. "She was with you then, right?"

"She was my cousin. That's how Jax knew her."

Wait, what? "I didn't know that."

"Jax doesn't like to talk about it."

"Do you know what happened to her?"

"No idea," he says. "I haven't heard from her in years. But I haven't really heard from anyone in my family since then."

"Oh, I'm sorry."

"It's okay, really," he says. He takes a stick and draws swirling patterns in the sandy soil. "Having the other Stags around helps. And there's Jax's mom, who cares . . . in her own way, at least. When the Stags got started, she gave us all the money we needed, which was the craziest part to get used to. We got the houses. Got the car. A bunch of guys we'd known in school were our first recruits. The way we had it, the Stags were supposed to be different than the other groups." He scratches at the back of his head. "I guess it's not really turning out that way."

"Well, it kinda is, right? I saw on the news that people are talking about our flyers."

Micah bobs his head. "Yeah, I guess."

We look out onto the water. The cool air goes right through my yoga pants and hoodie. I cross my arms and try to keep warm. He takes off his beanie and scrunches it in his hands.

"Like that Boar at Mission Dolores . . . I didn't even blink.
I didn't take any joy in it, but it didn't bother me either. I'm
just going along at this point, but I don't know what for. What
happened to Bri was really fucking horrible, and at the time
it convinced me that staying in the Stags was the best way to
go about making it right. Now I don't know. At least you've
got your brother's memory to keep you grounded."

"I guess. But it's not like what I plan to do is exactly moral."
I blot my eyes with my jacket again. The fog bank creeps
toward us from over the water. "Wait," I ask, voice rising. "Do
you know who did it? Who killed my brother?"

"No, I'm sorry. I'd tell you if I did, I swear."

"I'm not sure Jax is ever going to tell me," I say sullenly. "I
can't figure out what he wants."

"I'll talk to him about it, if you want," Micah replies.

"Really?"

"Yeah, of course."

I sigh. "That'd be amazing. Thanks."

He ruffles his hair. "In the meantime, I'm going to tell you
my secret to surviving the Wars."

I sit up. "What?"

"Think of an after. Envision your life when you're done
fighting whatever it is you're fighting."

Peace, I think first, though it feels so cliché. Me and my
parents happy, for once. And my dream trip—swimming in
crystal-clear water, eating foods with ingredients I've never
seen before, meeting family I never knew I had. I hadn't
thought about it in a while, but I still want to go.

"What are you thinking?" he asks, so I tell him.

"I know it's probably not everything I'm thinking it is.
The Philippines has a ton of corruption, and sometimes isn't
the safest of places, but . . . I don't know," I say, smiling and
shrugging at the same time. "I've just always wanted to go."

"You will," he says. "I'm sure of it." Reaching into his jacket pocket, he pulls out a business card. "When I'm out, I'm getting one of these dogs. I had one when I was a kid."

I take the card when he offers it. It's for a breed of dog I've never heard of, but the smiling puppy on the card is enough to make me smile. "Why don't you get one now?"

"No yard. Also, no time. When this is done, I'm going to get a dog and move back up north."

"Where are you from?"

"Auburn. North of Sac. Moved to SF when I was ten."

"Cool." I dust off a few stray leaves clinging to my leggings. "I don't know that much about that area."

"It's beautiful," he says. "And quiet. And just . . . open." He tugs at the end of his beanie. "I want to go home, or at least somewhere with more trees. More rain."

I nudge his arm. "No bougie hipsters?"

He laughs. "Fuck no. No hipsters, just big rivers and crazy tall trees."

We spend the next minute tacking on entity after entity, escalating each time and making each one more ridiculous than the next.

Finally I say, "I think we just described Narnia. Or Candy Land."

"Well, maybe that's where I'll go. Narnia, not Candy Land, obviously," he says. Micah looks back at the water. He lifts up his hands and makes a picture frame with his fingers. "There'll be sun there. Perfect sun, all the time."

He puts his arms back down and stares at the sea. There's light on his cheeks, in his hair, in his eyes. "See? It's fun to think of afters. Keeps you sane."

I smile, my heart lifting. I really hope Micah gets his after.

And me? All this time I've been waiting to get into the Wars, and now I'm here. I've never really imagined what would be next. Maybe I can try to get my GED, then go to college like normal. I had looked up a few schools in the area but wasn't sure what I wanted to do. I didn't see myself pursuing baking as a career—I wanted to keep that fun and carefree. So many of my classmates had their shit together and their lives planned out, but Mom and Dad reminded me all the time that it was okay I didn't 100 percent know what I wanted to do yet, which I was grateful for even before Leo died. *We could all go on the Philippines trip together,* I think. *Do something together, for once.*

"Thank you, Micah," I say quietly. "I really needed this."

He smiles back. "That's what I'm here for."

18

When we get back to the house, I check Matthew's phone. Still nothing.

"Please say something," I say to no one, tucking the phone back in its place. I spend the rest of the evening with Matthew on my mind. I still can't believe he'd think I would set him up, but it feels stupid and feeble to keep texting as much. I need to talk to him again, in person.

So the next day, when Jax, Nianna, and Micah tell me they're going to meet with the Boars, I send Matthew the text that it's now or never.

A minute passes. Then another.

Then the phone lights up, his text a single word:

Where?

Yes! Okay. It has to be somewhere close enough to me that I can get there quickly and get back, but also far enough from the safe house that I don't compromise it.

The Sunset District. It's in Stag territory, and practically a straight shot north of where I am. Even with traffic, it's the best I've got.

Adrenaline racing, I reply:

Green Apple Books in the Sunset. I don't have a lot of time. Come alone.

He responds: I will. Be there as soon as I can.

Like the night I left to go see Mom, I move quickly—because if I hesitate, I'll change my mind. Slipping Matthew's phone into my pocket, I bounce the other one in my hand and debate taking it. If someone texts me while I'm out, they'll know right away something's up when I don't answer. But if I take it, Jax will know I've gone.

"Fuck it," I say, and I chuck the phone on my bed. I grab the rest of what I'll need—my wallet, an extra jacket—and toss them in a backpack, the former clinking against a lone can of spray paint that I must have forgotten to take out after some night of tagging. Swinging open the side door, it smashes into the garbage and recycling bins stacked against it.

"Oh, come on," I grumble, finally shoving them out of the way but creating a ton of noise in the process.

I call a taxi and wait in the shadow of the house. When it finally arrives about ten minutes later, I give the driver the address and watch as Holloway House fades from my sight.

After what feels like hours, we roll into the Sunset. This is picturesque San Francisco: pastel houses with white stairways touching down to the street. As we get closer to Golden Gate Park, the houses give way to bakeries, yoga studios, and pizzerias. The bank on the corner stands next to a dentist's office and a Jamba Juice.

Finally—Green Apple Books. My parents used to take me here almost weekly when I was a kid. The iconic green storefront looks unchanged from my memories. I pay the fare and step out, a rush of brisk wind greeting me like an old friend. Shivering, I go into the store and inhale the warm, welcoming scent of books. The orderly chaos of the bookstore's endless stacks makes me want to forget why I'm here. I scan the aisles and when I spot Matthew's unruly dark hair, adrenaline surges in my veins.

Peering around the corner, I pause a moment to see if he's

really alone. *Matthew wouldn't lie to you,* I think. But the Wars have made me wary.

I clear my throat as I round the corner, and then pretend to browse through a book. We're standing next to each other, both frozen.

"Hey," I say quietly.

"Hey," he replies.

More silence. I shift to let another customer by, and Matthew moves a little, too. A circle of bruised skin surrounds his eye.

"I'm so sorry," I say. Matthew pretends to read the back of the book in his hands, emotionless. "How are you?"

"How do you think?" he says, setting the book back in its place. "They fucking beat me—"

"What else did you want me to do?" I fire back. "I meant what I said. If they'd found out the next Young Heron leader was there *alone* they would have done worse."

He ignores it. "So?"

"So?"

"Val, for fuck's sake. Are you joining TRUCE?"

"No," I say.

"Then why am I here?" Matt says. "Look, I'm running out of time. The Herons keep asking me to do more senior shit. No one even asked about my black eye because they all figure I'm living up to Aaron's reputation and fought someone." He sighs. "They're insane, and none of them are going to join. I even tried to get one of the new recruits, but he was too much like me. Nothing was going to make his parents prouder than being a Young Heron."

I shake my head. "Your parents aren't like that. They'd have let you say no."

He chuckles. "You don't know them. Why do you think we never had dinner with my parents, or hung out with them for more than a few minutes at a time? I wanted to keep you away from them."

"Okay," I say, racking my brain for any memory of us hanging out with his parents once we had started dating. *Did they even know?* "You don't want to let go of TRUCE, which matters to you. And I won't let go of Leo. So we're at a stalemate."

"You and me maybe, but we can figure this out," he says. "Look . . . you—the Stags, and the Boars for that matter—are running out of time. Camille's family is threatening to bring her home if she doesn't get this alliance of yours under control. We found one Boar safe house, right? The next one might be yours, and if you're with them, I won't be able to help you."

"Them being the Stags?"

"Them being criminals," he replies sternly. "Jax has a rap sheet a page long. His second, too."

"Micah—"

"Obin, yeah. Him. He's been with Jax since day one. The moment either of them slips up, it's years in prison. But—" His eyes go wide and Matthew grabs my hand, tugging me down. "Aure's here."

Fuck. "You said you'd come alone," I whisper.

"I did, I promise. She must have followed me."

I dash around to the next shelf over, watching the front entrance like a hawk. Sure enough, Aure strides in, hair in a sleek low ponytail. Matthew greets her loudly, drawing looks from the other patrons. Then they switch to whispers, but I make out enough words.

Orders. Permission. Rules. Phone.

My breath catches—Matthew would obviously have two phones like me, right? I do my best to look as calm as possible, all while eyeing the exit. There may be other Herons out there. *I should have brought my gun.* All I have is the stupid can of spray paint. I take it out anyway, remembering from some self-defense class that anything can be a weapon.

Deep breaths, I think. Jax wouldn't panic, and neither can I.

Aure and Matthew keep talking. Aure says for them to go.

"I'm going to have to tell her," she says.

"Hey, hey," Matthew replies in a calm voice. I know that voice—it's one he used to use with me. Then comes the sound—so unique and unmistakable that it makes me shatter on the spot.

Lips on lips.

Moments later, the two of them appear around the corner. His hand is in hers.

I crouch down farther, curling into a ball as if that will change what I've seen, as if I can change what I've finally realized—Matthew has been lying to me, about so much. That night on our birthday was him playing me, already working for the Herons like he's sworn he's not.

I swear I don't make a sound.

But by some twist of fate Aure looks over her shoulder, and her eyes meet mine. She whirls, dropping Matthew's hand. "What the fuck?"

Bursting from my crouch, I sidestep a low half-shelf of books and shove the thing over, toppling it. The heavy books thunder to the ground but Aure dodges it. I'm three steps from the exit when she grabs my hair, yanking me back, and I shriek.

"Stag bitch," she says. "What the . . . fuck are you doing here?"

My answer is to lift my hand.

Shaking the can once and praying it's enough, I spray brilliant cyan paint over my shoulder and straight into her face.

Aure screams but doesn't let go. Suddenly Matthew's there, too, and for a moment her grip falters. I take it—tearing away from them and the shouting patrons of my childhood bookstore.

Back on the street, I bolt straight down Sixth. Sprinting

past figures on the sidewalk, I swing my backpack around and shove the spray can back inside. Keeping my face as low as I can manage, I scan the streets for any sign of the buses that I know frequent this section of town.

Finally I see one—two blocks ahead. Racing toward it, I spare a second to look behind me. No one seems to be following me, but that doesn't mean no one is. I take my chances, hopping into the bus just as it starts to pull forward. I pay my fare and take a seat. My trembling fingers are stained cyan. That doesn't stop me from putting my hands to my face as tears slip from my eyes.

Aure may not have put a bullet in me like she probably wanted, but she may as well have. Curling my arms tighter around myself, I silently scream into my hands. The movement of the bus rocks me as I crumple into nothing.

Matthew lied, about everything. He kept me from getting into the Herons. He lied when he said he still cared about me. Whatever we used to have between us is truly gone.

But my anger and hurt aren't.

I get off at Glen Park and get onto a BART train, then call a taxi for the last leg home. It may not be enough to trick the Herons, but I'll get back at them soon enough.

Sneaking back in the side door, I grab my Stag phone and go upstairs. *Just explain where you were,* I think. *Then give Jax the phone.*

But the kitchen and living room and Jax's room are all quiet. Relief sweeps over me and I wash up. It takes a few scrubs for the paint to come off of my hands and from around my eyes, but even when the color is gone the shock isn't.

It's like I don't know what to do with my body, my tired limbs. What is Matthew thinking right now? He hasn't texted. Would he say he was sorry? Would he explain anything? Would he explain her?

When I finally hear the front door open, I head straight toward them. Nianna's the first to see me.

"The hell happened to you?" she asks as she sheds her jacket. Jax steps inside a moment later and meets my eyes.

"I need to talk to you," I say.

"Right now?"

"Yes. Please."

Jax gives me a look like I'm a movie trailer that's barely piqued his interest, but he tilts his head toward the basement anyway. When he shuts the door behind us, I pull out Matthew's phone and hold it in my palm like an offering.

"What is this?" he asks.

"Matthew Weston gave it to me," I say. "He sent it through my parents." *Okay, now the shitty part.* "I-I've been talking to him. He wants me to join TRUCE."

"How long have you been talking to him?"

"A few weeks. Since right after New Year's."

"Did you tell him anything about us?"

"No," I say. "I swear. You can read the texts." I motion to the phone again, and he takes it. "I should have given it to you right away, I know. But you wanted me to spy on them, and Matthew believes that only I have been using it. He wouldn't suspect I'd give it to you."

"You seem very sure," Jax replies coolly.

"Matthew wouldn't suspect this of me. I'm sure."

Jax nods, saying nothing. I fill the silence with babbling. "I'm sorry, I know I should have given it to you sooner. I don't know why I didn't but I am now and I—"

"Shh," he says, putting a finger to my lips. "This is good, Valentine. We can use this. Do the others know you have it?"

"No."

"Okay. We'll deal with this," he says, putting the phone in

his pocket. "Now, you want to tell me why you look like you haven't slept in days?"

I answer dutifully, telling him how I left—again—to meet with Matthew. I tell him everything Matthew said, including his getting desperate. Skipping the part about the kiss, I recount what happened with Aure.

"Wait, you sprayed her in the eyes?"

"Yeah."

"Shit," he says. He starts laughing. "Jesus, Val. You could have blinded her or some shit." From anyone else in any other situation, that would not be praise. But this is Jax, and blinding another human being is cause for celebration. "I'm so gonna mess with Camille about this. Saint-Helene was one of her best. She's going to be *pissed*."

"Good," I say.

"You sound mad."

"I am. I'm pissed. Matthew Weston is nothing but a liar to me now." I am no longer Matthew's by any definition, and he's no longer mine.

Jax grins, his hazel eyes sparkling with what I can only guess is unmitigated satisfaction. "Theresa likes to say that grief will only soothe the pain." He lifts my chin until I'm standing straighter, looking directly at him. "But anger gets you places."

Jax goes through every text. I'm next to him on the couch, hands on my knees like he's a teacher grading my test. He reviews the call log, eyes scanning back and forth.

"And there's nothing else?" he asks coolly.

"No," I reply. "Well, not in the phone. Matthew told me at the store that Camille's going to lose her position if she doesn't find us. That's why the Boar safe house was raided. We're next."

Jax nods. "We lie low. I'll tell Ty. First let's tell the others."

I ball my hand into a fist, pressing my fingernails into my palm. "Do we have to?"

"It'll be all right," he says.

He calls the group to the kitchen.

"What's going on?" Micah asks, scratching the back of his head. Nianna's eyebrows rise—she's surprised he doesn't know.

"I want to let you all in on something," Jax says. He sets the phone on the table. Its screen reflects the lamp above, a flare of light on the black surface.

"Whose is that?" Mako asks. "That's hella nicer than mine."

"Valentine?" Jax says. "You wanna explain?"

I don't have much of a choice. I clear my throat. "Matthew Weston gave me this phone. He sent it to my parents, and I got it from them. We've been talking for the past few weeks." Nianna's jaw drops. "I didn't tell him anything about the Stags. Jax checked the texts and I swear on my brother's memory I never revealed anything about the Stags' plans." I let that hang in the air a moment, reading their reactions. Today I found out that the Young Herons have been getting shit for our alliance with the Boars. They're looking for us."

"Which means no one leaves without my say-so," Jax cuts in. "We'll lay off our work with the Boars for now. Tagging's fine, but nothing more. We'll use the time to ride the wave of the reaction to the protest and flyers downtown. Boost it on social and see how it plays out."

"You're not usually one for waiting," Nianna says, tightening the knot on her bandana.

"And I'm never one for stupidity," Jax replies with a glare. "We lie low. That's an order."

19

The next week fades like the sea engulfed in fog. Jax and I meet whenever Matthew texts, but it's the same thing: that he's sorry. That he had to play along with the Herons, same way I'm playing along with the Stags. The last text stops me short.

"I'm not pretending," I tell Jax as he hands me the phone to respond. Jax decided I should continue to respond so nothing looks suspicious.

"I know." He sips a dark beer. "You giving me this is enough."

I type my reply:

I saw what I did. You've been lying to me this whole time.

It doesn't feel good to have Jax privy to this—my heartbreak making me feel like I've been hollowed out—but I let the betrayal win. Matthew has to be out of my life if I'm going to find Leo's killer.

I hand the phone back to him and go.

Days tick by, but I stay focused. I stop wondering if Matthew's texted back, or if Jax is responding as me. I go out and tag with the others whenever Jax lets us. I stop calling home. I work out even more, using the exertion to keep me grounded. Nianna even lets me join her for morning yoga, but only after

SHANNON PRICE

I ask three or four times. Now that Matthew's completely lost my attention, I've found it easier to bond with the Stags. I'm bolder, more forward with my attempts to click with them. So far, I think it's working.

By the time February arrives, I'm a sharper shot and have more or less memorized all the faces in the binders. There's one week of nothing but rain, keeping us indoors. Mako finds a deck of playing cards in one of the boxes downstairs. He, Kate, and I sit in a circle on the floor, our wineglasses nearby. After a couple rounds of Egyptian War, I offer to teach them a game called Hotel.

"So many rules," Mako says, chuckling as I shuffle the cards after a practice round.

"It gets easier," I say. "One or two rounds and it makes sense."

"Why's it called Hotel?" Kate asks.

"Technically it's 'Oh, Hell.'" I deal out the cards. "But we couldn't say that around my brother, so we made it Hotel."

Kate smiles. "Your kid brother played this? Dang. Babe, we gotta step it up."

"Leo was really smart," I say. "He could do almost all his homework by himself. After I nagged him, of course."

"Dang, that's a good kid," Mako says. "I hated homework."

I feel my chest begin to tighten. Kate shifts so she's scooted closer to Mako's chest. "I'm really sorry he died. How he did," she says. "It's not fair."

I meet her eyes and wonder if she's thinking about her mom. "No, it's not."

Nianna strides in from the kitchen, a sheen of sweat across her brow.

"Good workout?" I ask.

"Yeah," she replies, voice breathy.

"That's a cute top," Kate says. "Nice color on you."

Nianna looks down at the green workout shirt. Kate's right—the verdant shade complements her skin tone. "Thanks, dude. Theresa sent it to me."

"Ooh, what brand?" Kate raises her eyebrows. "Like, Prada gym clothes?"

"Didn't recognize it."

"Probably some fancy French label."

"Knowing Theresa, probably. What are you guys playing?"

"Hotel," I answer. "Wanna play?"

She opts to go shower instead, and the rest of us resume playing.

"Damn. I want to be Theresa," Kate says, her eyes alight. "She's, like, crazy rich. And *beautiful*."

"Not as beautiful as you," Mako chimes in, earning him a smile and playful smack from Kate.

"I guess she hasn't been around in a while," Kate goes on. "Nianna's met her a few times, me and Mako just once. We're overdue."

Overdue. Like the devastating earthquake every geologist in California says is coming, but I keep that to myself. The way they all talk about Theresa puts me on edge, like it's some royal visitation, but it makes me curious, too.

Nianna comes back out and sits with the rest of us. I deal her in, and we spend the rest of the afternoon bidding on rounds of cards and shouting at each other when we lose. I win the first two games easily, but Nianna gives me a run for my money on the third.

"Dammit," Kate says as she throws her cards down. "I thought I was getting it."

"It takes a bit of time," I say reassuringly, but she's already getting up. "And it's just a game."

"Whatever" is her reply. "I'm probably just too stupid to get it."

"Hey," says Mako, just as I say, "Kate, that's not true."

The door to her room slams, and I try and distract myself from the ugly pit in my stomach by gathering the cards back up. Mako goes after her and comes back a few minutes later, looking dejected as a kicked dog.

"Is she okay?" I ask.

He takes a huge breath. "She'll be fine. Just went to take a nap." He finds the beer she was drinking and finishes it in one gulp.

"I know this might not be my place," I say quietly. "But have you guys ever talked about her seeing a therapist?"

Mako nods. "She doesn't want to go."

"I think it could really help her."

"So do I," he says. "I bring it up sometimes, but she says she's not ready."

I set the deck aside. "Okay. Let us know if we can help ever." Next to me, Nianna nods her assent.

"Thanks," he replies. "It's fine, though."

Nianna gets another bottle of wine, and slowly the conversation turns from somber to normal.

"This is kind of a weird question," I say, once we're a glass or two in. "But how did you guys find me that night I was recruited? Like, did you know I was going to SFO?"

"Oh, God," Nianna says. "We staked out your place for hours. Seriously, Val, who stays home all day on their birthday?" She waves her hand emptily, smiling. "Anyway. We waited. Mako here was about ready to just call your house and creepily tell you to come outside."

"No, I said a doorbell ditch," he interjects. "I wanted to leave a note to tell you to come outside."

"Whatever," she replies. "When you finally left, we followed you. Jules, Cameron, and Kurt stayed behind in case we lost you."

"Worked out though," Mako says. "We got you in the end, didn't we?"

Something about hearing the word *we* is so comforting. I'm part of this now.

When we finally call it a night, I head to the basement feeling really good—slowly but surely, I'm fitting in. Jax has to see that.

I'm so close, Leo. I'm not sure what he would think of me, think of this. But I hope he's looking down on me, proud.

I'm not standing still anymore, and I'll never just stand still again.

The rain finally lets up, and Nianna and I go to the Mission to hang up some Stag posters and tag, if we can. I still feel nervous being alone with her after she yelled at me about not really being a Stag, but we're both desperate enough to get out of the house for a while that when Jax gives the okay to Nianna, she doesn't object when I invite myself along. She invites Kate, too, but she didn't want to get out of bed.

"I'm worried about her," I tell Nianna as we lock the door behind us.

"Yeah," she replies. "Me, too. She comes and goes."

We take the train and exit at Sixteenth and Mission. A billboard announcing that the SFPD is hiring has been marked up with black and red paint, mustaches and googly eyes drawn over the faces of the officers. Their motto reads: ORO EN PAZ, FIERRO EN GUERRA. *Gold in peace, iron in war.*

We walk up Sixteenth and I catch the smells of melted cheese and warm dough from the *pupusería* in front of us. My mouth waters. "Do you want to get food?"

Nianna gives a half shrug. "Sure."

We get a table facing the street. I order three *pupusas*—two mushroom and cheese and the other just chicken. I usually just get two, but I am in the mood to stress-stuff my face with greasy food.

"I don't think I've eaten here before," Nianna says.

Leo loved this place, I want to say, but it comes out, "They fixed it up since I was last here."

The waitress brings us our plates just as I'm tugging my hair into a ponytail—the stuffy air is making me sweat. The *pupusas* shine with marvelous grease.

Nianna takes a bite. Her eyes go wide. "Holy shit."

"Told you. The best."

The sound of cars rolling by carries in from the street as we eat. From somewhere far-off, a siren wails. I finish the chicken *pupusa* and move on to the other ones. Nianna refills both of our waters. Not for the first time, I admire the tattoo on Nianna's wrist. An arrow suits her: always looking forward, always looking to make her mark.

"What do you think you'll do after the Wars?" I ask. "What's your after?"

She slouches down and thinks. "There's never been an after in my head. Never been a person with a lot of options."

"You'll have them soon."

"I could go live with Theresa, I guess. Maybe travel abroad."

"Where would you go?"

"Ireland. I've been thinking about it. My dad was from there, and I think I have some distant relatives there."

There is so much more I want to ask her—but I don't get my chance. A fire truck blasts by on the street, its lights spinning. Nianna turns, her eyes following, and both of our phones buzz.

"Shit," she says.

We don't think, just move. I grab my jacket and slide an

arm through, racing for the door. Nianna beats me to the street.

"It's Jax," she says. "Herons just sent a message through IRIS. Says to watch the fireworks."

"Fuck."

We follow the truck.

Nianna and I shoulder our way into the growing crowd. She stops at the corner and puts her hand in front of me like she did the night Jax shot Michael Hennessy. A firefighter is shouting for the crowd to back up.

It's a house, a beautiful Victorian with white trim and shapely bay windows. Smoke pours out of the windows and rises into the afternoon sky in thick, black plumes. The front door has been pushed open. Across the street, an EMT puts a mask over the mouth of a little boy. His mother, red-faced from crying, strokes his hair. Two more kids cling to her legs, the whites of their eyes bright against sooty cheeks.

I put my hands to my ears. It is all noise. Noise and light and a biting smell I know will knit into my clothing surer than the finest thread.

I look at the pale faces of the crowd, their eyes reflecting the bright orange flames. A few houses down, a news crew is setting up a broadcast. The reporter has a pamphlet in his hands, the Boar logo clearly on it.

"I don't understand," I say. "The IRIS said it was the Herons." My Stag phone buzzes and so does Nianna's. We read Jax's text together.

"It is the Herons," she says. "They're framing the Boars . . ."

". . . by burning some innocent family's house down?" I say, my voice rising in question as we look back over to where the fire engine is pouring water onto the flames.

I listen in on the news reporter as he speaks to the camera.

"We're getting early reports this may be associated with the so-called Red Bridge Wars that, as many here in the city know, have been getting increasingly popular with the city's youth in recent years."

"Damn these gangs," an older woman mutters from behind me. In her hands is a canvas bag bursting with groceries. "It's enough to make me sick."

"It's enough to make me leave," says a beefy guy next to her. "I don't want my kids growing up with this shit." There's a murmur of assent.

Nianna tugs me by the elbow. "Come on. Let's get out of here."

Nodding, I turn to follow her—when a hand clamps down on my shoulder like a steel trap.

"You're one of them." The beefy guy spins me gruffly, pushing my shoulder so hard I bump into Nianna, who bumps into someone else. "You've got one of their tattoos."

Oh fuck. I put my hair up back at the restaurant.

It's as if someone whispers hate into the ears of the crowd, and each one is a willing listener. I try to shove my way through, but someone yanks my hood back, sending the zipper straight into my neck. Locking eyes with Nianna, I silently beg her to go, to protect herself.

"We didn't have anything to do with this," she says, eyes afire. "And we don't want any trouble."

"If you didn't want trouble you shouldn't have joined the gangs," a youngish Hispanic guy shouts back. Beside him, his girlfriend looks equal parts embarrassed and scared.

"Come on." Nianna grabs my hand as she barges past the Hispanic guy. We make it a few feet before others start shouting. A shrill voice starts screaming for the police, and we really start moving.

Hands grab at me, my sweatshirt, my hair. Beside me,

Nianna's thrown a punch and is spitting fire at a guy who yanked her bandana off her head.

We're not going to get out. *No, Valerie,* I tell myself. *You MUST.*

Just there—a break. I dart toward it, Nianna right behind me, and we're running back toward the BART station. Something heavy collides with my skull and my vision swims as I fall onto the ground, causing a group of teen girls to jump back and yelp. As Nianna pulls me up I touch my hand to my head and my palm comes back bloody.

"Shit," Nianna says, seeing the red. I let her lead me away, checking to make sure no one is following. Adrenaline sparks in my blood as we dash back around a corner. We duck into a gift shop and hide ourselves behind the window display.

"You okay?" I ask. My hand shakes as I put it to my head.

"Fine." She notices me holding my head. "Are you—oh shit." Nianna swears under her breath and hands me her bandana.

"Here."

"I'm fine."

"Oh, shut up and let someone take care of you for once." She works the fabric around my hair and ties the knot. The lotion on her skin makes her hands smell like cherry blossoms. "Come on," she says. "Let's get out of here."

We take the long way home.

20

When we get back to Holloway, Nianna opens the front door to a screaming match.

"For fuck's sake, Jax, listen!" It's Micah. "This is what we want. We should be helping them."

Jax and Micah stand on opposite sides of the kitchen table, both barely acknowledging us as we come into the room. There's a piece of paper on the table that's been ripped in half, the bottom of it soaking up the contents of a spilled glass of water.

"What's going on?" Nianna asks.

"That." Micah points to the paper. As I get closer my stomach drops—it's the letter John Kilmer sent my parents.

"Where did you find that?" I ask.

"It was in our room under all Jax's shit," Micah replies. He looks hurt, but more confused than anything else. He looks back to Jax. "TRUCE can give the city what we've always wanted to give it. Only they've got money, and *actual teams* working on it. I can't believe you didn't tell me about this. I can't believe you can't understand what I'm saying to you!"

"If the Wars are going to end, they will end *my* way," Jax fumes.

"Can't you put your pride aside for, like, a second? Let's at least watch the press conference tomorrow. To see what it's about."

"ENOUGH!" Jax shouts, punching his arm out to the side so it smacks into the fridge, sending the boxes and bottles stored on top crashing down. I yelp as glass collides with the floor and explodes across the hardwood floor, spilling all the way to my shoes. I teeter on my feet and Nianna catches my elbow, steadying me.

"TRUCE is a fucking trick," Jax seethes. "There will be no coming back from it. The Herons and their money win the day. They'd win the whole war. No. Fuck TRUCE, and fuck you, too, for getting your goddamn self all swoony at the idea. We're going to end the Wars the way *I planned it*—with the Herons running with their tails between their goddamn legs, the police admitting all they did wrong, and me standing on top letting them all know I did what they failed to do—bring justice for the city, and for Brianna. Don't tell me you've forgotten her, because I fucking haven't."

"I have not forgotten what happened to Bri," Micah fires back. "But the Stags aren't bringing peace, not at this rate. We're just adding to the chaos."

"It's not chaos, it's a reaction. Which is better than the nothing that was happening before we aligned with the Boars," Jax replies. "The Young Herons ignored us before. They dealt with the Boars, but mostly ignored them, too. There was no threat. *I* brought the threat. *I* did this. So you shut up, and remember who is in charge here."

Jax heads to his room, dark and fuming as storm clouds. When the door opens and slams shut behind him, I look over at Micah. He has his hand over his eyes, body hunched as he leans against the countertop as if he doesn't have the heart to keep himself up.

"Are you okay?" I ask him.

He doesn't say anything. Just nods, though I know he's lying.

It's in the stillness that I hear someone crying. Kate?

"I'll clean this," says Nianna. She indicates my head. "Go wash that."

I nod, stepping over the glass best as I can. My head continues to throb, but instead of going to the bathroom I drift toward Kate and Mako's room. I knock on the door. "Kate? Are you okay?"

There's a pause. "Come in."

She's huddled on the bed, the sleeves of her gray sweatshirt dotted with tears. Mako's on the bed with her, one arm around her shoulders.

"Hi, Val," she says. She points toward the general direction of the kitchen. "My parents . . . they'd yell at each other like that. Took me right back."

"Shit," I whisper. "Can I help at all?"

"I think I got— Wait, are you bleeding?" Mako interjects before Kate has a chance to answer.

"We ran into some trouble in the Mission."

"Boars or Herons?" he asks.

"Uh, neither actually. Angry citizen."

Mako groans and tightens his grip around Kate. She shrugs him off.

"I'm fine, Val. Thanks for checking."

Her tone is a slammed door, and when I lock eyes with Mako he gives me the tiniest of nods. "I'll be right back," he says to Kate.

Shutting the door behind him, Mako tilts his chin to the living room. "I could only half hear it," he says. "But I heard the Young Herons have a way to leave the Wars?"

"More or less," I say. "Jax doesn't trust it."

"What's the way?" Mako asks.

I try to remember the details of the letter. "Um, treatment programs, mental health services, reduced sentences. Things like that."

The lump in Mako's throat goes up and down as he swallows. "For anyone?"

"Bit eager there, surf boy."

Jax rounds the corner of the hallway, eyes blazing and a beer in his hand. He must have come back to the kitchen for it, I realize, dread sinking in. "You want out?" he asks.

"I didn't say that," Mako replies.

"You sure as hell got close."

"Let's not do this here," says Mako, shouldering past me until he meets Jax closer to the kitchen. *Away from Kate.* Finally, he raises his head to meet Jax's eyes. Mako's taller by at least an inch or two, but right now he looks like a boy sitting up tall to prove he's a man. A soldier before a general.

"Tell me you want out," Jax says. "Look me in the eyes and tell me you want out. And I'll send you over to Kilmer."

Mako's chest rises and falls with heavy breaths, then Jax punches him across the jaw. My hands fly to my mouth with a shriek.

"Disloyal son of a bitch," Jax says. "Tell me you want out. Man the fuck up and tell me!"

Blood dribbles out of Mako's lip. He mumbles something.

"What's that?"

"I don't want out."

"Louder."

"I. Don't. Want. Out."

"Good." Our leader then turns and gestures around the room. "What about you? Nianna? Valentine?"

I sit very still. "No one leaves the Wars."

"Damn right no one leaves the Wars." He goes into his bedroom, the door slamming behind him. I hope he stays there for good.

Mako walks over to the sink and spits out blood. He lets the water run, rinsing it away. "I can't get out," Mako whispers. "But she could."

Nianna, still brushing glass into a dustbin, says nothing. Stepping gingerly around her, I put a hand on Mako's shoulder.

"Hey . . ." I say.

"I'm fine," he says. He gives me a fake smile. "Go wash that cut. It's starting to look pretty bad."

I sigh—I don't want to just leave him, but he's got a point about the cut. "Okay."

Exhausted, I take a shower and very carefully wash the dried blood from my hair, scalp, and back. I run my fingers over the ridges of the cut before blotting it with a towel. My head is light from the lost blood, so I carefully tug my clothes back on and open the door. Micah's standing there, waiting for me. He has the torn letter from Chief Kilmer in his hand.

"Why didn't you tell me about this?" he asks, giving the paper to me.

"I told Jax," I respond defensively. "I thought if it was important he'd tell everyone else."

"Jax will never admit how big this is. How it might end things for good."

"Micah," I whisper. "If you want to leave so badly, why don't you just go? You've been here, what, four years? Three? Whatever. If you just talked to him . . ."

"There'd be more of that," he replies, pointing toward the kitchen. "You know that."

My shoulders slump. "Yeah. But still, there's gotta be something."

"Look, you don't know Jax like I do," he says. "Once he

sets his mind on something, nothing sways him. Believe me,
I'm sure he's halfway through thinking of a plan to dismantle
TRUCE right now."

I lean back into the wall. *Matthew.* Everything he's worked
for. Surely Jax couldn't just *undo* that, right? Then again, this
is Jax we're talking about. The guy could blot out the sun with
his ego, but I know there's an unsettling genius in his eyes. A
determination to carry out exactly what he wants.

"The press conference is tomorrow," I say. "Maybe if Jax
hears about it then, he'll come around."

Micah shakes his head. "Yeah, sure."

The next day, the Stags gather around the TV.

On the screen, Chief John Kilmer waves his hand at the
press, getting them to quiet down. Dozens are gathered—
reporters, policemen, and businessmen already checking their
watches. Somewhere in that crowd is Micah. Before he left, I
asked if he wanted someone to go with him.

"Jax only said I could go so he wouldn't have me in the
house," Micah had responded bitterly. "No way he'd let you
go."

"You're right," I responded, and I meant it—but it doesn't
mean I'm not a little antsy about having Micah out there alone.
Glancing over at Jax, I try to read his emotions, but he's focused on the TV.

On the screen, the press conference is getting underway.

"We are proud to announce this joint initiative between
the San Francisco Police Department, the City of San Francisco, and the Weston Corporation," Kilmer says. "The
TRUCE Initiative will make the city safer by offering am-
nesty and rehabilitation programs to gang members from all
groups. We are transparent in our goal. We want peace."

The lines around his eyes have gotten worse. His salt-and-pepper hair has gone full silver. His beard is less police officer and more tired pirate. I take a certain bit of pride in seeing him like this. He's worn down. Older.

I wonder just how different my life would be if it weren't for high-and-mighty John Kilmer. What if he hadn't walked away from Leo's investigation so quickly? It was written off like nothing: another casualty of the Wars.

Kilmer clears his throat and goes on. "Gang members need only to surrender themselves at a police station and enroll. Arrests will be formalized, with sentences given in proportion to the crimes. All those who participate will be allowed into treatment centers for addictions and mental health facilities aimed at easing PTSD.

"We understand that those in the deepest circles of this bloodshed will not come forward," says Kilmer. "And we have no intention of letting any violence go unpunished. The Weston Corporation and their affiliate, Olympus Enterprises, have been generous with their time, their money, and their technology. This cooperative effort has led to multiple leads on various gang members, all of which are ongoing."

The camera zooms out again. A ticker tape crosses the bottom of the screen, giving the highlights of his speech. Full coverage tonight at 5 P.M.

"At this point, I'd like to invite Mr. Tomas Olvera to the stage," Kilmer says.

Jax and Nianna suck air in through their teeth at the same time. I've studied the binders enough to know why.

A muscular guy with buzzed black hair comes to stand by the podium. A Boar tattoo is clearly visible on his skull. Tomas is six months in, maybe seven. He looks different than his picture.

"Like many of our city's young adults, Tomas joined the

Boars," says Chief Kilmer. "But effective today, he is no longer a member of the gangs. As the first initiate to the TRUCE
program, Tomas will answer for the crimes he committed in a
safe environment, focused on rehabilitation and public service."

Jax laughs and Mako echoes with a chuckle, but his eyes
spark with curiosity. I look at Kate. She's tugging at a knot in
her hair.

The coverage winds down. Reporters shout questions,
which Kilmer answers. The Stags' interest dwindles. Nianna
flips through channels and lands on a food competition. I
watch as three competitors try to make a dessert out of bub-
blegum ice cream, chocolate milk, and bean sprouts, but the
distraction doesn't take.

Matthew got his one. He's so confident in TRUCE that he's
let his family name go onto it. *That has to count for something.*
Micah gets home. He and Jax talk in their room a while, then
Jax comes down the stairs.

"Nianna, go get Mako," Jax says. "We're going to meet
with Ty and some of the senior Boars."

Nianna tosses the remote onto the couch and grabs her
jacket. Mako joins them in the hall, a black hoodie pulled over
his slicked hair. From what I can tell, none of them are armed
as they leave, and I mentally cross my fingers that the Boars
are as trustworthy as Jax thinks.

Micah shuffles down the hall a few minutes after.

"You didn't want to go?" I ask.

He gives me a shrug. "Jax didn't ask me."

"Oh." I switch gears. "Did you see any of the Boars or Herons there? At City Hall?" I ask.

"No," Micah says. "It was just press."

My friend's eyes are hollow, and it makes my chest hurt.
"Hey," I start. "I really am sorry that I didn't tell you about
TRUCE. It never crossed my mind."

"It's fine."

"Are we okay, though?"

"Yeah." He gives me a quick smile as if that'd seal the deal. "We're fine."

"Okay," I say. I tilt my head to the door. "I'm sorry Jax is still giving you shit."

"We're gonna give each other space," he says. "He'll come around. But I've already said sorry. The rest is up to him, like it always is."

Later that day, I catch Kate as she leaves the bathroom. A hot-pink towel is wrapped around her pale limbs.

"Can we talk?" I whisper. "In a minute. Take your time."

"Eh, I don't care." She waves me into the room.

Their floor is covered with discarded articles of clothing and old dinner plates. The bed's unmade, but I smooth out the cherry blossom–patterned comforter as I take a seat. Neatness isn't exactly Kate's or Mako's forte. The former hums to herself as she slips on her bra and underwear—a matching lilac set. Kate lets the towel fall completely, and just like that my brain has other things to focus on.

A dark line of straight, straight scars runs from her thigh to her hip. If I didn't have them myself, I'd probably be shocked. We're two of a kind.

"So, what's up?" she asks, pulling on a loose sweater.

"I was thinking about TRUCE," I say, watching her face for any clues to what she's thinking. "I think it sounds like a pretty good idea. What do you think?"

Her face clouds with instinctive resistance. "Val, don't be dumb. No one leaves before their time."

"I think this is different. The Westons have so much money,

Kate. So much it's stupid. I grew up with it. Well, not with it. But looking at it."

She grabs at a pair of black pants and pulls them on. "So?"

"So, I know whatever plan they have is real. No bullshit." I take a huge breath. "I think you should go for it."

Kate scrunches her hair, creating silky waves. "It's not going to happen."

"What about Mako? I know he wants you out."

"I don't have anything to go back to," she says. "My dad's a loser, and my sister's in Arizona and she doesn't talk to me. My mom's dead. I'm almost done, anyhow. Once I'm out, I'm safe—really safe. Theresa's got connections to last a lifetime. Isn't that why you joined?"

"No," I reply. "I joined for my brother. Jax knows which Boar killed him in that crossfire."

Kate goes very still, both her hands frozen on either side of her head. "Val . . . you know Leo wasn't just caught in a crossfire, right?"

"What?" My heartbeats are thunder.

"The Boars picked him to get back at the Herons for beating up one of their own. She was in a coma for, like, seven months before she died."

Holy shit. "But Leo was a kid. And we're not a Heron family."

"Aren't you, though?" She puts her hands on her hips. "Matthew Weston was too protected to be a target. But the Boars saw how close he and Leo were. They thought—hey, how can we hit the Herons right where it hurts?"

"Kate, what are you saying?"

"Matthew Weston was in line to lead the Herons like his brothers, yeah? The Boars wanted to keep him out of it. The Boars shot your brother because Matthew Weston loved him. It's *his* fault Leo's dead."

"How would you know that?"

She sighs—but not enough to make her anger ebb. "Jax got drunk and told Mako once. Just ask him." She brushes by me and goes into the hall, shutting the door behind her.

I don't know how much time passes. The air gets cold. Doors open and shut in the hallway, but no one comes for me. I'm unimportant. Unnecessary.

On the bones of a ghost, I go into the bathroom and take a shower that lasts an hour. Maybe two. I don't have my knife here in the bathroom, but I scratch at my scars until the skin breaks. But this time, it doesn't help. Doesn't take everything away.

I stay there even when Mako knocks at the door, and later breaks it in. I don't shut off the water as he shouts, as he taps at the closed shower curtain.

Somewhere through the clouds of steam, I hear Kate tell Mako that I know now and to leave me be a while longer.

When I finally muster the courage to leave the safety of the shower, I get dressed, blot my hair, and head straight for Jax's room. I knock three times.

"Jax? I need to talk to you."

He comes to the door. He searches my face for clues, then frowns. "What's up?"

"I want to call Matthew Weston," I state. "I need to. Kate . . . Kate just told me that my brother died because of him and I need to know if it's true."

After a beat, Jax nods. "Let's go downstairs, so no one else hears."

He retrieves the phone, and we head to my room. I stare pointedly forward, avoiding Kate's gaze as she looks up from the TV. *Fuck you,* I think, then feel bad. I'm glad I know now, but she didn't have to deliver it in such a cruel way.

When I'm ready, Jax hands me the phone.

"I'll put it on speaker," I say, fingers already tapping the phone to get to the right setting.

"You don't have to," Jax says. My head snaps up. He nods, mouth pulling into an amused smile at my reaction. "I trust you."

My heart pounds, and I force myself to stop staring at his stupidly handsome face. I have more important things to worry about.

I call. It rings once, then twice. *Will Matt even pick up, after what happened in the Sunset? Please, please ans—*

"Hello?" Matthew says.

My body fails me, and can't seem to breathe, let alone speak. "Val?"

"I need to ask you something," I stammer. Leo. My Leo, my sweet baby brother. I relive the last time I saw him—at the kitchen table with Mom setting down his cereal. Blue striped shirt. Neon-green shoes with knots I tied.

"What is it?" Matthew asks, and I slam back to the ground.

"Did you . . ." I say. Jax reaches out and brushes his fingers against mine. I take the invitation and slide my fingers into his. "Did you know that the Boars killed Leo because of you?"

"What?"

"They targeted him because you were close to him," I stammer, tears falling freely now. "They were trying to scare you, or something."

"I don't know what you're talking about," he says. "Who told you that? Are you sure they're telling you the truth?"

"I have no reason to doubt it," I reply. "Matthew, for the love of . . . did you know?"

He breathes into the phone and my heart threatens to burst out of my chest until—

"Yes. They told me when I joined."

"And yet you didn't tell me!" I say, covering my face with my hands. "Fuck you, Matthew. I have nothing more to say to you, ever."

I hang up. "I want to be alone," I say to Jax.

He takes my hand and gives it a squeeze. "Stay down here. No one will bother you."

He walks up the stairs, leaving me alone. I cry and cry until I don't have any tears left before fading into an uneasy sleep.

I don't know what Jax told the others, but when I finally return upstairs the next day, they're overly gracious in their niceness. Mako and Kate prepare breakfast, insisting I don't lift a finger.

Mako sets down the pancakes between a pitcher of orange juice and a bowl of fruit salad—apples, bananas, and raspberries. A spark of nostalgia catches in my chest.

Snagging a handful of chocolate chips from the cabinets, I pick through the fruit salad so my plate is nothing but raspberries. I take one and flip it bucket-side up then shove a chocolate chip into it.

Matthew. This is his favorite dessert. Raspberries and chocolate chips. It is one of the many things I loved him for—the simplicity. He didn't want his mother's crème brûlée, her Swedish princess cake, or her poached cinnamon pears drenched in white wine. No. He wanted raspberries with chocolate chips.

I smush the berry against my plate and don't eat it.

We eat and Nianna joins shortly after, pulled from her room by the smell of butter and sugar. Even Jaws makes an appearance inside the house. He doesn't eat, just leans against the counter drinking a bottle of water.

I'm wiping a pool of syrup off my plate when Jax saunters into the room. "Morning, lovelies."

"Morning," I reply. Jax lifts my pancake from the stack, folds it in half, then takes a bite.

"That is the weirdest fucking way to eat a pancake," says Nianna, and even with last night's news weighing me down, I can't help smiling. As I take another forkful of my own breakfast, she points to me. "See, Val is civilized."

"I'm just living in the future," Jax says defensively. "Pretty soon you'll all be eating pancakes like this." He makes a motion like he's dusting off his hands to show he's finished. He tilts his chin to me.

"Almost done?"

"Mm-hmm."

"Good. I want to take you somewhere. Just you and me."

"Oh, okay," I say. "Give me twenty minutes?"

Jax nods. "It's a date."

"Where are we going?"

"You'll see."

I finish eating, then change into jeans and a nice sweater, then tug a black jacket over it. I wish Jax hadn't said it was a date, because now I'm second-guessing everything. Should I wear makeup? I'll wear makeup. I slap on some foundation and eyeliner. A crescendo of excitement builds in my chest and I almost poke my eye out with the mascara wand. I can't focus.

Jax wants alone time with me—that has to mean he's ready to tell me who killed Leo. All this is finally going to be worth it.

Minutes later, I'm climbing into the car with Jax. Recklessness flickers in his eyes as he turns toward the freeway. He takes the on-ramp too quickly and I tighten my seat belt.

"So, are you going to tell me where we're going?" I ask.

"We're going to pay our respects."

"To who?"

"Stags who came before you."

I notice he says *you* and not *us*. Jax is the beginning and the end.

We head north on Highway 1 toward the Presidio, the same way Micah and I did a few weeks ago. This time the sea does nothing to calm my nerves. As we cruise past the polished homes of the Marina District, the Golden Gate comes into view. It really is a beautiful bridge. If you came halfway around the world to see its sleek cables, sturdy beams, and graceful curves, you wouldn't be disappointed.

Jax drums his fingers as we wait for a parking space. With every passing minute, I expect him to snap and start shouting at the other cars, but he just waits. He even hums to himself.

We park. Jax pulls up the hood of his sweatshirt as he gets out. I sidestep a group of tourists, inciting a glare from a jogger whose path I inadvertently crossed.

Clouds loom above the sprawling green of Crissy Field. To the left is a white-walled building called the Warming Hut with a gift shop and café. My mouth waters at the smell of bacon-wrapped hot dogs sizzling at the stand nearby.

The Golden Gate cuts across the water toward the Marin headlands—a splinter of red in the vast blue. Tourists mill about in groups, snapping selfies and adjusting their camera settings. Jax stops and offers to take an Indian couple's picture. They thank him, and he grins at my confused look. "What? I can be nice."

"Never said you couldn't." We both smile.

Jax leads me out onto the rocky sand as lacy white foam washes up and back, up and back.

"Why are we here?" I ask.

His shoulders slouch as he takes a seat on the sand. "Needed to be away from the house for a while." He takes out a cigarette, lights it, and inhales. "I come here to remember Stags who died."

"Oh."

Not sure what to do, I sit next to him. Mako said Jax takes care of his own. I bet he thought he'd protect them, too. *I know that feeling.*

"How many have died?"

"Do you really want to know?"

I take a beat to think. "Yes."

"Two. One was in a hit-and-run down in SoMa. Another was jumped in the Tenderloin while he was lighting a cigarette. Coward fucking beat him up in an alleyway. He died in the hospital. Boars took credit for both."

Credit. "Jesus."

"He wasn't there."

It takes me a second. "This doesn't seem like a time for jokes."

"I choose my moments." He winks. "Besides, Will—the one in SoMa—was a bit of a jokester. He'd have laughed."

He pulls down his hood, running his hand through his long hair to push it back. As he tilts his face toward the sky, my eyes run along his square jaw, roughed up right now with a hint of scruff. Even with unpredictable moods, I don't doubt that Jax's actions are entirely planned. Purposeful chaos. It's probably why people are so drawn to him.

"What about Brianna? Nianna told me," I say, seeing his look. "Why didn't you look for her? Or bring her back to the Stags, send her money or something?"

"That wasn't Nianna's story to tell," he replies.

"We don't have to talk about it. Sorry, I shouldn't have brought it up," I say hastily. *He's in a good mood, let's not ruin it, Val.* "Why do you come here to . . . honor them?" I ask. "You could pick anywhere, like the places they died."

Jax tilts his head at the bridge. "It's our namesake. The Wars could have been called anything. Some reporter came up with the Red Bridge Wars, and it stuck."

I nod—a Seattle reporter, if my online research was correct. Like any good native, I'm offended it doesn't get the name of the paint right.

As if on cue, Jax says, "Of course, it's not red. The paint's called International Orange."

My throat shuts like a slammed door.

"But you probably knew that."

Somehow I reply that yes, I did. The wind bites at me again, and my lip trembles. Jax asks me what's wrong, and I shake my head. I think I say my brother's name.

Right away, Jax puts his arms around me. I hate that he does. I should be better than this, stronger than this.

I hate that Jax kisses my head and whispers into my ear that it's all right. I hate that I'm calming down now with my head on his chest. I hate that I like hearing the beat of his heart. I can feel his blood pulsing, pulsing, pulsing.

Jax chooses his moments, his actions. So I'm choosing mine. I push him back enough that I can look him in the eyes. "You said you'd help me," I say. "Well, help me."

"With what?"

"Getting revenge on the Boars." I shrug and look at the sky, the bridge, then back to Jax's face. "I've studied the binders. I go to the range all the freakin' time. I gave you that phone. So why won't you tell me who it was?" He frowns and pulls away—and I know I've made a mistake. I shouldn't have questioned him.

"I'm sorry," I say quickly. "But *please*. It's been months, and I just sit in the house. I know you wanted me lying low because of the doxxing, but there's gotta be something I can do to earn your trust. And whatever it is, I will do it. Please."

My voice trails with the final word. Without thinking, I reach out and curl my fingers around the fabric of Jax's sweatshirt, pulling myself that much closer. Whatever is between us—or whatever I think is there—has to matter to him.

"You know what I like about you, Valentine?" he asks.

"What?"

"You're determined as hell." He smiles. "As soon as you gave me the phone, I knew. But we can't get your man until this treaty with the Boars plays out. There's too much at stake here. But I have a plan, and I know where to find the guy when we're ready. I'm sorry, Valerie."

It's how he says my name, that's what does it. Realizations rush to my mind at once, like someone's unlocked a door in my mind that I didn't know I had. I'm not just a Stag to him. I'm the girl he marked to join the Stags years ago. I'm the girl he hugs from behind, and checks on after she's gone to bed. It's not coincidence. Jax, for all the talk, has a weakness, and it's me.

Jax likes me. And I like him. *So what am I waiting for?*

I tug Jax closer again and kiss him square on the mouth.

He responds instantly, arms enveloping me in a wild, fierce embrace. I know Jax well enough to know his emotions are hurricanes, and this one is for me. His hand goes to the back of my neck, raking my hair and keeping my lips close on his. I fall into him, kissing him back.

We finally part, Jax sneaking one more gentle kiss on the delicate skin of my neck. Shivers race down my spine, in the best of ways.

"I've wanted to do that for a long time," he says.

"Me, too," I say. Then, smiling, I add, "Now what?"

He puts his arm around me, steering me back to the car. "Now we go home. Because if I get to kiss you like that after just telling you I have a plan . . ."

He trails off, but I get his meaning loud and clear—and blush something fierce because of it. This is nowhere near love and not something that the old Valerie would ever do. But Valentine?

I lean my head into Jax's shoulder. Valentine is free, and she doesn't have a goddamn thing to lose.

We get home, and Jax gives my hand a final squeeze before going to shower. Nianna and the others are in their respective rooms, but Micah is chilling on the couch looking at his phone.

"May I join you?" I say.

"You don't have to ask," he replies. "Sit."

"Thanks."

I'm scanning channels when Micah's phone rings. He takes it out and frowns at the number on the screen.

"Who is it?" I ask.

"I think I know, but . . ." He trails off, stepping over to the front door and going out onto the patio as he answers.

I can only take calls from other Stags, but of course Micah would be special. He takes his call out in the inner garden. The contestants on TV are down to their final minutes, but I'm not thinking of them. I'm still thinking about the bridge, still thinking about the kiss . . .

The door opens again. Micah's shoulders are hunched as he grips the phone tightly in his hand. He glances toward the bathroom, then back at me. "Can I talk to you?"

"Yeah, of course."

He motions for me to follow him to his room, and the ridiculous part of me marks the occasion—this is the first time I've gone inside his and Jax's room.

In one half of the room is a twin bed with a red quilt neatly tucked over it. The air smells vaguely of pot and cigarettes, but mostly of boy. Sagging lines of Christmas lights are hung in a scallop pattern along a bare, tan wall. Along the other wall is another bed—larger than the first, because Jax is Jax. To my surprise, it's also made.

Then I see it.

The IRIS machine is smaller than I thought it'd be. It looks a lot like the contraptions in old sci-fi movies: a metal box with a number pad on one side and a low tray for the messages to print into. The light on the top is orange and dull like a fire long burned.

The walls are bare, save for one poster: an image of a woman, clothed in the sea and standing on a pile of skulls. Her ample breasts and body are rendered—to my surprise—without a trace of sexual undertone. She's classically beautiful, like a marble statue.

"It's the only thing we could agree on," says Micah when he sees me staring. He wipes the back of his nose with his sleeve.

"Jax discussed his décor with you?" I reply, but one look at Micah's face erases my levity. "What's wrong?"

"That was Theresa. She said Jax's uncle is in the hospital." He lifts up his phone then chucks it onto the bed. "He's having heart surgery."

"Jesus," I say. "Why did she call you?"

"Guess she called Jax and he said he wasn't going to go see him."

"Why not?"

"I'm not sure." Down the hall, the bathroom door opens. "Guess we're about to find out. Jax!"

Our leader comes into the room, smiling and shirtless. When he spots me, his expression changes. "Hey, V," he says. "Welcome to our room."

Micah sits forward on the bed. "Dude, your mom called. You didn't tell me your uncle was having surgery."

Jax rolls his eyes. "For fuck's sake. She can just visit him herself."

"Open-heart surgery is pretty serious," Micah replies. "I think you should go. He's family, isn't he?" I catch the small sting in his voice. *Micah's family rejected him once he joined the Stags.* It must feel so unfair.

Jax rolls his eyes. "I barely know him. Theresa's overreacting."

"It sounded bad," Micah counters. "You're really not going to go? He bailed us out that one time, back in high school."

"You go then. You've met him. Say I'm busy or something." Jax goes back down the hall and leaves Micah and me alone. Micah flops back onto his bed and puts his hand to his eyes.

"I'd just feel bad, you know?" he says. "He really did bail me and Jax out one time. Another time he had us over for Thanksgiving when Theresa was in town."

"Which hospital is he in?"

"San Francisco General."

I take a moment to think. "That's not that far. I think you should go."

"Yeah?"

"Yeah. Like you said, it's the right thing to do."

He peels himself off the bed. Steadily his movements get faster. Minutes later, he's zipping up a backpack. We walk down the hallway together. Micah opens the front door, and a blast of cold air hits us.

"Gah, it's cold," he says, swinging the door shut again.

"Fuck. And my nice jacket still smells all smoky from the pro-test."

"Take mine," Jax calls from the couch.

"What?"

"Take my jacket, bro. It's on a chair in the kitchen."

Cautiously, Micah ducks into the kitchen and returns with the jacket in hand. He slides the soft leather over his lanky frame. He stands up straighter in it.

"All right, I'll be back when it's done." He smiles at me.

"Okay, see you," I reply.

"See you."

And then he goes.

21

The night comes and goes, but Micah doesn't come back. How long does open-heart surgery take, anyway? I do a quick Google search—three to four hours. That's a long time to have your body cracked open and gaping.

A shiver runs down my back. I'd be a mess if Mom or Dad were going through something like that. I can't imagine what Micah's feeling right now, even if Jax's uncle isn't a blood relative. Maybe I should have gone with him for support.

At lunch, while the rest of the Stags chatter like normal, I keep my eyes on Kate. She pushes the noodles and veggies around her plate before dumping it in the trash.

Leaning close to Nianna's ear, I ask, "Is Kate okay? She barely ate anything."

"She gets that way sometimes."

"We should say something."

Nianna gestures toward the bathroom. "Be my guest, but we've tried tons of times." She shakes her head. "I know you love her. We all do. So we just have to make sure she knows that."

"You're right," I reply, still not convinced. "I guess that's all we can do."

I go back to my room and lie down dejectedly on the bed. I didn't think I'd get so attached to the Stags. I've always known I'd be in the Wars for a year, but I imagined being in a larger group, not this small family. I feel for them. For Kate, who smiles to my face, but I've heard her crying in the shower. I feel for Mako, having to watch her internal struggles swirl ever faster. I wonder what that kind of love feels like.

I feel bad for sharp-eyed Nianna and her steadfast loyalty.

And for gentle Micah, who's seen it all and chooses to stay.

The afternoon passes, the world outside still. It drizzles at one point, before the fog descends and everything is gray. I spend the evening reading downstairs—some fantasy book I found in one of the boxes. It's just getting to an interesting part when the upstairs door opens.

Jax stomps down the stairs, a red cup in his hand. "Micah won't fucking pick up."

"Did you text him?"

"Yeah."

"Can't you track him?"

"No signal. He must have turned off the phone." Jax exhales, making a frustrated sound.

I shiver. "Maybe there's no service at the hospital?"

"Maybe," he replies, not believing it. "It's always the nicest places with the shittiest reception."

"It's Micah," I say. "If he could text, he would, right? I bet you'll get like six in a row once he has service again."

Jax nods. "Yeah, you're right. I'm just nervous."

Me, too. But I keep it to myself. It was me who told Micah to go, after all. I look around the room, eyes settling on the pool table. "Let's play pool. C'mon."

"Really?"

"Yeah, I still haven't played."

Jax doesn't look enthused, but he gets a cue from the wall. We break. I'm stripes, he's solids. He's a better player by far, but I manage to hit a few balls into the correct pockets.

Jax stays quiet as we play. Each time our eyes meet, he immediately looks away. I fuck up my shot completely and swear under my breath. "Sorry. Not very good at this."

"You're good at other things," he replies.

I exhale a half laugh, knowing my cheeks must be totally red by now. When I look up, he's watching me, body tense. I think back to the fire in my chest when we kissed at the bridge, and I think he's thinking about it, too. My limbs are light with anticipation as he slowly sets down his cue and comes around the side of the table toward me.

"I won't do anything you don't want me to," he whispers.

Steady, Val.

"I know."

My heart beats so hard that I can see the blood pulse underneath my skin. I am not Valerie Simons. I am Valentine. Valentine the Stag, the godless heathen.

Jax lifts me onto the soft felt of the table. The fluorescent lights buzz over our heads as he reaches around and pulls my hips forward until I'm leaning backward, my legs dangling over the edge. He snakes a hand up between my legs, pressing right where he should, and I don't resist.

Our lips meet—he tastes like power and danger and cigarettes. We're back by the bridge, back to feeling blizzardy. I want him. I'm scared, but I want him, have wanted him for a long time, and not solely for an ulterior motive.

Jax carries me to the bed, then lays me down gently.

I clear my mind as best as I am able, and fall freely into his touch. I let go of the soot, the grime, the fear.

The rest is just a bonus.

22

I wake up with Jax next to me, calm as a fragile sea.

Shifting ever so slightly, I slide the lower half of my body out of the bed and sit on the edge, looking back at him.

How many people see this side of him? The unguarded, unprotected side. When Jax is awake, he's constantly three steps ahead, unfazed by us mortals.

I relive last night—the unexpected gentleness, even hesitation with me until he was really sure I was okay. That I wanted him, too. Which I did.

Which makes me totally unsure of what to say when he wakes up.

His eyes search mine, like I'm a galaxy that he needs to explore.

"Hi," he says.

"Hi."

"You okay?"

I nod. "You?"

He nods back. "We don't have to tell the others."

My heart sinks a little. Am I so embarrassing that he wants to keep it a secret?

His eyes widen. "Not like that, Valentine. I mean . . . like, it can be ours."

Ours. The first thing Jax and I have for just the two of us, without Micah or any of the other Stags.

"Okay," I say. "Just for us."

He stands up and gets dressed without another word, and I do the same. The air between us may as well be a hundred-foot wall—how can someone be so close but so far at the same time? We head toward the stairs, and I'm dying for the awkward silence to end when Jax pivots.

"I'd scream to the heavens how much I care about you, if you want. You just tell me when." Then both his hands are on either side of my face and I'm kissing him back, pulling his fucking gorgeous body closer to mine. We part, breathless, and he goes up the stairs, shutting the door quietly behind him.

When I'm alone again, I fall slowly into routine—pulling off the sheets and throwing them into the washer. I lie back on my bare mattress and stare at the ceiling, reeling. Looking at my phone, I take note of the time.

It's 6:57 A.M. *Ours.*

I kill time with a workout in the now even smaller gym space near my bed. Every time I feel like stopping I picture Jax's face when he saw me, remember the feeling of his hands on my skin . . . and I blush like crazy, then keep going.

After a shower, I eat a bowl of cereal and watch Jax and Nianna battle it out in Mario Kart. Nianna whoops in victory as she crosses the finish line.

"You're losing your touch, Jax," she says. "I never used to win."

"Shut up," he replies, smiling. His eyes meet mine for a beat, then he's back and focused on the TV. "Let's play again."

Our leader comes back and routs her the next two rounds,

much to her chagrin. Jax yawns, and hands the controller to me. "Your turn, Valentine. Don't fuck this up for us."

"Oh, God," I reply, grimacing as I take it. *Did he mean to say* us?

Nianna checks her phone as the round starts. I've never been amazing at video games, but I used to play this with Lyla and her friends at sleepovers and the like, so I know a trick or two. Nianna and I are well matched and she's winning until her phone lights up and she glances at the message. Immediately she pauses the game.

"Oh no," she says.

"What?"

"Have you seen Kate today?"

"No," I reply, my sense of dread growing. "Why?"

"Mako just texted me. She told him she was out tagging with me, and she told me she was with him and Jaws at 24."

"What?" I say. "Where would she go?"

"I don't know," Nianna replies.

The air in the room seems to transform, and Jax is on his phone in a flash. My heart pounds as he waits for the screen to load—presumably the tracking app for all of our phones.

Sweet, sweet Kate. Whatever her demons are, they're winning the war for her mind—any one of us knows that as well as we'd know the sun in the sky.

My blood freezes with Jax's next words: "She's at the bridge."

"Oh my god," I say. *Kate. Not Kate. No no no.*

"Let's go!" Jax says, the panic in his eyes betraying his usually enigmatic expressions. For once, I know what Jax is thinking, because I'm thinking the same horrible thing: we won't make it in time.

We run out the door, not even stopping to tug on jackets. Nianna takes the passenger seat as I slide into the back then slam the door. Jax slams the keys in the ignition and backs the van out, tires squealing. The ride is a desperate whisper of a wish. *Please, no.*

Jax drives. Nianna stares at her phone.

I count every moment where I must have failed. All the moments that could have led to these hateful, heart-wrenching minutes. Her confession about her mom. Her erratic, lengthy sleeps. Like she was looking to escape something. It's clear now—she was already on the edge.

Mako. That poor guy. I text him practically every mile. `We're going as fast as we can. We'll get to her. Keep calling her.`

I can hear the thunder of my own fear as we finally, finally reach the Golden Gate Bridge Welcome Center. Jax nearly hits a group of tourists as he parks the van up on the sidewalk, bursting out of it before they have the chance to yell. Nianna and I follow right behind, but Jax is a force of nature sprinting wildly toward the bridge. He shoves people out of the way, howling at cyclists to clear a path, his girl's about to jump. I give up on muttering apologies and instead scream ahead, begging the people to let Jax through.

"Move! Move!" I yell.

Then I see her—her hair bright against the gray of the fog. She's on the bridge, safe, hair swept off to one side. Suddenly I realize it isn't off to the side—it's cut. Locks of gold surround her boots, and when Jax sweeps her in his arms, the strands flutter like feathers. A pair of scissors lies next to her shoes.

She's crying. "I'm sorry. I wasn't going to do it. I wasn't." Jax says something I can't hear and she nods. "I know. I'm sorry."

Jax releases her eventually and Nianna and I both grab her in a hug. Words tumble out of our mouths like a blurry snowfall.

"I'm so happy you're okay," I say.

"We love you," says Nianna.

Kate nods. "I know, I know."

"Anything you need, we're here. Any way we can help."

"I know, I know. I'm sorry."

Looking up, I lock eyes with Jax, who's just finished sending a text. *Mako.* Or Micah.

We huddle there for who knows how long, ignoring the looks of the tourists trying to amble by. Finally the cold gets to us, and we take our windswept hair and snotty noses back toward the parking lot. My hands are numb as I hold Kate's, Jax flanking her other side. We move the car, Jax finessing an excuse to the park ranger who put a ticket on it. *They'll want to call the police,* I think, but I guess Jax talks our way out of that, too, because the ranger just takes the ticket off the van. I catch her telling Jax she's really happy that it turned out okay.

A gut-wrenching scream cuts through the quiet: "Kate!"

Mako runs up, his cheeks red from crying and eyes wide and worried. She runs to him and fresh tears spring from my eyes as the two of them collapse to the ground, so tightly wound together that even an earthquake couldn't shake them apart.

It starts to rain, and Jax finally nudges the reunited couple into the van with the rest of us.

"Where's Micah?" Nianna asks me, clicking her seat belt.

I texted him, but he didn't reply yet. "He probably texted Jax." Nianna's frown tells me it's as stupid of an answer as I thought, but I brush it off. He didn't have service last night either. Micah would head back to the house once he saw the texts. We're all together, *alive* and safe. The past twenty-four hours have been so wild. I feel like a ship caught in a whirlpool, spinning and spiraling endlessly until finally breaking free. *Deep breath in, deep breath out.* I check the time—6:21 P.M.

I doze on the ride back, mind and body wiped out by the events of the past day. We pile out of the van, and Nianna fiddles for her keys. I'm daydreaming of the steaming bowl of clam chowder I'm going to make myself when we get inside and then—

"Why is the door unlocked?" Nianna says, pushing it open.

Kate screams.

I follow her gaze and my smile dies—possibly forever—at the sight of Micah's body on the floor.

23

Jax is inconsolable.

We've abandoned Holloway House and are holed up on Beale. The gilded lobby mocked us with its shine when we stumbled into the apartment like abandoned dogs.

It's a small apartment that still smells new. It's not fit for more than two people, with white walls and large furniture that dominates the room.

From my place on the couch, I curl up tighter, my throat raw from sobbing. I can't unsee it. The reflection of my face in the blood. His limbs splayed awkwardly, covered in the tattoos he so carefully designed. The wings of the Herons spray painted on his back.

The world will tell us that he got what he deserved, that we got what we deserved. They are wrong, so wrong. Micah wanted out. He wanted a loyal dog and pine trees and breathable air.

Jax wails from the next room. Pounds on the walls. Screams—then goes silent again. I have never known a person less worthy of comfort yet so sincere in despair.

We should bury him, I beg Jax silently. *Bury him properly. Give him honors if those exist. A twenty-one-gun salute. Anything and everything and—*

Nianna clears her throat. "We'll have to tell his parents."

I nod, numb. We have nothing but the clothes on our backs, a few necessities stocked in the kitchen and bathroom, and each other. There's nothing to be said, so we don't say anything. A cough here, a sniffle there. The room is warm thanks to the thermostat, but suddenly I can't stand that either.

Without a word, I get up, pull open the sliding-glass door, and go out onto the balcony. It's a tiny triangle with metal-and-glass railings so clear I could reach through them and fall into the open air. The lights of downtown give me just enough of a glow to see where I'm stepping. The symphony of cities echoes from far below me. Cars honk. Crosswalks beep. And none of it matters.

Micah can't be dead. But he is. My body buckles and I vomit over the railing. I don't stop until there's nothing more, nothing left inside me but bile and anguish.

Soul and feet dragging, I join the others inside. There's a knock at the front door. Three short bursts, followed by two slow ones. My heart leaps to my throat, but a moment later I remember that the pattern is Stag code. Mako opens the door. Jaws carries the IRIS machine with all the reverence you'd give an armed bomb. He places it on the counter and plugs it in. The lights stay dark—no new messages. The Young Herons aren't even going to gloat about it.

I crawl back into my corner of the sofa, eyelids getting heavier once I lie down all the way. I unzip my sweatshirt and drape it over my shoulders, but it's about as good at being a blanket as it is at bringing me any comfort. Closing my eyes, I imagine myself back home in my bed, Mom's protective arms around my shoulders.

But I'm here. And I'm sick with despair.

I'm not sure if any of us actually sleeps. Mako lies on the floor right next to Kate. They rest with their hands entwined.

When I stretch out, my toes touch Kate's. She moves hers away. Nianna is the last one standing. The sliding door opens and shuts, and in the quiet I hear her voice, her crying. *She's calling the others,* I realize. They have to know Holloway isn't secure.

Dawn comes, bleary and unwelcome, and I'm the first awake, but I feel as if I've been up all night. My arm aches from how I slept on it. Turning onto my other side, I watch the morning sunshine fill the room. My first day on this planet without Micah on it, too.

When I finally get up, I walk silently over to the kitchen to see what we're working with in terms of food. Even though I don't want to eat, I know I need to.

A twelve-pack of beers, a half-dozen eggs, and an old chunk of cheddar cheese are all that stare back at me. The cabinets aren't much better—crackers, a stale box of cereal, coffee grounds, and a jar of peanut butter.

I make sandwiches out of the peanut butter and crackers, smoothing the spread onto each one slowly. I make enough for myself, then more. Somewhere around the last few crackers, I cry again.

Over by the door, Jaws clears his throat. When I turn, he motions to the crackers, and I bring some over to him. He takes one and chews it slowly.

"Why are you here?" I whisper. He cocks an eyebrow. "I mean, no offense, but it's pretty obvious that you're older than the rest of us. Why are you here? Don't you have a family? Wife, kids?" I motion to the others. "Don't you have something you'd rather be doing that watching out for us?"

"Jax's mother is an old friend. She helped me get into this country. Now all I see is suffering. All of you suffer. I try to keep the suffering out. I failed. I am sorry."

Jaws takes another cracker sandwich. Then he pulls the gun from its holster and turns it over in his hands, murmuring to himself like he's praying, as if there's a god who'll pity him, pity us.

Jax comes out of the bedroom around eleven. He says nothing and goes straight for the bathroom, where he showers for an hour. When he turns off the water, he disappears into the bedroom again and shuts the door behind him.

Mako gets us all sandwiches from a deli downstairs. When he comes back, Kurt is there with him, red-eyed and hollow. He gives us each a hug. "I can't believe it," he says when he gets to me. "I just can't."

I don't want to eat, but I force the bread and turkey down, chewing slowly. Each bite pulls me a little closer toward being human, which isn't saying much.

Jax opens the bedroom door. Mako tosses him a sandwich, and he catches it.

"What are you going to do?" I ask him.

Nianna nudges my shoulder. "Give the guy a second."

"No. Jax, what are you going to do? What are *we* going to do?"

The man in front of me is changed. Unrecognizable. The arrogance is gone.

There is only anger.

"First," he says. "We'll say goodbye. Then I'm going to find who did this and rip out their fucking throat."

"Are you going to call his dad?" asks Nianna.

"I got ahold of him for all of ten seconds. I told him it was me, and he gave me some choice words about his son's decisions then hung up."

I flinch—Micah was his *son*. How could anyone be so heartless?

Jax goes over to IRIS, and the rest of us watch, mesmerized, as his hands fly over the keypad. He holds down the pound sign. The machine buzzes. Message sent.

"Let's go to Holloway," he says. "We'll get the guns and anything else you want to keep."

My chest tightens. The blood. Micah's body. "I can't go in there."

Jax looks to Jaws, still at his hallway perch. The latter nods. "Micah's out."

"Where?"

"With a friend," Jaws answers in a tone that must be the gentlest he can muster. "We'll go see him. Soon."

Jax travels to Holloway alone. Says he won't have any more of us dying for his sake. He'll take the train after us. "They wanted me, they fucking got me," he said bitterly as we left for the station.

We get out at Balboa. It's pouring rain and none of us are prepared. Water weighs down my sweater so much that by the time we make it to the house, it's nearly off my shoulders.

The door is open. The door is never open.

I turn and throw up in the bushes. Mako pats my back and I tell them to go ahead.

The three of them go inside as I rip petals from the flowers. Kate opens the garage door, its squeaks and screeching more jarring than before. My room feels frozen and immovable, like a still-life painting.

Shivering, I change into fresh clothes, then pause and look around. There's nothing here I want—not even my knife, which would have been the first thing I turned to before. But Micah wouldn't have wanted that. He would have wanted me to reach out, be stronger with people around me. *I'll do better,* I promise. *Just as soon as we find who did this to you.*

It takes most of my courage to go up the stairs and into the room. It takes the rest of it to pass the couch. Not a drop of Micah remains. I keep walking.

The door to the bedroom creaks.

His bed is made. Of course it's made. I was there, but seeing it sharpens my pain: he'll never sleep here again. Opening the closet, I dig through his pile of laundry until I find the right jacket. I find what I need in the right-side pocket and tuck it into my own.

We leave Holloway for good and take a series of buses to the edge of the city, a part that I'm not familiar with. A man in a dark jacket waits at the front door of the funeral home and lets us in. Next to him are Cameron and Juliet—the former his usual sullen self, and the latter totally silent. She hugs Nianna first, then pushes her back with a shake of her head.

"Closed?" Jaws asks the man. The mortician nods and unlocks the door. Jaws shakes the man's hand, and he isn't subtle enough for me to not see a stack of money changing hands.

Micah's body lies in a casket of warm-colored wood. Chairs line the edges of the room and low lights above us provide just enough light to be considered appropriate. Vases bursting with flowers give off a weighty perfume. My body falls against the wall and I sink to the ground, feeling sick. "*I don't like small places,*" Micah had told me. "*Never have.*"

This can't be real. He can't be dead.

"Take all the time you need," the mortician tells Jaws.

In the corner is a small stand for people to light candles.

Kate goes over to it and lights one, then a second. She keeps on lighting them, and we watch until all the candles are glowing.

"There's not enough." She starts to cry, standing so still, as if moving would make it worse. Mako gets up and puts his arms around her. "Babe, there's not enough."

"I know," he says softly. "I know."

We stay a while, sniffling and silent. The flickering candlelight casts wild shadows on the wall, and when I can't bear to look at the casket anymore, I watch the shadows move and change. Kurt, Juliet, and Cameron arrive separately, and we trade hugs and muffled sobs into each other's shoulders. *None of this is real. It can't be.*

Juliet puts her arm around me. "He was such a good one."

In the corner, away from us, Jax sits alone, his face buried in his hands.

We finally crawl back to Beale, heavy with exhaustion. Jax tells Kurt and the others to stay in the Mission in case the Boars need them—Beale's too small for us all anyway.

Over on the polished counter, the IRIS machine is lit up. For reasons I don't know, I follow behind Jax and read the message with him.

"All right then," he says. "It's done."

I take the note. *Golden Gate Park. Friday at midnight.* I get to the end and frown.

"The Boars are coming too?"

"They're part of the Wars," Jax replies. "I need them there if we're going to end this, once and for all."

"Do you think you can?"

He doesn't answer right away. "I don't know."

A cruel part of me wants to say that this wouldn't have happened if he'd gone to the hospital himself. But even though I want to scream it, I know it's too unkind of a thought to give life to. It's nothing he doesn't already know. Nothing he won't live with for the rest of his life. There's no group he can join, no place he can run to get rid of this guilt, sure as the Stag tattoo on his heart.

Instead, I say, "You're going to kill Camille."

He kisses me on the forehead and I don't care that everyone sees.

"I'm going to kill every Heron there."

24

Morning comes, and we're still empty. A collection of up-turned bowls.

Around eight, the doorbell rings, and I jolt up. Jaws leaps to action; his gun is cocked before he stands. My body tenses—Kurt and the others went back to the Mission for the night. We didn't make plans for the morning.

"We posted that we didn't want visitors," Nianna whispers. "This is a private building. Which means . . ."

Jaws looks into the peephole—one of those safety ones where you can't tell when someone is looking out—and immediately puts his pistol down.

He opens the door like a bellman. "Good morning, Ms. Canne."

A woman walks through the hallway with short, quick steps. She's dressed in an ivory dress that hugs her petite frame just where it should. Gold jewelry hangs off her ears, matching the necklace around her throat. She carries herself the way Matthew's mother does, walking on money and led by a heart that's weathered much.

"Theresa?" Nianna gets up slowly, then gives her a hug. "What are you doing here?"

Theresa stiffens, her nostrils narrowing as she inhales. "I heard what happened. I came because I know my son, and I know he loved Micah more than he ever bothered to say out loud."

She greets Kate and Mako by name. Then she sees me. Her lips part, and for a moment, she seems to forget where she is and what her name is.

"I'm Valerie." I stand and adjust my disheveled clothes. She waits for me to offer my hand.

Her skin is smooth and cool as a river stone. "Theresa Canne, though I'm sure you guessed that by now."

Kate gives Theresa her seat while Nianna hurries to fetch a cup of coffee. Theresa takes in the state of the apartment. It must belong to her. All the Stags' holdings belong to her.

"Mako, you are looking fit," she says, smiling cheerily. "Kate, don't let this one get away."

"I don't plan on it," Kate replies. It's an empty compliment followed quickly by an awkward silence. The language of socialites means nothing to us. Theresa shifts in her seat, crossing her legs tighter.

"Theresa, you said you heard . . ." Nianna starts. "We've asked that he be cremated."

She closes her eyes. "That boy was always the kindest. Gentle, and friendly to everyone."

There's a loud *thump* from the closed bedroom door.

"I suppose that's him," Theresa says.

Nianna nods. "Want me to get him?"

"No, I'd like to."

She knocks on the door twice before going in. I hear Jax say something, followed by Theresa's steady reply. The door clicks shut and Kate exhales sharply, slouching as she does.

"She looks amazing," she mutters. "Hasn't aged a day."

"Jax doesn't seem surprised she's here," I say.

"They're like that," Nianna replies. "It's one of the few

ways they're close. Jax always seems to know when his mother's coming to visit. It's weird."

When Theresa comes back out, she walks over and puts her hand on my arm, giving it an almost imperceptible tug. "Valerie, I wonder if I could have a word."

I swallow. "Of course."

We go out onto the balcony. The wind blows Theresa's perfect waves of pale blond hair as she stares out into the sky-line. She keeps one hand on the railing and the other at her side, not bothering to brush the strands from her face. There's something unsettling about that.

"Jax told me about you," she says. "A long time ago."

"I haven't known him that long."

"No, of course not. It was years ago. I remember. I was in the city on business, and I got the feeling Jax needed me. A mother knows."

I nod like I agree. I'm very sure Mom never once sensed I needed her. *If she did, I would never have started cutting like I did.* Then again, she had her own grief to grapple with.

"When I arrived, Jax was standing on this very balcony. He told me a little boy had been killed."

My blood turns to ice.

"And that the boy had an older sister."

The earth stops turning.

"I have a lot of time to myself," says Theresa. "I've often wondered what you might look like, or if you would join the Stags when your time came." The shape of her eyes is just like Jax's. "Do you regret it? Joining."

I press myself against the railing behind me. "I would have joined no matter what anyone said. My mom told me not to. So did my dad. But I had to."

"Because of your brother."

"Yes."

Theresa shifts so that she is facing me. She cups my chin in her hand, raising my gaze from the ground. "Tell me."

"I'm sorry?"

"Tell me what happened. I want to hear it in your own words."

There is a universe in her eyes. I wonder if she can see the glacier of pain in mine. My life since Leo died—chewing on exhaust fumes. My life, a permanent hydroplane.

Blood pounds in my head. I squeeze my eyes shut like a child waiting for a monster to disappear. Only when I open them again, Theresa is still there. Her very presence changes the feel of the air. I stare hard into her eyes—they're blue-green, like the calmest mountain lake, only I get the feeling there's something sinister in their depths.

"Tell me," she says again.

The memory unlocks. Micah's dead; what does anything really matter anyway? Even my deepest shame has changed to something inconsequential.

So I tell her all of it—well-worn words and realities I've lived with each day for two years. I recount that day the way I've recounted it a thousand times in my head and to Lyla and, more than once, to John Kilmer.

It had been warm that day—the sky was overcast but un-usually bright given the time of year. I didn't even bring an extra jacket to class.

Dad was at work. Mom was up in Napa visiting our grandma. Both of them fussed over whether I was responsible enough yet to drive on my own, but I had my license and Mom's old Lexus. I got home around three, but Leo didn't wrap up his music class until four so I set my alarm and took a nap.

The ring of the house phone startled me awake. That was

strange. I remember it was strange that the home phone would be ringing because it almost never did. My room was dark as I shot up and grabbed at my phone—4:31 P.M.

I'd overslept.

I sped toward Marina View Elementary. The wind had picked up as fog swept in from the west, bringing with it darker rainclouds.

I made the last turn and spotted a pair of women huddled together, clutching each other's hands. One of them was Leo's teacher, Mrs. Miu. I swear to God I'll live the rest of my life and never forget the look she gave me. The unmitigated panic in her recognition.

A police officer directed traffic away from the usual lot where I signed Leo out. Rolling down my window, I blinked into the first sprinkle of rain. "S'cuse me? I'm here to pick up my brother."

"All the kids have been relocated to First Baptist across the street." She pulled out her radio. "What's your name?"

"Valerie Simons. Picking up Leo Simons."

The officer didn't move. Her radio buzzed, but she didn't budge.

"Miss Simons, I'm going to have you pull over just past that tape."

It was weird that I was the only car she was letting get close. I knew it was. All these things I knew, even in the moment, were unusual. Still, I eased around an ambulance and parked. Another officer was waiting for me.

"I'm here to pick up my brother," I said over the rain. I opened the door. "His name is Leo Simons. She said they were at the church . . ." It was hard to hear over the sound of the rain, the cars, and the crackling radios. Even the flashing white-and-red lights of the ambulance added a special friction to the din.

"Miss Simons, I am sorry to tell you, but there was a shooting here about an hour ago."

"Oh my god. Is everyone okay?"

Her face changed. "I'm very sorry—"

"No."

"Ma'am—"

"Leo?" I screamed.

I pushed past her and staggered toward the school like a wounded animal. Ducking under the yellow police tape, I saw the faintest stream of red running down the hill—a living watercolor of our shared blood. The rain brought it to my boots, swirling into a crimson pool as I came to a halt.

Six people stood around a small body. A camera flashed. A pair of legs shifted, and there was my brother, *my* brother—his tiny arm and tiny face exposed as a coroner pulled back the tarp. They didn't notice me there until I screamed.

I screamed until my throat was raw, until my stomach was weak with horror and I couldn't hear anything else but the pain emitting from my chest and into the dark, dark clouds. A paramedic caught me just before the concrete came rushing up to meet my skull.

If only I'd done something else. Anything else. If I'd gone online instead of napped. If I'd gotten Starbucks with Lyla like she'd suggested. If only I'd decided, hey, let's get the little bro early today and sneak in some In-N-Out for dinner.

But no. I overslept.

I rebury the thoughts like I've done before. The scars on my leg flare to life, molten metal at a forge of memory.

"I should have been there. I should have been on time." I wipe my nose. "That's what gets me. All I had to do was be on time. But I wasn't. I wasn't and that's why he's dead."

"That is not true."

"Yes, yes, it actually is." I cross my arms and curl myself

inward as if that would stamp out the pain in my chest. "If I'd been there on time, or early—"

"Valerie."

Theresa stares at me sternly. "Thank you for telling me," she says. "God knows the world could use a little more honesty. And because it does, I'm telling you it was not your fault. An accident, if anything."

I nod numbly in reply. I've heard this spiel before, from Mom, Dad, Matthew, John freakin' Kilmer, everyone. Everyone told me it wasn't my fault, it just never took.

But now? Micah is dead, Leo is dead. All I have are the Stags.

I take a deep breath. "Theresa, may I ask . . . why do you do it?"

"Do what?"

"Fund the Stags. Fund the Wars."

The spot between her upper lip and nose twitch, and for a split second her face is something sinister. "I love my son. This is what he wants. It makes him happy. What kind of mother would I be if I kept him from that?"

"Yeah, but still."

Her gaze goes from stern to malicious in an instant. "I see what you're thinking—that I am complicit in this. Well, I am. That is a decision I made a long time ago and I stand by it. My son is my life. I have every right to do with my money as I please, and giving Jax what he wants is what I please."

I nod again, looking away. I have a sudden vision of Theresa lifting me up and over the railing.

Theresa inhales so deeply I wonder how her lungs can contain it all. She lets it go and shakes her hand as if we've been discussing something frivolous. "Anyway. Keep your head down and I'm sure you'll finish your year just fine."

Nodding, I try to think of something complimentary to say. "Jax looks after us well."

"Jon."

"What?"

"My son's name is Jonathan Anthony Wilde. Where on earth he got 'Jax' from, I'll never know."

Jonathan Anthony Wilde. I wish I could un-hear it. Jax needs to stay a god in my eyes. My leader, not a human being. Not somebody's child.

"I won't ask you to forgive him," she says. "Or me, for that matter. Clearly you think my actions are wrong. That is your choice. But I will ask you to forgive yourself. I'm sure you've been told to. But truly—it's time."

She angles around me, so close that for a moment all I breathe is her refined perfume. I am not sorry to see her go. Through the glass, I watch as she gives each of the others a hug, then leaves.

Nianna opens the slider. "Jax wants to start planning."

I know the spot they've picked: the Music Concourse at Golden Gate Park. Between the de Young Museum and California Academy of Sciences is an open plaza with fountains, gnarled trees, and rows of green benches. Families go there. Tourists go there. It's beautiful and safe—and Jax is going to bathe it in blood.

"I'll meet Camille and Ty here." Jax taps his finger on the middle of the stone columns. "We'll talk, pretend to make some kind of treaty. Ty will be in on it, and his guys will be around. The Young Herons, too."

"When will you make your move?" Nianna asks.

"Right away. I've said I want a negotiation. I'm not going

to give them one." Jax goes quiet, and very still. I study his face, waiting for him to say more and wondering what he's thinking. Is he expecting to die? Something catches in my chest, like a hook on my heart—I can't lose another one. There's no room left in my head or heart for any more pain.

Mako buys more food from the deli, and we eat. I chew and taste the salty, then sweet. All of it bitter.

We drag ourselves toward sleep. Tonight, Mako and Kate squeeze onto one side of the couch. Her face is curled against his chest in a way I'd guess might make it difficult to breathe. She won't move, though, not for the world.

Jax goes into the bedroom. When he doesn't shut the door behind him, I let myself in. He faces the bed like he doesn't know what it's for.

I put my arms around his waist, leaning my forehead between his shoulder blades. He doesn't say anything, doesn't move.

So I take his hand and guide him to bed. We curl our limbs around each other. I kiss his cheek. My lips remember the feel of his skin, even after all these days. Even after *this* day. Jax rolls onto his side, facing away from me. I lean my forehead against his back.

Jax shifts rolling over until his face is next to mine.

"I have something to tell you," he says.

"What is it?"

"The guy who killed your brother. It's Ty Boreas."

His words should shock me. I should be paralyzed with a wave of emotions as the knowledge hits home, but I'm already so exhausted, my whole body an open and aching wound, that instead I start crying and ask, "Why?"

"It was Elliott Boreas's final test for his little brother before he handed the reins to the Boars over to him. He wanted to make sure his brother would do anything to get back at the Herons." Jax sighs, shuddering. "The day Ty told me was the day I left the Boars. It had been coming for a while, but killing an innocent kid to hurt the Westons was the last straw.

"I begged Brianna to come with me. She said no, at first. She knew what happened to deserters and didn't want to take the risk. Finally she caved and . . . you know the rest. After she was kidnapped, we went to the police. Did everything right. She had to tell them everything, every detail. But as soon as we told them we were Boars who wanted out, they took us less seriously. They said they'd follow up with us and never did, even when I called in.

"Brianna stopped talking to me. Later, I found out she went back to the Boars. They got her hooked on some drug, and she couldn't quit it. Then she disappeared. I've hired investigators to find her. They all say she moved to LA and never came back."

Jax isn't crying. He's a hard guy to read at the best of times, but right now even more so. So I let my tears flow for the both of us and for Brianna.

Memories come back like embers fanned back to life—me, Matthew, and Leo in the living room, my brother laughing until snot ran down his face as Matthew spun him around like an airplane. The vision shifts. Matthew at the funeral, holding my hand. He didn't say anything then. He never, never told me the truth.

My leader lets me sob into the bed as each wave of realization erodes any confusion I ever had. Ty Boreas killed Leo to get at Matthew, before Matthew was even a Heron. Before Matthew was mine, or pretended to be. I have to believe the memories of those six months were real. Everything else was just a fantasy I built up in my head.

My mind jumps—Ty Boreas. I was so close to him, literally. Fuck honor and rules. I could have done it weeks ago. That stupid, guilty look that gave me pause. Did he recognize me and want to apologize? Did he want to laugh in my face, let me know the truth right there? He must have bragged about it, must have told someone. That's how those Boars knew about Leo the day I was tattooed. They'd heard the legend and wanted to drive the hurt home.

Jax places his hand firmly on my shoulder.

"Tomorrow," he says. "When I take my shot at Camille, you can take your shot at Ty."

Revenge for Leo, innocent of everything. Revenge for sweet, kindhearted Micah. Freedom for all of us.

"I'm ready," I whisper back. "Let's end this."

Finally, a smile. "Let's end this."

25

The black day arrives. I can't sit still, so I focus on each task as if my life depended on it. Go to the store with Mako, get breakfast. Eat. Think. Plan. Anything to pass the time while remembering that today's the day I get my revenge.

We take the M line to Forest Hill then transfer to a bus. The road is winding with rows of houses on one side and dense trees on the other. The bus turns, and we're in the Inner Sunset.

We get to the park at 7:17 P.M., leaving us hours until any of the other gangs are set to arrive. But I already feel them. I feel them coming. Focusing on the ground beneath my feet, I manage to keep my calm.

Micah. Leo. This is for them. *This is what I want.*

I stand by Jax. "There's not much cover."

He lights a cigarette. "Just stick with the plan."

His eyes are hard and focused as he scans the Music Concourse not once, but twice. A park security vehicle stops at the crosswalk. Mako and Kate take a selfie, playing the carefree tourists. The car rolls forward. Kate deletes the photo.

"You and Kate behind those benches." Jax points to the other side. "Nianna and Mako there. Jaws in the pillars behind." There's a catch in his voice, and I feel it like I would a punch. We're all used to him saying Micah's name, too.

We drag our feet, not knowing whether to say good luck or goodbye or both.

Nianna steps up next to me. "You look nervous."

"I'm fine."

"Valerie?"

"What?"

"I'm sorry for what I said. About you not being a real Stag."

"I'm sorry, too. I should have been more open from the start."

I turn and walk away, the gravel crunching under my feet, and a faint feeling from the back of my mind ricochets forward. That's the first time she's called me by my full name. The only one who ever did was Micah.

Mako and Kate's ritual is hard to watch. Their usual quick peck is slow, and they both linger. They're breaking, like at the end of *Casablanca*. I can almost hear the whir of a plane waiting to take her away.

They pull apart, and I take Kate's hand. He whispers one last thing in her ear. I want to say something, but there aren't any words. I don't say goodbye to Mako. If I looked back at him now, I'd lose all my nerve and tell them to run, please run, and be happy.

Logic says I can go. Loyalty says I can't. I couldn't protect Leo, and I couldn't save Micah. I've lived with guilt long enough now to know its every whisper, the way it turns its head, the way it kisses and kills.

I know I'll never be free if I run now. This time, I have to do something.

Dozens of sycamore and elm trees spread their bulky limbs toward each other like synapses between neurons in the brain. Even though they're tipped with green buds, the trees look nightmarish, like something out of a Tim Burton movie.

Jax takes a spot next to an aisle. Behind him, an elderly

couple huddles together. There's a group of teens hanging out on the steps in front of the columns. The girls squeal in ripped skinny jeans and oversized sweatshirts.

I hate them. I wish I were them—carefree.

Looking at the far side of the concourse, I can just make out the shapes of Kurt and Cameron. Juliet is over by the Cal Academy. We are making the Stag presence known.

Mako's stationed a few rows back and to the right of Jax. Nianna disappears to the far side of the columns to guard the opposite side. Jaws paces the perimeter of the stage we've set, circling it in slow, weighty steps. When the security car comes again, he melts into the shadows of the columns until it drives past.

Kate and I take turns sitting on the bench and crouching down behind it. The benches are flimsy—no way they'd stop a bullet—with curling green armrests that remind me of Disneyland. Silly things you think about when you're about to die.

There is nothing to do but wait and listen.

Buses load and offload passengers. Crows call to each other from the trees. The clang of a nearby flagpole's line, tossed in the wind—I hear all of it.

Kate and I trade places. Blood rushes back into my legs as I stretch out. Down below, Jax starts on what must be his fourth or fifth cigarette. Farther down, Nianna and Mako pace around their post and each other. Getting here so early seemed like a smart idea. It gave us something to focus on.

But we still have hours to go.

Next to me, Kate makes a small noise in her throat. She shifts her gun. Then, out of nowhere, she laughs. "I just remembered what this place is called. It's the Spreckels Temple of Music."

"Really?"

"I read that somewhere. Spreckels Temple of Music.

Spreckels. Like sprinkles." We both laugh—nervously, desperately. Then she adds, "Hey, Val?"

"Yeah?"

"I'm sorry for how I treated you. I know you were just trying to help."

"It's okay," I say, reaching over to give her hand a squeeze. She takes it and squeezes right back.

That's the last we say for a while. I think about calling Mom and Dad to say goodbye. Or maybe just to hear their voices. I decide not to.

Micah knew this would happen—me, choosing not to reach out. I didn't get why he thought that then. I do now. I've changed. I don't want to call home and have my parents realize that for themselves.

Stars poke out in the dark mantle of night, and I shiver again and again. The flavor of the air changes. Nighttime sets in, and every sound sharpens my senses until I'm a living, breathing X-Acto knife.

The Boars come first, their figures appearing from behind the museum. I watch as they hurry past a sculpture of three colored figures with their hands over their heads. I spot Adam Yglesias alongside a burly guy who keeps his head down, hood up. Quick, purposeful strides tell me the Boars mean business. Do they want peace, or revenge? Aren't those our only choices, now? A few of them walk down near Jax, giving him a wide berth.

I notice the first Heron at the columns. Even in the low light, I recognize Aure's pale face and fine features. She's dressed head to toe in black but a white undershirt peeks out at her wrists.

Matthew appears by her side. He's dressed just like Aure—as are the five other Herons crowded around them. Matthew says something to Camille, and she shakes her head.

Then Aure goes down the steps with the others toward the benches, leaving Matthew with Camille beneath the coffers of the half dome.

Has Matthew risen in their ranks so fast? Or was Aure demoted because of what happened at Green Apple? I try to think of it like Jax would, and not like I would. *Camille is playing to their position and history as a show of strength*. To everyone else, Matthew is the next Heron leader, so it's only natural he be up there.

Over at the benches, our leader stands up. He stretches and kicks at a loose stone on the ground then goes up and stands across from Matthew and Camille. Jax is grinning but not in a cheerful way. More like a maniacal, you're-going-down way.

I find the handle of the gun in the holster around my leg.

"Wait for the signal," Kate urges.

"I know." But she doesn't know what Jax and I planned.

Suddenly, worry for Jax burns in my chest. Jonathan Anthony Wilde—Theresa's precious baby boy. He'll be in the middle of it all. What if someone's coming here with a vendetta against him?

I take careful breaths as I watch the leaders talk. Kate whispers to wait for the signal, and I nod each time. I wish I'd called home.

Then something happens.

Police cars materialize from the roadway, their headlights blinding in the pitch-dark. *Oro en paz, fierro en guerra.*

"Oh my god," Kate says, pulling herself up from the ground. "Val, we're—"

"Surrounded." Caught in the oval bowl of the concourse. Police floodlights come to life with dull pops. The trees around us cast misshapen shadows over the benches. Over me and

Kate. Over Jax. They'll take us all and the Wars will be over, all my chances at revenge for Micah and Leo lost in red tape.

Without another thought, I sprint toward the platform just as police megaphones tell me what I already know: there's nowhere to run.

26

I don't know who takes the first shot, but when I fire Ty falls and I stagger at the feeling of a weight being lifted, and a new one crashing down. It's done. *I'm done.*

Jax fires, too, and Camille falls back. Somewhere behind us, a Young Heron shrieks. Matthew dives, shouting as he pulls out a gun, but the Boar next to him lunges forward and punches him hard in the jaw. Another shot rings out, and I swear to God I hear Jax laughing.

I have to run. I have to run right fucking now.

The police rush in from the other side of the pavilion. Two officers slam Adam Yglesias down from behind, but the Boar leader screams bloody murder and somehow lands a punch. In the frenzy, I keep my eyes on Matthew as he disappears around the other side of the pavilion.

I sprint to the left side of the pavilion and bound up the steps to the columns. Garbled sounds from the police megaphones blend with the gunfire. I want to drop my gun and run, but instead I press my free hand into the column. It's ridged, like a soup can. More stupid little things to notice when you're about to die.

Adrenaline thumps through my veins. I can feel it pulsing, feel *myself* pulsing, radiating. My hands shake and I am dead but so, so alive.

Someone races up the steps behind me. I turn—but not soon enough. A Young Heron twice my size rounds the other column and slams his fist into my stomach. I choke on my own bile and double over. He yanks the gun from my hand.

"Fucking Stag!" His spit lands hot on my cheek.

I shove him forward, but he hardly moves. He lunges at me again and I snap my knee up. He grunts as I hit his groin, but he keeps his grip on me. He slams me against a column. I pivot to do the same to him, but he just laughs. He puts the cold lip of a gun against my side. A shadow materializes from behind him. I give the Young Heron's arm a final, desperate shove as Jaws shoots.

But not fast enough. The shot leaves me deaf and the pain leaves me blind.

Agony. Absolute agony. I look down at my hip and see red.

"Jaws!" I scream as life rushes from me.

"Go," he says, leaning down to pull me back on my feet. I take a few steps toward the safety of the dense trees beyond. He turns back, looking for more Herons or police, and then someone shoots him in the chest.

I watch his body hit the ground.

My ears feel stuffed with the densest cotton, ringing at the same time as I stumble backward until I'm in the half-street between the temple and a thicket of trees. There's a break in the static: someone yelling.

"Weston!"

Jax races after Matthew. Their bodies rush deeper into the park, swallowed by the night, by the leaves and woods.

No! I can't leave Jax, not now. I find a steady gait somewhere between a fast walk and a jog. My fingers are slick with blood, and the wound sears my side with pain. I can feel it right at my hip—a chunk of my flesh missing—but I can't stop. Not now.

Within seconds, I've lost them in the shadows cast by the streetlamp ahead. I press on. The footpaths by the main road are easiest to run on, but they'd leave me wholly exposed. I cut across a bed of grass, watching, listening, and begging God to help me find them.

A gunshot sounds from up ahead toward Stow Lake. I take a few more breaths before I straighten up and hobble toward the sound.

I hear a car door slam from the street to my left, and I freeze. A band of police cruisers waits in the dark. A cop stands beside the first one, a walkie-talkie in his hand. The lights spin in a dizzy wash of color. Another wailing—an ambulance?—gets closer. I duck into the nearest tangle of foliage. My wound oozes more blood, and I want to lie down, to be still. The chopping of a helicopter sounds from overhead as sweat trickles down my forehead.

"Over here! Here!" a woman shouts, and I brace myself to be found.

But she's not yelling about me. An officer comes into view, her arms tucked under the armpits of a limp body with lithe, pale limbs. The second officer carries the feet. My heart seizes.

They place Aurelia Saint-Helene on the ground. The first officer shouts for the ambulance then leans down and places two fingers at Aure's neck. The officer shakes her head.

The tears are hot on my cheeks as I take my chance. *She was kind, once.*

Turning away from them, I make a beeline for the next row of trees beyond. If I can make it toward Stow Lake, maybe I'll have gotten away in time.

Fog descends in weighty clouds as I reach a staircase. The earthy, wet smell of the lake fills my nose. I'm so close. Gripping the railing, I ease myself up as quickly as I dare, but each step is steeper than the last. Sweat drips down my forehead, my chest, my back. Between breaths, I try to listen for sounds of my being followed. I don't catch any.

Leaning against the metal bar, I take off my jacket and pull at the thin inner lining until it tears. I grit my teeth and tuck the bundle of fabric between my waistband and my shredded skin. I cry out—but hell, any bandage is better than no bandage. I don't know how much blood I've lost. I don't think I want to.

The trail splits. I can't decide left or right so I pick middle—which keeps me in the foliage but means another blast of pain from my side. I suck in a hissing breath and look out onto the glassy surface of Stow Lake.

Directly ahead, across the water, comes a shout.

There's another shout—I've been hearing those screams for the past two days.

"Jax!" Head light and heart reeling, I dart for the path to my right. It's out in the open, but it's the quickest way to the falls.

I take it.

My footsteps seem to echo in the silence—there's no other sound, until a matching set of footsteps sounds from my left.

Someone is running toward me. I take in his height and hair. Even in moonlight, gold is gold.

Jax throws his arms around me at once. I shake and cry, and my side radiates pain, but here he is. I decide then and there that I love Jax. I love him because Micah loved him, and because he doesn't say anything as we hold each other. We're back at the bridge, the two of us, him comforting me. His hand is on the back of my head, the other at my side.

Jax kisses me, soft and forgiving, and I lean in for a minute before I pull away.

"Where's Matthew?" I gasp.

"Somewhere by the falls," he says. "I lost him. Stay here. I'll find that fucker and—"

"No," I say. "Let me." Jax exhales, and the shrill moment stretches. I pull away from him. "He won't hurt me."

"You don't know that."

"Yes, I do. I can do this."

He sighs, but nods. I walk closer to the waterfall beyond. The lake's surface is still, broken only by the insects skittering across its surface. The sirens are still blaring from the concourse, but I can see their light flashing in the distance. I don't have a lot of time.

"Matthew?" I call out, keeping my gun at the ready. Silence. "It's me."

I count the beats of my heart. *Boom boom, boom boom*. Finally—

He steps out from a wall of calla lilies. I take in his cropped hair, the Heron white of his shirt beneath his jacket. Most of all I take in the gun in his hand, which he doesn't let go of as he approaches.

Looking at him, my heartaches outnumber the stars. Neither of us move. I think how far we've come from that night at the Young Heron headquarters, where nothing kept us apart. It wasn't all that long ago yet I feel I've changed so much, like every cell in my body has become something different—more driven, more alive. The Stags gave me grounding, gave me a voice. So I use it.

"Did the Herons kill Micah Obin?"

"Yes."

"Why?"

"Camille put a hit out. It was supposed to be her last move before she went home to Japan."

My voice shakes. "Micah was innocent."

"He'd been a Stag for years. You think that guy didn't kill

anyone? You think he didn't ever send someone to the same hospital where we found him?"

The hospital. Of course. But what hits me hardest is Matthew saying *we*.

"*That guy* was my friend, you asshole. He went to that hospital because he was kind and selfless."

Voices shout in the distance. Even without him in my sight, I know Jax is telling me that we're running out of time.

"Matthew, we're getting nowhere." I keep my eyes on the gun. "I mean, what are we even doing?"

"What do you want me to say? You're the one who hasn't put down her gun."

"But what if I did," I say carefully. "We can both do it."

Second pass like years. One. Two. Three.

Matthew starts to lower his arm. Suddenly, Jax steps out from the bushes behind me, gun raised. "Not so fast, Weston. You people killed my best friend. You killed my *brother*!"

Matthew raises his gun again, but his aim is less steady. "It was you we were going for."

"Jax," I say, but he doesn't look at me. No one in the world exists except him and Matthew, and nothing I can say or do is going to change it.

"Say his name!" Jax yells.

"I don't owe you anything," Matthew replies. "I didn't kill him. I didn't give the order."

"You have the goddamn tattoo," Jax fires back. "You people hurt my girl, you rape this city, and you *killed my brother*." His voice is unnatural. Inhuman. Fear and adrenaline keep me upright, but not much else. "I'll give you three chances to admit it. I want you to fucking own what you did."

"I didn't kill him," Matthew says.

"That's one. Say. It."

Matthew looks to me. "Val, get away from him."

"No," I reply, putting both my hands out like *stop*. I move in front of Jax. "It doesn't have to be like this."

"You know it does," he replies. He looks back at Matthew. "That's two."

Matthew puts a second hand on his gun, steadying himself. "I didn't do it."

"Yes, you did."

Before I have the chance to protest, Jax lunges and puts his whole body in front of mine. Two shots ring out, like the beats of a heart.

Then silence.

27

Ten years ago I moved into my grandmother's old house. I hadn't wanted to leave my school, my friends.

Then I met a boy, and he was in my class. I met a boy, and we grew up at each other's sides. I met a boy, and in time I fell in love with him. Our stories were intertwined. I loved that.

But that story ends here—with rage and a bullet and a broken heart.

Because Matthew Weston just fired a gun at me, or at Jax, and maybe I'll never know for sure. But I do know that Jax is clutching his arm as blood spills from between his fingers, and Matthew is on the ground, unmoving.

Gripping the back of Jax's sweatshirt, I scream as my ears ring with a blank, high-pitched tone.

I don't move until I'm sure it's over. When I open my eyes, I start to go to Matthew but Jax grabs the side of my head and pulls my forehead to his.

"What have you done?" I say. Tears slide down my face, onto my lips. Salt and sorrow.

"I ended it. It's done."

"I have to look at him."

"No, you don't."

"Yes, I do."

Jax releases my cheek. I take a shaky breath, then look.

Matthew lies on his side, totally still. I think I can handle the sight but I just *can't* and instead I fall to my knees, my body bending into itself. My heart shreds itself in half over and over until there is nothing. The night is so cold.

"He fired first," Jax says, crouching beside me.

"I know," I reply, but the voice doesn't feel like my own. This person is empty, and broken. Gently I reach out and try and look at Jax's arm, but he pulls it back.

"I have to go now. Give me your gun."

When I don't move, he takes it gingerly from my hands. "Let's go," I say.

"No." He lifts his good arm and pulls my head close, kissing my forehead. "I have to go, alone."

"Jax?"

"Goodbye, Valerie." Then he goes.

I call his name, aware I may be marking myself to the police. I'm alone, me and Matthew.

Somehow I make it over to him. Put my head on his chest and wait for the steady beat of his good, good heart even though I know it won't come. The fabric of my jeans soaks with his blood.

I am gutted.

I do not know how long it takes them to find me, and I don't know how they do. Mako lifts me like I'm dead, and I smell Kate's perfume as she checks my pulse.

The godless heathens leave the dead and take me home.

EPILOGUE

Gravel crunches under my feet as I walk toward the house. Barking carries into the cool, pine-filled air.

A woman opens the front door. She's in an oversized sweatshirt and jeans. I pull out my ponytail and let my hair cover my neck. Just in case.

"Hi," I call out. "Are you Leah? We spoke on the phone. I'm Valerie."

Leah shakes my hand. "Good to meet you. Find the place all right?"

"Yes, the directions you gave were perfect. Thank you."

She leads me through the house and into an expansive backyard. The dogs swarm me, sniffing and nosing my hands. Leah points to a smaller pen where the puppies are kept.

"There are three males and two females up for sale. You were looking for a male, right?"

"That's right."

The puppies are so adorable it hurts. They bounce around the yard, yipping and following one another. Leah catches my smile.

"Yeah, they're cute as buttons. Great parents, too. AKC certified, both of them. Let's see—the ones with purple, green, and yellow ribbons are males."

Yellow catches my eye first. He's a feisty one that never

stops moving. Purple joins him, and they yap and skip with each other a while. Two of their sisters—Pink and Red—join in on the fun.

The last of the puppies whines by the door of their shed, his nose poking into the air. It's a short step, maybe five inches, down to the dirt. He sticks out a paw tentatively. He waggles it around a moment then tumbles forward. Green gets up quickly and scampers toward his siblings.

Leah lets me wander around the pen, picking up and snuggling with each, but Green's won my heart. He squirms in my arms and I wince—the scar in my side isn't quite done healing—as Leah gets out the paperwork. I sign my name, pay her the adoption fee, and head out to the car.

"I'll call in a couple days, in case you have any trouble with him."

"Thank you. I think we'll be fine."

Nianna opens the car door, and I set the puppy in her lap. "Holy shit, he's cute."

"You should have come in and seen the others."

She pulls him closer as I start the car. "What're you gonna name him?"

"I don't know yet." I flick on my turn signal and get on the main road. It'll be another two hours back to Berkeley. At least for now, the puppy seems content to turn around and around in Nianna's lap. He whines a little, then settles down.

"Do you think he'll ever come back?" I ask her. "Jax."

"Honestly? No."

No one's seen Jax since that night four months ago. No one has any other numbers for him, and Nianna said Theresa hasn't returned her calls. Kate and Mako are gone, too, moved to his aunt's house in Hawaii.

"It can get a little boring there," Mako said when he told

me his plan. "But I think we could use some boring. My family is so stoked to meet her." Then, he showed me a small square box, winked, and slipped it back in his pocket.

Nothing has been easy, but I've done what I had to do to heal. I let go.

I cried until my eyes and body were so dry I swore I'd never be able to create tears again. I ran a fever for a day, and then ached for two more. I was wrecked for weeks. I only ate because Mom made me—even then, it was three bites at a time. I stayed in bed, slept as much as possible, and refused to open my blinds. I said goodbye to my brother, my first love, and Jax in one terrible, beautiful go.

Which isn't to say I never think about it. I carry them with me—my golden three—when I'm at the grocery store picking up the oatmeal brand Dad likes, when I'm putting scar cream on my leg, and when I stare at my ceiling and listen to the trees rustle outside. They are my first thought when I wake, and I've learned to make that okay. I let them inspire me, push me from my bed to my floor and then, slowly, all the way up.

Jax was there for me, in the end. That's why he took my gun with him. If they found him, it'd be him who shot Ty, and not me. That last part is the hardest to swallow, but I disconnect from it as much as I can. I had to. I was justified, wasn't I? But even if all that is true, who am I, that I could kill someone? What kind of monster does that make me?

I'm enrolled in therapy, twice a week. It's not the same place I went to for Leo, and I'm glad for it. Some days all I do is cry my eyes out. Other days I sit there and she talks to me, trying to coax out answers. I think it's helping. At least Dr. Stauffer was in favor of me getting the puppy. She even said I could bring him to our sessions once he's been trained.

I know neither a dog nor therapy is a quick fix for the shit I've done, and the shit I've seen. But I owe it to everyone giving me a second chance to at least try. Matthew, Micah, Aure—they won't ever get this opportunity to heal and change.

Lyla and I are on rocky ground. Despite my best efforts, the time apart seemed to create barriers between us. We've hung out—exploring Berkeley bookstores and quirky shops downtown—but it doesn't feel like it did before. When she talks about books and classes and the cute guys in debate club, I find myself just nodding along. We lived in different worlds too long, but I haven't given up, and make an effort to set up as many hangouts as I can.

Over in the passenger seat, Nianna keeps her hands around the puppy, scratching his ruff. She's wearing more makeup now than I've ever seen on her: plum lipstick and a healthy smear of eyeliner. She is both herself and not herself, and I could ask her what brought on the change but decided it's better I don't. She's living with some family friends, sleeping on their couch until she figures out what to do next.

"I like your shorter hair," I say.

She tugs at a curl until it's straight then lets go. "Thanks. I feel lighter." She closes her eyes and scratches the puppy's head again. "Every bit helps."

When we pull up to the BART station, Nianna gets out of the car and secures the dog inside his crate in the backseat. Walking back to the window, she adjusts her backpack on her shoulders.

"Good luck with the fur baby."

"Thanks," I say. "See you Sunday?"

Nianna's not too far from me—just a BART ride away in Oakland. We meet up here and there. Sometimes we get food. Other times we just drive. I thought it'd make it worse to stay in touch, but it helps. We both have a lot of rebuilding to do.

I feel the tension between Mom and Dad each time we all share a room. One child dead, and now me—a former gang member without a high school diploma. It's less that they're scared of me than that they're unsure how to handle me. Part of why I joined the Wars was to make amends for my mistakes, but in doing so I've driven a wedge between my parents and me that refuses to budge. We've forgotten how to talk to one another, how to be a family. So I do everything I can to try to return to normal. I clean the house and have coffee with Mom in the mornings. I help with dinner and do the chores I did before. One evening over dinner, I mentioned going to the Philippines, and both of them lit up like stars.

"It has been years since I went," Mom had said quietly, after a pause. "And your *kuyo* has been begging me to come."

"Let's look at ticket prices after we eat," Dad replied, taking her hand and giving me the most sincere smile I'd seen in weeks. The sight made me start sobbing on the spot, and my parents held me tightly until I calmed down. *I'm living both our afters. Mine and Micah's.*

We're planning to wait a few months at least, until the puppy is trained enough to be left with someone while we're gone. But it's going to happen, and I can't wait.

I put the car into drive and give Nianna one last wave. I adjust the paper crane on the driver's side dash.

"All right, Obin, let's go home."

The pup looks at me with kind eyes as water begins to come into mine. I let the tears fall as I turn toward the new house in Berkeley. Mom and Dad were as ready for a change of scenery as I was. Getting out of the city was one of the first things they suggested to me when I made my way home.

Moving out of SF was the first step. I don't know how many more it'll take for me to heal, but at least I'm climbing.

Through a gap in the trees, I spot a gray shield of fog rolling in from across the sea, ready to engulf San Francisco in its chilly protection. It won't reach here, though. Here, there are trees and kinder winds, a chance of warm sun.

We'll find it again, the sun.

ACKNOWLEDGMENTS

There are so many talented, compassionate people who drifted in and out of my life as this dream of mine—and my pile of shelved manuscripts—grew, and I have kept a running list since the beginning. Now it's time to take that roughed-up Post-it and make it official. To everyone on these next few pages and the ones I have inadvertently forgotten, I want to quote a beloved movie from my childhood: I would have been lost without you.

Enormous thanks to Elana Roth Parker—my fearless, badass champion of an agent. Your wisdom and patience saved my sanity multiple times, and I can say very sincerely you surpassed all my expectations of what working with an agent would be like. You are the agent of dreams. Thank you to Laura Dail and everyone at LDLA—you are all rock stars!

Thank you to Diana Gill, who saw my story and knew exactly how to nurture it to make it sharper, stronger, and more vibrant than ever before. A huge thank you, too, to Kristin Temple, Charlene Adhiambo, and all the amazing folks at Tor Teen. You have made me feel like a welcome member of a family since day one and I am so grateful for all the work you've done for me.

Thank you to #TeamElana—Alexa Donne, Leigh Mar, Anna Bright, June CL Tan, Lily Meade, and Deeba Zargarpur—

for the rants, check-ins, and support even before this book sold. Much love to the Stripy Tigers of SUISS 2014 and Mama Tiger, Ruth Gilligan, who gave me an international tribe of writing buddies that I could rely on any day.

Thank you to the *Santa Clara Review*—you guys are my family. Thank you for believing in me before I had the sense to believe in myself. Thank you especially to Professor Kirk Glaser, who always knew how to push my writing further.

Thanks to Casa 151, whose antics and love helped shaped who the Stags came to be; and to the women of Measure UP, who made my life into a real-life *Pitch Perfect* in all the best ways. I love all of you. Stay beautiful.

I could never forget everyone at Counterpoint Press: thank you especially to Megan Fishmann, for taking a chance on a wide-eyed intern and for being one of the best cheerleaders I know. Thanks, too, to Jack Shoemaker, Kelli Adams, Jenn Kovitz, Andy Hunter, and Rolph Blythe for your guidance and support during my time as a publicist.

Endless thanks to Bethany Onsgard, Deborah Kenmore, Kelly Winton, and Jenny Alton: you are my favorite canaries in the coal mine, and the brightest, kindest, and most hilarious coworkers a person could ask for. In the immortal words of a card I may or may not have once accidentally mailed to a very famous author: stay cool. And to Nick: I knew you were a rarity long before you were gone, and I am grateful to have known you as long as I did. I love you so much. I hope I've made you proud.

A tremendous thanks to Peter Gibbs, Drake Bonin, and Christina Estrella-Lemus—thank you for all the laughs and unedited hilarity, and for being sincerely kind souls. To Zach Waterson, I'll forever yell your name and push people out of the way to hug you when you arrive at parties. Thank you for being you.

Thank you to "5quad"—you wonderful, weird, and hard-working bunch. Thank you for your enthusiasm, love, and constant check-ins about my book (and for putting up with me when my answer to the last of those was "UGH"). Shout-out to Jon Slocum, who made me laugh every damn day and who let me tell him about any book gossip I saw on Twitter. You are the best.

Special thanks to Samir Khanna, the Jack Donaghy to my Liz Lemon, for the honest talks and for teaching me that thing about time. Much love to Tasha Yglesias, Ari Jones-Krause, David Jones-Krause, and Sahand Emanian—I'm so glad I answered that Craigslist ad.

I would be a mess without the marvelous Natalie Grazian—we've come so far from the SCR office, haven't we? Thank you for reading this book in its early form and letting me bounce ideas off you. Thank you even more for the sanity checks and for being one of the few people on the planet I can be totally real with.

So much love to "Moo" and Hannah, for being beacons of love and support since the start. I admire both of you and love that you never questioned my typing into the night, even when I was supposed to be on vacation. Abundant love to the wee ones—Abigail, Anna Grace, and Audrey—who are constant sources of love and light.

Huge thanks to Richard for all the sage advice through-out this book's journey and beyond. Love to Meese Patly and family for helping shape the person I am today.

Thank you to my sister, Nicole, for being my first beta reader and champion. Thank you for the strictly professional comments ("PUPPIES!") and for enduring all my late-night wait-isn't-this-a-plot-hole texts.

My life would be a lot less bright without Gaston, my lost-and-found love—I'm so glad we made it to "found."

Thank you for the meals you cooked, dishes you washed, and errands you ran just so I'd have more time to work on this book. Your unflagging support of me and my dream through every triumph, pitfall, and stress-cry has meant the world. I love you. You are everything.

Last but not least, thank you to Mom and Dad for encouraging my creativity every day of my life. Thank you for letting me try out whatever activity I wanted to, whether it be drawing, painting, or singing—and finally, writing. I'm beyond lucky to have parents like you. Thank you, *mahal kita*.